Doris Farrand's Vocation

Isabella "Pansy" Alden

Anglocentria
Aurora, Colorado

This is a work of fiction. Names, characters, places and incidents are products of the author's imagination or are used fictitiously. Any resemblance to actual persons, living or dead, or to events or locales, is entirely coincidental.

A Note from the Publisher . . .
Doris Farrand's Vocation was originally published in 1903. This edition has been reproduced with every effort to retain the flavor of the original with minor changes to update spelling and punctuation. You'll find this book reflects many of the feelings and attitudes prevalent at the time of its original publication. It may contain references that reflect mores and opinions that directly conflict with today's prevailing sentiments.

You can learn more about Isabella, read free short stories and view a complete list of her published books at:

www.IsabellaAlden.com

Doris Farrand's Vocation

Chapter 1

Athalie was the milliner of the family. She was trimming a hat for Doris, or was "fussing" with it, which was the word that she applied to her work. Doris was near at hand and was occasionally appealed to in the way of advice. She was, however, giving much more heed to her book than to the hat. Doris liked pretty hats, but not so well as she did fine recitations, and she felt that the work was quite safe in Athalie's hands. Doris was the student of the family, and the one who usually had the pretty hats; not because she so planned, but because she was so busy with her books that Athalie said unless somebody else planned her clothes for her she would go in rags. That, however, was an exaggeration; rags, or personal disorder of any sort, could not be thought of in connection with Doris Farrand. Athalie bunched up the ribbon, stabbed it with a large pin, then held the hat from her and surveyed it with her head on one side, much as a bird in a cage examines a new thing brought to him. The result was that the pin was twitched out impatiently and the ribbon allowed to fall in straight lines to the floor.

"There are not loops enough," she said discontentedly. "I wish that for just once I could have all the ribbon I wanted; there is never enough of anything."

"Except dust," said Mrs. Farrand, who appeared from the next room with a duster in one hand and a whisk broom in the other. "There is enough of that, certainly. People living on this street will never need to be taught that things generally were made of dust, and are hurrying back to their original element. I am distressed to see how it has gathered in that front room since yesterday."

"I should let it gather," said Athalie, trying the ribbon in another series of loops. "I'm not going about forever with dust cloths and whisks. I think of making a series of signs that shall read, 'This room was thoroughly dusted this morning,' and then letting the dust lie there. How would that do? Mother, what am I to do about this hat? There isn't ribbon enough to make it look respectable."

This brought Doris's eyes from her book.

"Oh, never mind the hat," she said hurriedly. "It will do well enough. You always make things look pretty, Athalie; but don't worry mother about my hats."

"Child, somebody has to 'mind,' or you'll have no hat to wear for Sunday; and you wouldn't look well without one in church, more's the pity. It ought to be the fashion to go without hats. Think how lovely it would be if one could wear wreaths of roses on one's head instead. There are plenty of roses. Mother, that's another thing that there is enough of in this country, roses and dust. There is some contrast between the two."

"Yet the roses will all be dust in a little while," said Doris dreamily, her eyes still away from her book, looking into space.

"What a horrid idea!" said Athalie. Then she flashed to another topic.

"What are you going to wear to the reception, Dorrie?"

The girl let her eyes slowly travel toward her sister, and laughed. "What a wasted question!" she said. "My dress, of course."

Athalie groaned. "Oh, dear, it is really too bad! Mommie!"— raising her voice, for the mother had returned to the next room— "can't we possibly manage a new dress for Doris?"

"Oh, Athalie, don't!" There was real distress in Doris's voice. But Mrs. Farrand had heard and came to the doorway.

"Why, Athalie," she said, "wasn't it only yesterday that I was telling you about the increase in rent and the extra bill for coal?"

"Yes, it was; and I am thinking about bills, of course, as we generally are. There are always extra ones and unusual expenses; but still I can't see how Doris is to get on at school without clothes. Her best dress is simply not fit to wear to that reception."

"The reception isn't a necessity, Athalie." This was Doris's voice.

"No, I don't suppose it is. I presume we should all live and eat our three meals a day if you never went to another; but at the same time we both know it would be rather unpleasant for you to explain why you did not attend this particular one, since it is given by the President in honor of your own class, and you are a prominent member of that class. But even if we leave that function out entirely, the fact remains that you need a new dress. If you would help me the least bit, I could get mother to listen to reason. At Bostwick's they would be only too glad to have us start an account, and we could let it run until spring; by that time perhaps—"

But Mrs. Farrand interrupted, speaking with a positiveness that she rarely used in talking with her daughters.

"No, Athalie, I cannot give my consent to any such plan. We have had to let the bill for coal wait, and there may be other necessities before the winter is over. Besides, we have not reason whatever for believing that it will be easier to pay for an extra next spring than it is now. I cannot feel that for the sake of a dress, which Doris herself says is not necessary, we should humiliate ourselves to ask for credit. You both know what a horror your father had of bills."

"Well, then, I am sure I don't see how—" Athalie began, but broke off to say, "There's Richard."

The young man thus announced came in briskly, admitting himself, after a premonitory tap at the side door, in the manner of one much at home.

"Good morning," he said, hat in hand. "No, thank you; if I take a seat, I shall stay too long, and I haven't a minute to spare. I just dropped in to get a promise from Doris. You will go, won't you?"

"I think not this time, Richard."

The young man frowned.

"Well, now, why not?" he asked, with the air of one who had a right to question closely. But Doris was not disposed to be communicative.

"There are reasons," she said vaguely, and let her eyes drop again to her open book. The caller made an impatient movement and looked at Athalie.

"I wish you could talk your sister into a little reason," he said. "She is determined to make a nun of herself."

"What is it?" asked Athalie. "Where do you want her to go this time?"

"Why, only to town. We are making up a little party for the play at the Nordham, you know. That play is having a great run, and some of us haven't seen it yet. We have special rates for tomorrow evening and special seats, and it is an opportunity of a lifetime."

Athalie laughed. "You have so many opportunities of a lifetime, Richard," she said, "your life ought to be very rich."

"Oh, well, it is, for that matter. I mean it shall be. It is a duty that everyone owes to himself to make his life as rich as possible. I shall certainly not lose this opportunity, and I don't think Doris ought to. We could catch the midnight train out, and there will be a chance to sleep late the next morning, and no classes to miss; she could go as well as not if she only thought so. You help me reduce her to reason, Athalie. I am not going to take your final answer now, Doris; I shall stop tomorrow morning for it, and I'm going to plan just as though you had promised to go."

Still he did not go, but kept hovering about the subject, trying to draw Doris into an argument until she cut short the interview, so far as she was concerned, by gathering up her books and announcing that it was time for her to go at once. Richard's path lay in an opposite direction, so he stayed to urge upon Athalie the duty of bringing Doris to terms. That young woman believed that she understood the obstacle in the way, but she kept a discreet silence with regard to it. She and Doris and their mother might talk of clothes together; but not even so intimate an outsider as Richard should hear of their perplexities.

It as not until the sisters were in their room for the night that Athalie tried to further Richard's plan.

"Is it clothes this time, too, poor little girlie?" she began, with a tenderness in her voice which reminded one of a mother. There were times when this girl, who was only four years the elder, felt more like a mother than a sister to Doris.

The younger one shook her head, smiling.

"No, Athalie, I sometimes think of other things than clothes."

"I should say you did! I am sure no one can accuse you of thinking too much of them; but I thought perhaps the girl were planning to blossom out tomorrow evening. Why don't you go, then? Richard is awfully anxious to have you; his heart seems to be quite set upon it. What is in the way? You haven't had an outing for some time."

Doris was standing before the mirror brushing out her hair for the night. She arrested the brush midway to think; then, with it still in her hand, turned slowly toward her sister, the troubled look on her face deepening as she spoke.

"I don't know. Does there seem to you no reason why I should not go?

"Well, of course Richard ought not to be encouraged to spend money unnecessarily; still, to go with him will be the very way to help him avoid that. He will go, anyway, and take somebody; it might better be you than one of the girls who will lead him into all sorts of extravagances."

"I am not thinking of Richard, at least not of his money. There are other considerations." She spoke hesitatingly, as one at a loss how to express her thought.

"That train is due here at two o'clock, and is often late; it would certainly be three before we should get to bed. What sort of preparation is that for the next day?"

"But the next day will be Sunday," said Athalie, quickly.

"Yes, does that seem to you an argument in favor of the plan? It isn't as we used to think or as father used to. Do you remember when we were little girls that father objected to the school carnival because it was to be held on Saturday and it would be nearly midnight before we could get home?"

"Oh, well," said Athalie, "we were children then."

"It wasn't that simply, was it? Wasn't it because the next day would be Sunday and father wanted us fresh for the best that Sunday could give?"

"Yes, of course, and that applies now, as a rule; but an occasional outing would rest you and make you fresher for the next day, especially when there was no hard work for that day. Sunday is for rest, you know."

"For resting from theater-going?" said Doris, with a not untroubled smile. "I wonder if it is, and if most of the others are right and only—only a very few people are mistaken? I confess to a good deal of confusion of mind about many things. You are older than I, Athalie; you must surely remember very well what father thought."

Athalie looked almost annoyed.

"Of course I remember," she said. "You mean about going to the theater, I suppose?"

"That and other things," said Doris.

"But people's ideas change, you know. If father were living now, he might feel differently about many things. Mother does. Indiscriminate theater-going she, of course, thinks of as she always did; but an occasional play, which has a splendid moral lesson, it seems narrow-minded to object to in these days. Why, Doris, the very best people go to this particular play."

"Not all of them," said Doris, thoughtfully. "A few persons, even yet, hold to the same views that father believed in all his life. I have half thought sometimes that I would go back to them; I don't know—I don't do much theater-going, it is true; but Richard does more of it than I should think he would like. It is rather unusual, isn't it, for one who expects to be a minister?"

"He isn't a minister yet," said Athalie, with decision. "And you can't help what he does, in any case. Don't you see how impatient he is of the mere suggestion of advice? He won't take a hint, even from mother. I told him yesterday that I understood him well enough to urge him vehemently to a course that I wanted him to avoid. Richard will be sure to go tomorrow night, whether you go or not, and he needs you for ballast. I don't think you need to be anxious about yourself. There isn't the slightest fear of your being led into a life of dissipation; we are too poor for that, all of us."

"I might go on the stage," said Doris, speaking lightly for the first time. "Professor Blauvelt told me again yesterday that I had marked histrionic talent. A great deal of money is made in that way; often more in a single night than a teacher can earn in a year."

Athalie laughed and at the same time gave a little shrug to express aversion.

"Thank goodness," she said, "that you will never do anything of that sort."

Instantly Doris's face grew grave again.

"That," she said, "is one of the perplexities connected with this whole subject. Why, for instance, should I not go on the stage, if I have talent in that direction, which might be cultivated? If it is a good, safe place to frequent, why shouldn't it offer a good, safe employment for me or any other girl? Yet everybody shrinks from having their friends choose it."

"Of course they do," said Athalie promptly. "I hope none of the people even remotely connected with our name will ever be reduced to that."

"But why not, Athalie? We go to see the actors and praise their talent and admire some of them immensely. Why not join their ranks, if we have brains enough?"

The older sister turned and stared for a moment in speechless dismay. She was never quite sure of Doris in any line. Suddenly she broke forth:

"My goodness, Doris, what is the matter? You are not surely thinking of anything so horrid as that! It would simply kill mother to know that you had mentioned it as a possibility. What do you mean?"

Doris laughed and turned back to the mirror and her hair brush.

"I don't mean anything," she said lightly. "At least, nothing is farther from my present thoughts than the stage as a way of earning my living. I was simply trying to get at the logic of our position."

"Oh, never mind the logic," Athalie said, restored to composure. "I'm not a college-bred girl, remember, and cannot be expected to speak always according to the books. I know what I mean, and so do you. Of course, we like to see people do things sometimes that we wouldn't for the world do ourselves; that's natural, I'm sure. My advice to you is to go with Rich. You can keep him from spending more money than is good for him. If you refuse and he goes off in a huff and takes one of the Wilder girls, for instance, they will hint at creams and carriages and all sorts of extravagances. How those girls *can* go on as they do with young men is more than I can understand. I should die of shame if you talked even to Richard as they do to passing acquaintances."

Doris had no reply ready. Her sister, who while she talked had been moving around with her customary dispatch, was presently in bed and very soon thereafter asleep. Doris went about on tiptoe, completing her preparations for the night, and presently sat down before the little reading-stand on which lay a school text-book and her Bible.

Chapter 2

"That ye might walk worthy of God."

She did not open either book however, but sat with her elbows leaning on the table and her chin resting on her clasped hands. She was in what Athalie called one of her "brown studies." She had Athalie's question to answer to herself. "What is the matter?" her sister had asked, in a tone almost of dismay. What answer could be made to it? The young woman was conscious that she had some time ago reached a period of unrest, of dissatisfaction not only with herself, but with almost all others of her world. Had she been asked to state definitely the time when this feeling first took possession of her, she knew that she could have done so, although she had never tried to follow out the subtle waves of influence set in motion that Sunday morning months before. On this evening she went back to it in memory; that May morning with the air athrob with the breath of roses and honeysuckle and other rich perfumes of semi-tropical regions. Birds sang their ecstasies from the great oak trees, but a Sabbath hush had seemed to settle over all other sounds. She was in the great church again, in an upstairs class room; the girls were all there, and Miss Mayburn stood before them, open Bible in hand, and talked on her favorite theme, Paul. Miss Mayburn was an ardent admirer of Paul; she never wearied of talking about him. It was a silly speech of Daisy Blakslie's that, if Paul and Miss Mayburn had been contemporaries, he would never have remained a bachelor. Daisy Blakslie had a reputation for smart sayings to sustain; Doris believed this was why she was often very silly indeed. But Miss

Mayburn certainly knew a great deal about Paul. She had succeeded in awakening a genuine admiration for him in the minds of her class—those fluttery, irresponsible-looking girls in their gossamer robes with all the glories of the early summer foreshadowed in the tints of their fresh spring toilets. Doris remembered that she had that morning looked among the rows of faces in search of earnestness. Many of them belonged to college girls whom she knew as earnest enough in Latin or history; but she had often puzzled curiously over the airy indifference which seemed to take possession of them on Sunday mornings.

"Where is the lesson?" was a not uncommon question floating in undertone through the class. It was scarcely possible even to imagine such a state of things for Monday in a college class room. What would those grave professors, who were confronted on week days, have said or done under such strange circumstances? Yet here the study was in the Book of books, and Miss Mayburn was an acknowledged expert. What made the difference? Why did all those gay girls come to Bible class at all? This was one of Doris's mental questions, followed immediately by a personal one. Why did she? Still, her own answer—so far as it was an answer—was ready. She had always gone to Sunday-school. The old-fashioned "infant class" in her father's church was one of the vivid memories of her childhood. She had advanced by the usual processes from one department to another until here she was as a matter of course in the senior class. When the family removed from their old home to this college town, Doris had unhesitatingly accepted Miss Mayburn's invitation to join her Bible class, and had come into it with as little knowledge of the Bible, so far as its application to daily living was concerned, as was possible for one who had been supposedly a student of that book for fifteen years; for Doris Farrand's fourth birthday had been marked by her reciting to her delighted father an entire chapter from the Bible without a mistake. But she found in Miss Mayburn a different Bible teacher from any that had heretofore fallen to her lot. There was promptly awakened within her a desire to do something like intellectual justice to the text-book, and a realization of the fact that she had heretofore set it apart from other text-books as one not necessary to be studied. It was easy to become recognized as by far the best pupil in the class, though she blushed over this distinction, feeling that she had it simply because most of the others did not study at all. At the same time she was conscious of the fact that Miss Mayburn was not satisfied with her. She read the wistfulness in the teacher's expressive eyes that said to her as plainly as words could have done, "You might do so much more, and you will not."

"So I might, I suppose," Doris used to tell herself, as she mused over those wistful eyes, "if I had time and—it were worth while." Before allowing that last phrase, she made a distinct mental pause to consider whether or not it had in it a tinge of irreverence; she had been carefully taught in that regard. Then she went on boldly. "Why should it be worth while? I never expect to be a Bible teacher. I couldn't be that; but these other studies I expect to teach. It would take a great deal of time for me to know the Bible lesson as thoroughly as I am trying to know German, for instance; I don't know why I should. I know more of the Bible now than I can ever practice. Of course, I shall continue to study it, and I think I shall stay in the Sunday-school; at least, I shall as long as I can have Miss Mayburn for a teacher."

There was always a little tinge of self-approbation in her thoughts when they reached that point. Doris recognized that she was distinctly superior to many of the college girls in this regard. Some of them asked her openly if she did not find it a dreadful bore to be tied down to Sunday-school. For themselves, they laid that function aside with their short dresses and long braids. Doris always felt superior when she explained with a smile that she found the Sunday-school a pleasant place in which to spend an hour, that Miss Mayburn was recognized as a very superior teacher. She never asked any of them to join her; had she thought of it, she would have put it aside as a useless effort; most of the girls of her class were distinctly of another world. They themselves recognized the difference. "I suppose it is because your father was a clergyman," one of them said, trying to put into words the subtle atmosphere that she felt. She spoke respectfully, and Doris's eyes grew dim, as they often did at the mention of her father. She was only thirteen when he went away to the other country; but her memory of him was vivid, and her sense of loss, at times, intense. The girls knew this and admired it in her. They thought it did her credit that she respected not only her father's memory, but what some of them called his "notions." Doris had once overheard the word as applied to herself, and often thought of it. Were they simply "notions," or were they principles? Sometimes, as she grew older, she realized that she had got away from some of them, either above or below, which was it?

On the evening in question she went back in her thoughts to that May morning in which this special wave of unrest had enveloped her. Miss Mayburn had been dull that morning, or was the dullness in herself? Afterward she thought that it might have been; she had been up late the night before.

The girls of the class had been more listless sand inattentive than usual. One of them had whispered to Doris, in the midst of the teacher's earnest words, that she did wish Miss Mayburn would resurrect some other Bible worthy for a time and give Paul a rest; and Doris had smiled absently in reply, and been conscious afterward that her ears were listening for the warning bell that should close the dull hour. Then Miss Mayburn had said:

"Dear girls, I have something to tell you. This, I suppose, will be our last morning together for a long time, perhaps forever. I am going away to be gone for at least a year, possibly for much longer. I feel that I must tell you of my one deepest regret in going; that is, leaving my class with so little accomplished. I do not know that I could make plain to you with words how hard it is for me to go away feeling that I have so signally failed in my work."

Instantly they were all interest and excitement. She had surprised them and touched their hearts toward herself. It appeared that they were extremely fond of her. They did not hesitate to pour out their regrets and assurances of undying remembrance. Despite Miss Mayburn's earnest effort to turn their thoughts from her to the appeal she was trying to make for another, they persisted in holding her to her own personality and their regrets in losing her. Daisy Blakslie's blue eyes dimmed with tears, and the voice was tremulous in which she assured her teacher that she should not go to Bible class any more; she never wanted any other teacher. And then, after all that, Miss Mayburn had not gone. A sudden turn in family affairs, as unexpected as those had been which seemed to make her going a necessity, had changed her hastily formed plans, and on the following Sunday she was there, smiling her greeting to her class.

"A regular stage effect," Daisy had murmured, while Miss Mayburn greeted a newcomer. "Good-byes and tears and regrets and good resolutions all wasted. Here we are gain, with Paul as much in evidence as ever. Isn't it a shame?"

It had been none of those experiences which had impressed Doris Farrand. She heartily respected Miss Mayburn, and admired her intellectually, but the two lives had not touched closely enough for strong regrets over separation; at least, so far as Doris was concerned. In truth her first sensation over the news had been one of relief. Now that there would be no Miss Mayburn to call promptly with solicitous inquiries, she need not be so regular in her attendance at Bible class. Perhaps she might even drop out altogether. There had been times when she felt that Miss Mayburn was too solicitous. Thoughts somewhat like these had floated through her mind while she joined civilly in the outward expressions of regret; and then Miss Mayburn had said:

"There is just one phrase that I want to leave with you. If I could get even one of you to choose it for a life motto, I should know that God had owned and blessed my work. It was Paul's word to the people whom he loved, and for whose highest good he longed inexpressibly, and human language can get no higher. 'That ye might walk worthy of God.' Think of it, girls, what if we should? You and I? Can you begin to imagine what a difference it would make with us, with our friends, with the world of which we are a part? Think of being worthy of God; of something more than his compassionate love; worthy of his friendship, his companionship. Isn't it wonderful that Paul dared to hint at such a possibility? Isn't it certain that he was inspired, else he would have been afraid of the thought as blasphemy?"

There was nothing new in all this, of course. The idea was at least as old as the text which gave it expression. Doris Farrand had known that text all her life. It was one that she had laboriously sewed into a cardboard motto in her early childhood. The letters, she remembered, were of rustic design and were done in shades of blue, "Walk Worthy of God." Their intense individuality had not impressed her then as they did when Miss Mayburn quoted them. She found the words in her Bible that evening, and found that they were even more personal and individual. Paul had not said "you" but "ye," and as if to make assurance doubly sure had added that explanatory clause, "every one of you." Not some special saint, like his friend Timothy, destined from his birth to be a star in the religious world, but every member of that early church—people not noted for learning or spiritual mindedness. They, the beginners of the church, the veritable babes in Christ, were directed to walk

15

"worthy of God." What ought to be expected, nineteen centuries later, of her, Doris Farrand?

The verse had haunted her. Miss Mayburn's going or staying seemed to have nothing to do with it; she had been but the mouth-piece, the thought was divine.

"And reasonable," confessed Doris, as she tossed on a sleepless bed and considered the direction. "It is a perfectly reasonable requirement. If he gives his care, his love, oh, more than that, his companionship, what less could he ask than that we make the effort to be worthy of him? Who does, I wonder? If just one perfect man or woman could be found! Not perfect in the silly, schoolgirl sense, but just a complete man, putting first things always first, it would give one courage to make the attempt. But— do I know one who has reached even my ideal?"

The summer that followed this night of introspection might have been characterized, so far as Doris Farrand's religious life was concerned, by that one word, "spasmodic." There had been weeks together when she scarcely so much as thought of the phrase which had stirred her, but lived her full and, for the most part, happy life with as little consideration of the high position to which she had been called as though she were a humming-bird instead of an immortal. Then there came hours when a chance remark, made sometimes by a passing stranger, or a sentence from a book or paper that she caught up and glanced over while she waited, would recall her unrest, and for the time being overwhelm her with it. So wearing at these times did her self-questionings grow, that she told herself impatiently it would be better for her if she made no professions and had no ideals to be false to. Yet there had been professions that stared her in the face and goaded her with a sense of the contrast between them and her daily living. She could close her eyes and seem to be again in the old church, and hear the roll of words which she had so carefully studied that their exact arrangement came back to her.

"You take the word of God as your rule of life? You give yourself, soul and body, time and talents, to God's service? You do this intelligently, sincerely, freely and forever?"

"I ought never to have made such promises," she told herself irritably. "How could a child of twelve be expected to know herself well enough for pledges like those?" Yet even while she asked the questions, she seemed to see as in a vision that serious-faced child of twelve standing just in front of the communion table, while her father with a light in his eyes, the memory of which had stayed with her through the years, and a quality in his voice that seemed to her like a caress, had said as he held her hand in one that trembled, "I welcome you, my daughter, to all the privileges of this church, and to the life of usefulness and happiness which an honest adherence to the obligations which you have assumed will insure."

No matter if the words were a form so commonly used by her father in the reception of members that she was able, after this lapse of years, to recall each one: the look on his face, and the tenderness in his voice, and the tremble of his hand were for her, his little daughter. That dear father! She was nineteen now, and the father, who had been at once her incentive and her reward for all true living, had been long gone to the world which Doris hoped and believed was satisfying his highest ideals. But his "little daughter" was ready, at times, to confess with tears that she had not adhered to the obligations then assumed. When these spasms of unrest took hold of her, she was either utterly self-abased before her professions, or eager in self-excuse. Whichever mood possessed her she found equally uncomfortable and, on the whole, the summer had not been profitable.

Chapter 3

"That God would count you worthy of this calling."

She went to the city with Richard, as she had half believed that she would. Richard had a fashion of brushing aside her objections, and smiling, sometimes almost sneering, away her logic. At least there would be a suggestion of sneers. He never sneered outright at Doris; she would perhaps have been a stronger character if he had. She went with him under protest; she was always doing things under protest, she told herself irritably; but that was not quite true, such moods were only spasmodic. She was able to throw off her scruples, or to trample on them, and enjoy the Saturday night outing to the utmost. On the following morning she felt as she had foretold that she would. Her head ached, and she came downstairs looking so pale and miserable that Athalie suggested her omitting the Bible class, and her mother seconded the suggestions. Doris's reply was almost irritable; she was not going to fail Miss Mayburn because she had chosen to break the Sabbath on Saturday. She went away late, and without breakfast.

They talked her over, the mother and older sister, after she was gone.

"I wish that child could be persuaded to take life a little easier," Athalie said. "She will be all worn out before she is through with school. She has too large a conscience for these times."

"Or else ours is too small," said the mother, with an uneasy smile. Any talk of conscience had a tendency with her toward uneasiness; she was at once reminded of her husband, whose conscience had also been "large."

"No," said Athalie, in a positive tone, "I don't think so. Richard is right; one's ideas of things change with one's development. What we thought in the physical world twenty-five years ago about a great many things, we don't think any more. Why shouldn't our ideas in these other directions change, too?"

"Principles do not change," said Mrs. Farrand, quoting mechanically a phrase familiar to her ears, rather than expressing an inward conviction.

"No, but one's interpretation of principles may. Doris could be narrow, as narrow as a knife-blade if she chose; she has in her the material for the making of a first-class fanatic. If she should ever come strongly under the influence of people of one idea, I should tremble for her. But I don't know who there is to influence her in such directions. To be sure, there is Miss Mayburn; but she is a woman so set apart that I shouldn't think the child would ever hope or, for that matter, care to grow like her."

"I thought you liked Miss Mayburn," was Mrs. Farrand's irrelevant reply.

"Why, I adore her, of course, everybody does; but I don't care to have two of her—one is enough for a generation, or at least for a town. Won't you eat Doris's egg, mother? It will be wasted if you don't. So silly in the child to rush off to that Bible class without her breakfast, and looking like a ghost!"

From which it will be seen that Doris's home influence was not likely to develop her in "narrowness" or fanaticism. Athalie's comment on Miss Mayburn, also, would have found an echo in her sister's heart. Miss Mayburn was a woman to be admired, adored even, but not copied. In truth, Doris half believed that it would not be possible for ordinary mortals to copy her. To become a Miss Mayburn one must have Miss Mayburn's surroundings and history. She was quite past her youth, and was the only and idolized daughter of a beautiful home where very luxury and refinement that money could produce surrounded her. Money was lavishly at her disposal to do with as she would, and no one to question or disapprove. Why should not such a person live an ideal life? Doris confessed, on those occasions when her conscience insisted upon bringing forward Miss Mayburn as a witness, that, so far as outward appearance went, that young woman's life and professions matched. Even money, that most difficult gift for some people to manage, was being daily used by Miss Mayburn in a way to suggest that she looked upon herself as merely a steward. Doris was given to comforting her heart by assuring herself that money would not be hard for her to use as a trust; that there was nothing she would like better than to be able to play Lady bountiful, as Miss Mayburn did; and she believed, too, that she would be able to do it in the same gracious way without a touch of patronage. But suppose that good woman was compelled to go without a fresh pair of gloves, for instance, when she wanted to give a new pair of shoes to another; would she be so sweet and gracious and peaceful? In other words, did not unlimited money account for much of Miss Mayburn's serenity, as well as for her boundless benevolence? Still, of course, it was not all nor chiefly money. There were other things. Miss Mayburn was an old maid— Doris was too cultivated a young woman to use that word in conversation, but she let her thoughts linger on it occasionally— and once there had come into her life a great and bitter disappointment. Was it not possible that, but for this, she might have been just a commonplace, half-and-half Christian like the rest of the world? But here the girl always stopped, her face flushing in shame at her own thought. Was it possible that Miss Mayburn had been able to live a life of remarkable beauty and purity so that wherever she went the atmosphere seemed sweetened and brightened, simply because she had loved and been engaged to marry one who had deserted her almost upon her wedding day? Such a confession would mean that the grace of Christ was not sufficient until the joys of this life had either been drained to their dregs or been soured in the process of making. There was no recourse but to set Miss Mayburn aside as a rare exotic, not understood, and not to be accounted for by the ordinary processes of gardening. But she was the only one whom Athalie could summon as having possibly a narrowing influence. Certainly no such word could be applied to Richard Shipley's influence. In truth, that young man prided himself upon his constantly broadening views of life in general, and talked loftily about a wider horizon and freer air; though when his life had been trammeled by what he called narrowness, would have been hard for him to explain. It is true that his mother had been at one time in her life extremely "narrow," but he had early taken her in hand, and might have been said to have brought her up. Certainly now, after seven years of careful training, she had no ideas on any subject whatsoever that were not echoes of Richard's own.

The two young people, Doris and Richard, having played together as children, and quarreled together through their earlier years of school life, had been separated by Mrs. Shipley's removal to another town. When, after the passage of years, they found themselves together again in the college town where Richard was a junior when Doris was ready for the freshman class, Athalie said that they began where they left off as children, and played and quarreled together as usual.

It was certain that they dropped, almost as a matter of course, into intimate friendship. Immediately they were "Doris" and "Richard" to each other, and in a surprisingly short time their intimate friends on both sides learned to speak of them collectively. It was one of those cases of affinity which seemed to be taken as a matter of course, and all calculations having to do with them started from the standpoint of "Doris and Richard," without even a comma between.

Not that there was any definite engagement of marriage between them. Indeed, Mrs. Shipley had been heard to say that she did not like long engagements; that Richard would have three more years of study before him when he had been graduated from college, and no one could tell what might happen in four or five years. A man, especially, ought to have more sense than to trammel himself with promises of any sort. Those who knew Mrs. Shipley well smiled significantly over such statements. They knew that she was quoting Richard and that she always quoted Richard either consciously or unconsciously in all she said.

Still, they pleased her by commending the young man's prudence, and said that not many college boys, they were afraid, showed such excellent sense.

Richard Shipley's excellent sense did not, however, keep him from attaching himself closely to Doris Farrand and absorbing all her leisure—to say nothing of a good deal of time that was not leisure—so thoroughly as to afford small opportunity to other friends. Moreover, he ruled the girl's life, or tried to, and succeeded better than those well acquainted with Doris would have expected anyone to do. Richard was used to ruling; he was by nature and by cultivation an autocrat.

"What a minister he will make!" said those who admired him, and who knew that his intention was to study theology. "He will be able to control all his young people; they will think what he thinks, and do what he plans, as a matter of course."

But there were others who said that they did not think Richard Shipley was intended for the ministry. They were sure they shouldn't like to have him for a pastor. Why, he would think that he ought to be allowed to manage the personal and private affairs of all his parishioners!

A few of his acquaintances, when they came to know him intimately, were given to wondering thoughtfully why Shipley chose the ministry. The actual fact was that he did not choose it; it chose him. It may be said that this was the only step in the young man's life, since the day when, at a remarkably early age, he began to take steps, that he had not chosen or at least tried to choose, for himself. He was the son of a woman who had been reared in luxury, but who had been early left a widow in straitened circumstances. She had struggled along as best she could, holding on with tenacity to only one possession: her five-year-old boy. She had contrived to live on the pitiful sum left to them, until her son was twelve years old. Then the death of an eccentric and forgotten relative left ten thousand dollars in trust for the boy, the interest to be used in educating him, the principal to become his as soon as he was of age, provided he chose the ministry as his profession. If, at twenty-one, he was still undecided with regard to his life-work, the sum was to be held in trust for five years more, after which, in the event of his having chosen some other profession or occupation, the money was to revert to a distant cousin.

To Richard's mother there had seemed no alternative: her son must be brought up with the ministry in view, as a matter of course. It must be admitted, however, that she liked the idea. The profession was eminently respectable, was indeed in itself a passport to the best society, and it would insure Richard's being always good, so she thought, poor woman. Richard as a child took kindly to the idea. Indeed, his earlier years seemed to have been spent in preparation for such a life-work. At six and seven he had mounted unused carts, or milk stands, or a carriage block, and harangued the children of the neighborhood, or, failing in them, the hens and the cat; he had shouted to passers-by that he was preaching, and that when he got to be a man he was going to preach all the time. It may be said of him that at that early age he discovered what is also realized later in life: that it is easier to preach than to practice. Still, Richard was a good boy in the main. He was regular in attendance at Sunday-school, and prided himself on knowing his lesson better than the other boys did. There was a time in his life when he began to attend the mid-week prayer meeting regularly, and to take active part in the same, to the astonishment of many and the admiration of some. This was when he was still quite young; as he grew older, he was sometimes thoughtful, and occasionally even irritable over its being taken for granted that he was to be a preacher.

"I would rather choose for myself," he told his mother fretfully. "What business had that old man, just because he had wanted to be a minister and couldn't, to find a boy who happened to have the same name as his, and make him into one in spite of himself?"

"But you would rather be a minister than anything else in the world, wouldn't you, Richie dear? Think what nice times they have! Dressed up all the week, and going out to teas and dinners; and lots of weddings to attend, with great big fees, sometimes."

That was the kind of answer that Richard's mother could give to such a complaint! He had interrupted her snarlingly.

"Oh, yes, and funerals; they are always having to go and visit sick folks and dying folks, and attend their funerals."

"Well, of course, there are funerals everywhere; you can't escape them, nor sick people, whatever you do." She said it with a sigh; she had not escaped funerals herself; they had darkened all her life. But she brightened, and spoke consolingly.
"Still, even then, Richie, the minister is the most important of all the friends. They look up to him and take his advice; and there's a chance to do good, too. And then you know how you like to make speeches; besides his sermons, the minister is always being called upon to address all sorts of things. Why, I should think you would like it better than anything else in the world! You are just fitted for it; anybody can see that."

"I would rather be a lawyer," would Richard say obstinately. "They can make speeches, too, lots of them. A lawyer can be sarcastic and witty and make people laugh; and a minister has to be as solemn as an owl all the time. If I had been let alone, I should be a great lawyer, and a rich one, too." Then would the mother look distressed. In imagination she saw that ten thousand dollars, the interest of which made her life so much easier, slipping into the hands of a far-away cousin.

"But, Richie," she would say imploringly, "think! How could you get your education? Lawyers need fine educations, and you would have no money, and have to spend all your time earning a living. How could you possibly be a lawyer?"

But to his mother's intense relief, Richard would reply, "Oh, I don't expect to be." Still, he said it irritably, and added: "Of course I shall have to go on now, and be a minister to the end of my days. That is what a fellow gets by being poor and having to let other people pick and choose for him."

There were times, however, when the boy was magnanimous and admitted that he didn't dislike the idea of being a minister; that what he liked least about it was having the profession chosen for him, instead of choosing it for himself, as he quite likely would have done. At the same time he was sure that he might be a great lawyer if he had half a chance.

As the years passed, and Richard entered upon and finally neared the completion of his college course, his eminent fitness for the ministry was not so apparent as it had been in early childhood. Not that he was disreputable in any sense of the word. On the contrary, he was in some respects a model young man, and a fair student, easily carrying off honors that others had to work hard for, and being sought after in debates and other public functions requiring a ready tongue. But there were subtle changes in him, distinctly felt and not easy to define. His fondness for preaching had quite died out, which was well, of course; but there were a few who felt that along with his childish follies he had also put away or, as he expressed it, outgrown some ideas that would better have stayed.

Chapter 4

"Seek ye first the kingdom of God."

Perhaps none of Richard's friends felt the subtle change in him so distinctly, or deplored it so keenly, as did Doris Farrand. During the early years of their acquaintance, when they were children together, she had looked up to Richard as her leader in all matters having to do with her religious nature. She was one of the few always ready to listen to his sermons, and as he grew older she thought his prayers were wonderful. Her first thought, after the decisions were made which would bring her once more into daily companionship with Richard Shipley, had been that he had probably taken great strides in Christian experience. He was almost ready for the theological seminary, and she looked forward to meeting and being helped by him as she had been when a child. For reasons which she did not mention, as well as for many frankly spoken ones, she was glad that circumstances had made it advisable for them to move to the college town where Richard was studying, and come once more in daily touch with him. He had been as glad as herself to renew the old friendship, and had speedily dropped into more than his former intimacy with the family. But as the months went by, and Doris's spasms of dissatisfaction with her own life grew more frequent, there were times when she almost resented it as a personal injury that Richard Shipley had not taken the forward strides, religiously, which his early youth had promised. Instead of looking up to him, and being able to take her moral poise from him, she had often to admonish

27

him for carelessness and luke-warmness. Especially during this second year of their renewed friendship Doris felt that he had changed. "Developed," he called it. He said that the change she noticed was caused by his breathing better mental air; that he was getting a wider outlook upon life, and withdrawing from many of the superstitions which had trammeled his earlier days. Was he right? Was she inclined to be narrow, as he sometimes hinted? This was one of the girl's painful questions, which she found herself unable to answer so that it stayed answered. Of one thing she was almost certain, that whatever might be said of herself, she liked Richard better in the days when he was what he now called "narrow." Still, of course, if it was narrowness, prejudice, sentiment, and nothing more, she must get rid of such ideas, and must not trammel Richard.

To her surprise, almost to her dismay, a new student, the last person whom she would have supposed could have such influence, was contributing to her unrest. This was Garrett Randall, a freshman, who was a trial to Richard.

"It is an infinite pity that that fellow chose this, of all the schools open to him," Richard said, as he and Doris lingered on the piazza, and Garrett Randall passed with a nod for Doris and a familiar "halloo" for Richard.

"I don't see why," answered Doris, instantly on the alert for the honor of the college which was her present favorite. "I should think this would commend itself as the place of all others for him. It is so near to his home that he can go back and forth often, and it gives him such excellent opportunities for earning his way, that he can enter now, instead of waiting for several years longer; he is older than most of the freshmen."

"You have mentioned one of the objections to this college; I don't believe in allowing students to work their way through. A college man has brain work enough to tax all his energies, and has no business to try to do manual labor at the same time." Richard was using what Athalie called his superior tone, but Doris laughed.

"That will do very well," she said, "for people who have eccentric relatives to lend them a bank account; but what would become of the poor fellows who must earn their education or have none?"

"In nine cases out of ten it would be better for all such to be content with a common school education. But I don't care to argue about that; Garrett Randall is welcome to all the education he can get, which won't be much. He is at least ten years behind time in book knowledge, and a hundred years behind in the sort that is not found in books; what I meant to say was that it is an annoyance to me, personally, to have him choose this town to experiment in."

"But, Richard, I cannot imagine why it should be."

"That is because you are not acquainted with the fellow. He doesn't know his place. I have the misfortune to have lived for a few years, you remember, in the same town where, I presume, he was born and bred. For this reason, although we never met in society, and our surroundings and interests were as different as though we had lived in different worlds, he chooses to consider himself acquainted with me. He never fails to salute me in much the same way that he exhibited just now. However, I ought not to complain, when you have to receive a nod from the same source, without so much as a touch of the fellow's hat."

Doris laughed again, but not cheerfully; Richard's manner jarred on her.

"I have noticed that he is not what we call cultured," she said. "But really, Richard, do you think that ought to have so much consideration? I don't mind his friendly nods; I know he does not mean disrespect, and that he will learn all such important trifles in time. I suppose he feels drawn toward you because you are from the same locality as himself; the poor fellow is probably lonesome and homesick a good deal of the time. As for his brains, I think it will be discovered that he has some. Mr. Harvard, who has him in Latin, says he is working hard and making a fairly respectable showing."

Richard made a movement, indicating impatience.

"All right," he said, "he may be a second Cicero, if he pleases; I shall not hinder him. Nevertheless, it is decidedly disagreeable to have him assuming intimacy with me. He is not of my world, and there isn't the slightest probability that he ever will be. But, as I said, I don't care to discuss him. I stopped to tell you that we are to go to Hadley's tonight, at eight o'clock, to run over some of the music for the cantata. Hadley wants a few of us to come in and look at the more difficult parts, so as to be ready to lead the crowd. I told him he might count on us, I thought; I'll call for you a few minutes after eight."

Doris's expressive face suggested trouble.

"I don't think I can go tonight, Richard."

"Why not? There isn't another vacant evening this week, and the general rehearsal will be on Monday."

"I know, but this isn't a vacant evening. I told Mr. Holmes I would try to be out, and play the organ for him, if Horace Wells didn't appear, as he probably won't."

"Doris! The idea! You to play that wheezy organ, when it would be better for all concerned if it were never played. I think Mr. Holmes is asking a great deal of you. He must have dozens of girls in his congregation capable of grinding out those Gospel Hymns. Why doesn't he call on one of them?"

Doris laughed again. "Isn't logic one of your strong points, Richard? That is precisely what Mr. Holmes has done. I happen to be one of the dozen girls in his congregation that he considers capable."

"But you are comparatively a newcomer; there are scores of girls who have grown up with the old organ and are used to its horrors. Don't be absurd, Doris, and unaccommodating. You know how much your voice is depended on to lead. Hadley will be hurt and vexed if you fail him, and with good reason. He is giving a great deal of time to this affair, and the least we can do is to stand by him."

"We are all giving too much time to it." Doris was grave again. "I am sorry I promised to help get it up; I ought to have realized how it would interfere with regular work. I have been thinking about it more or less ever since I heard Dr. Bannister's talk yesterday. One sentence of his seemed to be for me: 'In apportioning our time, it makes all the difference in the world just what we count as of first importance.' He was looking directly at me when he said that, as though he thought it fitted my need."

"That is a very original and thrilling sentence!" Richard said in fine sarcasm, "I don't wonder that it impressed you. Dr. Bannister, my dear friend, is a fanatic, and everyone who has seen or heard much of him knows it. I hope our young man, Holmes, is not trying to live up to any such ideal."

"Richard, do you know how almost sure you are to brand as fanatics people who do not happen to agree with your views?"

"I presume I do," the young man said, complacently. "The truth is, I am extremely liberal; I pride myself on it; I intend to grow in that direction, if possible, and to avoid all narrowing lines of thought. Such being the case, it follows naturally that people who do not agree with me in broad thinking are narrow and fanatical. Isn't that logical? I shall call for you tonight at eight, or a trifle after; I depend on you not to disappoint me. Get Athalie to thump the old organ; she is always ready to sacrifice herself to relieve you."

Doris did not disappoint him. It half vexed her to think that she gave up her deliberate plans at his call; but Athalie was on his side.

"It would be absurd to inconvenience all those singers and annoy Mr. Hadley simply because you have promised to play that wretched organ," she said, "especially when I stand ready to take your place. Never mind if Mr. Holmes would rather hear you play than anyone else; so would I, for that matter; but he will have to tolerate me, and learn that you have other engagements, sometimes, besides those connected with the church." Athalie had no thought of sarcasm, but her sister smiled faintly over that last sentence. What portion of her time did she give to the church? Still, even her mother said gently that they must think of other people's convenience and be accommodating, and if there really was not any evening but this for the special rehearsal, why then— So Doris, who had begun the week with certain well-defined resolutions, allowed herself to be persuaded, saying nothing, not even to her mother, about having resolved, without regard to the organ, to be more regular in her attendance at the mid-week meeting. She was ready for Richard at the appointed hour, in the mood in which persons of her make-up find themselves when they realize that they have weakened along a line which had been deliberately marked out as the right one.

Richard did not find her company as agreeable as usual. During the walk home he told her frankly that he had never heard her sing so poorly as she had that evening; that part of the time her voice sounded as though she had no interest whatever in the music. She confessed that she had not much interest in it. Some of the songs she thought exceedingly silly, to say the least, even offensive to good taste, at times. Richard answered her loftily that sensible people were not expected to pay much attention to the words; it was the music that counted, and that was classic, every note of it. But Doris was obstinate.

"I don't care if it is," she said with spirit. "Some of the music I don't like, and the words are the silliest I ever heard set to music. I wasn't interested in any of it tonight. The plain truth is, Richard, that I ought not to have been there. I don't mind telling you that last Sunday I made a resolution to be a great deal more careful about Thursday evening engagements than I have been of late, and yet I let the first trifle that came in sight turn me aside. I presume it was that which put me in ill humor. One doesn't like to discover that one is a mere bit of thistle-down to be blown away by a passing breeze. There was no necessity for it; Mr. Hadley could have arranged this extra rehearsal for Friday evening as well as Thursday, if he had known that it would have made the slightest difference to any of us; he told me so. To be sure, he knows that most of us who have leading parts are church members, and that every church in town has its mid-week meeting set for Thursday; but we have taught him to think that we are just as willing to make engagements for that hour as for any other. He looked astonished tonight when I mentioned the meeting; that is as much as we have impressed our religious opinions upon him after a year's effort."

Then Richard Shipley took this fanatical girl in hand.

"Now, my dear Doris, you must let me speak a plain word to you. I am really glad to have the opportunity. Of course, I was talking nonsense this morning, in part; but in all seriousness I am afraid that you are inclined to grow narrow. Take this matter of the mid-week meeting, for instance. What reasonable person could expect that you and I, college students, with innumerable duties and engagements connected with college life pressing upon us, could be at all regular in our attendance there? The thing is utterly unreasonable, and no minister, even, but a fanatic like Dr. Bannister, would think of it for a moment. Why, Holmes himself is trammeled by that mid-week meeting. There are functions occurring continually in a town like this, that he would enjoy immensely, and that are sure to conflict with it."

"Why does he let it trammel him?" asked Doris, quickly. "If it is absurd and unreasonable to expect you and me to take notice of that mid-week engagement, why shouldn't Mr. Holmes ignore it whenever he chooses?"

"That is one of the misfortunes of his profession," said Richard, lightly. "The superstitions of a past and outgrown age are woven about him." Then, more seriously: "Of course, Doris, you do not need to be told that I am in sympathy with all church functions within reasonable bounds. I expect to attend the prayer meeting, for instance, whenever it does not interfere with my regular duties, nor with the recreation that I believe my system needs; but I distinctly decline to be bound by it, or to have any other person than myself lay down the law to me about it."

Whenever Richard became dignified and superior, Doris found herself inclined to laugh. It was an amused tone in which she answered him:

"Who has been laying down law to you, Richard? No one has said a word to me about prayer meeting, except that Mr. Holmes asked if he might call upon me to play when he was left in the lurch. It is myself that I find troublesome. I find that I still have some sense of the binding nature of obligations, even when self-assumed; and there are times when I find it difficult to keep a firm throttle on my conscience. I will confess that when you talk about needing recreation, I am disposed to smile. We both know that overwork isn't one of your temptations. As for the prayer meeting, I don't believe you realize that nine times out of ten you are absent. I realize it because I am not much more regular than that myself. But I am not trying to bind you, nor even to argue with you. I find my own responsibilities quite as much as I can manage."

The sentence, begun lightly, ended with seriousness. It was very trying to Doris to have to admit that Richard disappointed her.

"And he expecting to be a minister!" When she said this she was glad that she was alone and in the dark.

Chapter 5

"Ministering among yourselves as good stewards."

Mrs. Farrand's six o'clock dinner was waiting to be served. It was a very simple dinner as to its courses, and would be unpretentious in the serving; but the dining-room was so dainty in its appointments, and so cheery and homelike in its atmosphere, as to present an excellent picture of American home life. It was Tuesday, an evening on which they were rarely alone. Doris was the one who had first spoken of the privilege of hospitality.

"There is one thing, mother," she had said, "that I hope we can do this winter. We have no home friends to be running in and out and sharing our pleasant times with us, but ought we not to share them, occasionally? Can't we make little pieces of home sometimes for home-sick girls and boys, who must have days when they would give up all their college ambitions for a glimpse of their mother and a baked potato eaten at a home table? I was away from home, remember, for five whole months, and I know how it feels. Couldn't we be on the lookout, all of us, for people to whom we could lend a hand in this way? I don't mean having company, and a fuss, but just asking a person home with us whom we chance to meet, to share what we happen to have."

"And if we didn't chance to have baked potatoes enough to go round, and but three spoonfuls of pudding, I could do without the potato and you without the pudding as well as not, and give them to the guest," said Athalie, gaily. "But wouldn't he or she be a trifle discomfited if this little arrangement should chance to be noticed?"

Doris had joined her mother in laughing at this, but had immediately grown thoughtful; and while Athalie, thus launched upon one of her favorite themes, expressed herself freely as to the inconvenience of limited means and the impossibility, under such conditions, of being always ready for company, the younger girl considered her plan, and at the earliest opportunity presented it.

"Mother, how would it do to have a certain day in the week set apart, when it should be seen to that there were more than Athalie's three potatoes, and an extra spoonful or two of pudding, and have it understood that if, on that day, one or more of us should bring home a guest, no embarrassment would result?"

It was in this way that the "Tuesdays at Home" were evolved in the Farrand household. Doris's plan had met with instant approval, although Athalie had been merry over her including them all in it. "I presume mother will be constantly bringing home guests," she said, "and as for me, I shall never go out without finding half a dozen; there will not be room for yours." Doris had joined in the fun, and then continued her planning:

"It wouldn't cost a great deal to have company in that way, would it? I think it might be made pleasant and helpful to some who are far away from their homes; and perhaps to some who have no pleasant homes to remember."

"Richard, for instance," Athalie had said. "I am never able to understand how he can think his home a pleasant one with a woman like Mrs. Shipley at its head. Don't look horror-stricken, Doris, I don't mean anything dreadful; she is well enough in her way, but as a mother I should consider her an utter failure. That may be, however, because Richard effaces her so completely."

And then Doris had looked reproachful, and had replied in the half-injured tone in which she sometimes resented criticisms of Richard:

"I am sure, Athalie, Richard is very good to his mother."

"Oh, yes, and so am I good to the cat, and give her almost as much consideration as he does his mother. But I'm not blaming him, child; it is his way, and he doesn't mean anything by it, I suppose, nor imagine how it impresses others: He will come in for his share of dinners, without doubt."

"He comes now whenever he chooses," Doris said. "I wasn't thinking of him; he isn't one of the homesick kind. Perhaps there aren't any; but I think there must be; in fact, I am almost certain of two or three. I should like to have Garrett Randall come occasionally, just to give him something decent to eat, if for no other reason. He boards at that yellow house down by the ferry; a horrid-looking place, and I have heard that even of the kind of food they serve there isn't enough to satisfy an ordinary appetite. To be sure, they can't do much, at the price they ask; it is the cheapest place in town. I suppose that is why Mr. Randall goes there. Richard says they are very poor; his mother is taking in washing this winter, to help along. Wouldn't it be pleasant, mother, to have him here once in a while and give him a good dinner?"

Then Athalie had said, "I thought Richard did not like Garrett Randall?" And Doris had flushed, and answered with just a touch of coldness that she did not know why her sister should think so; Richard had said nothing against him. It was true he thought that a young man as poor as Mr. Randall should not try for a college education, but of course he knew that the young man himself was the best judge of that. She believed he thought, too, that this was not, for some reasons, the very best place for such young men; but he had certainly found no fault with Garrett Randall's character.

By that time Athalie, being sorry that she had spoken, made haste to soothe the feelings she had ruffled, and entered, with the mother, most heartily into the new scheme. Mrs. Farrand had been especially warm in her approval of it, and had said to Athalie, after

Doris went away, that it was exactly like her father's way of doing things. The tender smile on her face, as she spoke, emphasized her comfort in having a child of hers exactly like her father in anything.

From the first, the special evenings were a great success. Richard, being duly made acquainted with the plan, had heartily approved; and although he had been in the habit of inviting himself to dinner whenever he chose, and sharing the limited amount of pudding most cheerfully, he was nevertheless particular thereafter to come oftener on Tuesday than at any other time. Among the first to be invited had been Garrett Randall. From their first meeting, Doris had been interested in him because of the rugged directness with which he grappled the peculiar problems confronting him, and overcame obstacles which would have hindered many. Later, when she came to understand Richard Shipley's feeling toward the young man, she shrank from the plans she had half formed to help him, and then took herself to task with the severe statement that Richard would be ashamed of her if he knew that a chance expression of his could move her from a course that she believed right and helpful. It had been this thought which had made her mention Garrett Randall to her mother and sister in connection with her hospitable plans, so committing herself to his interests. It had been the chief reason why he had stood first on her list of guests. She had been careful not to include Richard in the same invitation. Richard had been with them at dinner the night before, and could come at any time; there was no reason why he should be compelled to a closer intimacy with Garrett Randall than his tastes suggested. Of course, they were very unlike in every way, and men, she presumed, felt those differences even more than women did.

Now another Tuesday evening had come, and Richard Shipley had invited himself to dinner, notwithstanding the fact that he had been there the Tuesday before, and once between. He had appeared at the side door with a genial good evening, and a frank confession that he was hungry for one of Mrs. Farrand's home evenings, and had not dared to mention the matter to Doris, lest she should forbid his coming so soon again. Doris had not yet come in; she had warned them that she must be rather late that evening.

"But I did not suppose she meant as late as this," Mrs. Farrand said, with an anxious glance out of the window. The anxiety was partly for Doris, as it was growing dark, and partly for certain dishes that were getting over-done. Just then Doris appeared at the gate, and Garrett Randall was with her. Richard's face at sight of him gathered in a frown. He tried at once to cover from Athalie's observing eyes that he was not happy in the prospect of another guest, but it was clear that his affection for Garrett Randall had not increased with the passing weeks.

The young man came in like a north wind, which was Athalie's favorite simile for him, loud-voiced and hearty.

"Halloo, Shipley," he said. "You're in luck, too, are you? It's great luck, I tell you, when a fellow gets asked here to dinner; but you can't appreciate it as you could if you boarded around."

Athalie laughed appreciatively. She told Doris afterward that to have a chance to watch Garrett Randall and Richard try to get on together, was as good as going to a play. Richard was dignity personified. He ignored the newcomer's greeting, and hastened to make some general remark about the weather, which, however, Randall appropriated as to himself, and made cheerful reply.

"It's doing its best outside to make any kind of a home attractive, that's a fact. This is the night for what the boys call a wet rain. It reaches the skin without any trouble, and there's a snarly little wind blowing that helps the general wetness to strike into your bones. But all that only makes a room like this the greater paradise for a fellow to drop into. I'm awfully glad to be here, Mrs. Farrand, and I appreciate it as the other fellow can't."

"You have an original and delicate way of estimating friendship, I see." Richard spoke in what Athalie called his acid tone. She made haste to cover the sarcasm.

"Are you boarding around, Mr. Randall? I thought that was a luxury sacred to the country school ma'ams of past ages."

"Oh, mine isn't their kind, Miss Farrand. I know about them; my mother used to teach school. They got so much pay, and board thrown in. There's no throwing in about my board, I tell you; it has to be paid for every week, and there's the rub, as Shakespeare said, or some of those old fellows. I guess it was Shakespeare; queer how he said things that fit in now, all the time. Did you ever notice it, Shipley?"

"Where do you board?" asked Athalie, hastily.

"That's the question—where do I? I try the Arcade restaurant for a week, and then I go to Peterson's or Greerdon's. This week it's Greerdon's, and it's six of one and half a dozen of the others. Whichever place I try, I'm half sorry before the first meal is over that I didn't go to some of the others."

His loud, genial laugh closed the sentence, but he added immediately: "That's mostly talk, you know. They aren't half bad, any of 'em. I can praise them all to the skies, on occasion. You should have seen the letter I wrote to mother last night. I had just come from dinner, and I made her think that the St. James in Buffalo, where she used to stop occasionally when she was a girl, was nowhere, in comparison with my surroundings. I wonder why St. James had so many more hotels named for him than any other saint? One doesn't hear of people stopping at St. Peter's, for instance, or St. John's; but St. James seems to figure in all the cities. Did you ever think of it?"

There was fun in his tone, but there was also interest. It was clear that his only historic association with such names, at least that came to him quickly, dated back to the first century. Richard laughed in reply, but Doris did not like the quality of the laugh, and made haste to introduce a new topic of conversation.

Despite Richard's dignity, it was a merry company. In truth, the dignity was reserved for the other guest. With the family Richard was genial, as usual, and led the conversation, as he generally did. "It is a blessing," Athalie said, "that Richard talks well; he talks so much that it would be dreadful if he had nothing to say."

The menu was excellent, affording abundant opportunity for young Randall's too outspoken praise; he ate with the relish, it might almost be said with the eagerness, of one whose appetite was not often satisfied. It must also be confessed that his table manners were not of the best: he ate his plate of bisque with a swooping sound accompanying each spoonful, and to Mrs. Farrand's suggestion that he try another plate, replied heartily that he could swallow another plateful of stuff like that without half trying. He took the chicken joint without ceremony into his large, strong fingers, and manipulated it with zest. Occasionally he even forgot what was evidently a newly acquired piece of knowledge, and conveyed his knife to his mouth loaded with food. In short, Garrett Randall distinguished himself that evening as a person who had had almost no opportunity to mingle with people of ordinary culture, or else as one more than ordinarily obtuse. Doris was painfully alive to all his breaches of etiquette. On the two other occasions when he had dined with the family, they had not been so glaringly apparent. The girl told herself that it was because they had not served soup, and certain other dishes that afforded opportunity for carelessness, and not at all because Richard the fastidious was there to observe, with a peculiarly trying smile on his handsome face.

Richard had spent his home life in what he called poverty, but he had been at all times in an atmosphere where good manners were the rule. A knowledge of the little proprieties of the table and parlor had been absorbed by him so early in life that he had forgotten the process of learning. Moreover, Richard loved culture, and made more of the proprieties than many do who are equally accustomed to them. To him it was torture to be associated with ungainliness in any form. Garrett Randall's onslaught at the peas, which he carried to his mouth with the spoon laid at his plate for the dessert, instead of using his fork, was a positive trial to Richard, while Athalie was simply amused.

When the dessert was set on the table, young Randall's show of ill-breeding reached its climax. He exclaimed over the dish as pretty enough to be used on the parlor table as an ornament, and actually smacked his lips in anticipation of its toothsomeness. Yet with the first mouthful, which was so large as to compel observation, he colored to the roots of his curly hair, and unceremoniously pushed his plate from him.

The habit of propriety kept the puzzled hostess from commenting, and made Athalie talk eagerly to Richard about the series of rare concerts that were soon to be given; though she said afterward that she wanted to ask their guest if a mistake had been made and his pudding been served hot, instead of ice cold. For a moment young Randall was evidently intensely embarrassed. He made no further effort with the ruby-colored mound before him, but managed to drink his tiny cup of coffee in one great mouthful, then glanced at the clock, and uttered an exclamation which brought Doris to his aid.

"Mother, I promised Mr. Randall that you would excuse him at seven, even though we were not through dinner; he has an important engagement." She went with him to the parlor to get a book she had promised him, and thence to the hall, where he made his eager explanation.

Chapter 6

"A man shall be commended according to his wisdom."

"I'm awfully sorry about that pudding; I don't know when I have been so cut up. I hope your mother won't think I didn't like it. I wish you would tell her about it; I didn't know whether I ought to, just then, or not. It was awfully good, but I can't touch that kind of thing, you know."

Doris smiled on him reassuringly, but was puzzled.

"I don't know in the least," she said. "Of course, you are not to eat puddings unless you choose, and it isn't of the least consequence, only I am curious. If you liked it, why mustn't you eat it? Do you mind telling me?"

"It was the wine," he said gravely. "I never dreamed of there being any in it, not at your house, you know, until I took that first mouthful. I wouldn't have taken it for a ten-dollar gold piece, poor as I am, if I had guessed; I give you my word for it."

Doris's face must still have expressed bewilderment, for he went on eagerly:

"You see, I have given my word. I promised my mother as sober a promise as I ever expect to make in my life; and besides, if you know anything about me, you know I have awfully good reasons for letting the stuff alone, without any promise."

Doris went back, presently, to the dining room, where the others were still lingering over coffee and nuts. Her face was flushed, and her mother noted that her eyes were troubled.

"Doris," said Athalie, "have you discovered what was the

matter with the pudding? Until I tasted it, I was in distress lest I had used salt for sugar."

"Yes," said Doris, "I discovered. Mother, ought we to have anything on our table that could possibly cause anybody to go wrong?"

"Dear child," said the startled mother, "of course not. What can you mean?"

And then Athalie exclaimed, "Oh, Doris; it was the wine sauce!"

"Yes," said Doris, gravely, "it was. His father was a drunkard. I did not know that; he has promised his mother that he would never touch a drop of liquor in any form. I would not have had him break his pledge in our house for anything in the world. Mother, he said he never thought about there being any danger here, because he knew we were minister's folks."

"Poor fellow!" said Mrs. Farrand. "I never thought of there being any objection to that pudding. It is an old-fashioned one that I don't often make; but when I do, I make wine sauce for it as a matter of course. Why, Doris, your father ate it, and he was very particular. We never served wine at our house, even when we lived in a community where it was somewhat the custom. But a few spoonfuls in a sauce seems very different. Still, we will banish it if there is any possible harm in it."

Richard had kept silence longer than was his habit; at this point he broke forth: "Dear Mrs. Farrand, in the interests of ordinary humanity let me beg that you will do no such thing. Your pudding was perfect; the absence of anything from it would be a mar. If I dare, I should like to suggest instead that fellows who have no knowledge of the first principles of propriety be banished from your table until they have taken a course in the common decencies of life. I want to ask you frankly if you ever before saw so uncouth a fellow. His manner of eating soup must have been learned from the pigs at the trough; and he hasn't even learned what to do with his knife! I did not dare to look in your direction, Athalie, while the shoveling process was going on, lest I should laugh outright."

Athalie did not join in the laugh which closed this sentence, and Richard made haste to add, looking at Mrs. Farrand:

"I trust you are not really troubled about the wine sauce. The idea of a few drops of wine in a pudding being harmful to any person is nonsense, of course; that is the crude notion of an illiterate country youth who doesn't understand even the first principles of common propriety."

"He understands morals, it seems, if he doesn't table etiquette, and knows how to keep a promise even when the doing so involves embarrassment." It was Athalie who made this almost caustic rejoinder, moved to opposition by Richard's dogmatic manner. His assumption of the office of general adviser often irritated her; she was conscious of something in her nature which antagonized his, although she liked him and looked upon him as her probable future brother-in-law.

"But even in that case," she had said to her mother only the day before, "it will be Doris that he will marry, and not you and me. Why need he think he must order *our* affairs for us?"

Richard laughed in response to her comment. "Oh, yes," he said, "I've no doubt that he is great on pledges, and a model in many respects; but it is an infinite pity that he couldn't have some lessons in decency before he has to be tolerated in refined homes."

That Richard had been tried that evening was evidenced by the persistent way in which he returned to the topic, ignoring all efforts at pleasanter themes. At last Doris was moved to the defense.

"You are hard on him, Richard," she said. "He is ignorant, but not coarse; there is not a suggestion about him of what I call coarseness. What he lacks is in the line of outside trifles easily acquired; he shows that he has not had opportunity as yet to acquire them."

"Not even to discover that gentlemen do not address their young lady acquaintances by their first names," said Richard, with almost a sneer on his handsome face. Doris's face flushed. She had noticed the slip of Garrett Randall's tongue over her name and had expected to hear of it.

"Even that," she said coldly, "is pardonable. I remember that Mr. Randall has been brought up in a country neighborhood where the girls and boys are on just such familiar terms, and the habit of his life holds, that is all. I am certain that he meant no rudeness; I have been called 'Miss Farrand' by young men who had not an atom of real reverence for womanhood in their whole make-up, and I am sure that Garrett Randall has." Richard was stung by her words beyond the limit of endurance.

"Oh, if you like it," he said loftily, "of course there is no more to be said. I was not aware that your friendship had progressed thus far, and I was simply trying to protect your mother and Athalie from having to come in contact with boors on a basis of equality."

Immediately the flash in Doris's eyes recalled him to his senses, and his tone changed to a light and careless one.

"Don't let us quarrel before people, Doris; we do enough of that in private. Mrs. Farrand, you have no idea what a close rein she keeps on me, and what new and startling ideas I have daily to cringe before. She is becoming a young woman with hobbies, and is out of sorts with me half the time because I cannot keep pace with her, although I am blundering along after her in my masculine fashion. Here's Randall, for instance, at whom I have been poking fun, just in the way of reaction. Of course I know there isn't a worthier fellow in the world, and I am all the time trying to smooth the way for him. You may be sure I am able to vouch for his real worth, or I should not have let Doris come in contact with him at all."

Mrs. Farrand was gracious and met this concession halfway, encouraging Richard to continue.

"In spite of my wicked words, I even admire your self-sacrificing kindness in admitting the boy to your table occasionally. I know his home surroundings, and can imagine what it must be to him. Even a second-course dinner is new ground to him, and when it comes to a third and fourth, I don't wonder that he lost himself entirely over the pudding."

"What kind of a mother has he, Richard?" asked Athalie.

"Why, a very worthy woman, who works hard at whatever she can get to keep the wolf from the door. I, who have old-fashioned ideas in some directions, should admire Garrett a great deal more if he were to go to work and support his mother, instead of struggling for an education that he will never especially adorn. I have frankly told him so, with as good a result as one could expect in such a case. He is bent on learning by experience the folly of his course; so I shall lend a helping hand, as I have opportunity, even though I can't hope to keep pace with Doris."

He meant what he said, and Doris knew that he did. She was already mentally excusing him for his disagreeableness, reminding herself that to one so accustomed to the refinements of life, and so sensitive to any lapses as Richard undoubtedly was, Garrett Randall could only act as an irritant. The girl knew instinctively how that familiar "Doris," on the lips of another, had jarred him. He could not realize that Garrett Randall had simply been copying him, unable to see why she should not be "Doris" to the one as well as the other. If Richard in his willingness to lend a helping hand could only see it to be his duty and privilege to give the poor fellow a friendly hint, now and then, about just such small matters, what might he not accomplish? It was something of the sort which she had suggested to him, and to which he referred when he called her a young woman with hobbies. The suggestion had been put down as a task that was impossible for him, and also utterly useless. A fellow who could not take on the small proprieties of life of his own accord, simply by using his own eyes and ears, could never make passable use of them after they were patched on by someone else.

It was reflection over expressions of this sort which had caused Doris to think of Garrett Randall in connection with those Tuesday dinners. If Richard was right, and the young man had only to use his eyes and ears in order to acquire a certain kind of culture, why, then, it stood to reason that he ought to be given opportunity to use them such opportunity as cheap boarding-houses did not afford.

Her first attempt at hospitality with young Randall had convinced her not only of his need of just such help as she could give, but of the exceeding disagreeableness of bringing Garrett Randall and Richard the fastidious to the same table, at least for the present. She thought she had planned skillfully to avoid this. Her scheme on two occasions had worked well, but the third invitation had not been arranged for beforehand.

On her way home, late and in haste, trying to manage her strap of books and an umbrella in the "snarly little wind" which was blowing, Garrett Randall had overtaken her with brisk step and the quick instincts of the true gentleman.

"Let me have the umbrella; I'm caught out without one, as usual. Give me the books, too; they are awfully heavy. Why do you carry around such a lot of them?"

Then Doris had remembered swiftly that it was Tuesday evening, and there were no guests at home, and that Richard was in town and would not be out until the late train, and had pressed her invitation to dinner. But Richard had changed his plans since morning, and was the first person she saw when she entered the dining-room.

The result of the encounter had been so disagreeable to Doris that she could not at once get back to her natural manner. The "quarrel" which Richard had professed to fear at the dinner table was continued after they left the dining room, and were alone. At least the talk which had led to it was continued. Doris was at first unusually quiet and constrained; and Richard, after trying vainly to bridge over the space between them, plunged headlong into trouble by accusing her of giving more heed to that country boor than she did to him, her lifelong friend. A lively discussion followed, during which some plain truths were spoken. Richard announced that he thought young women ought to keep their philanthropic schemes for the benefit of their own sex entirely. When men were concerned, they should be careful not to permit themselves to descend from their own social spheres. Leave such efforts, when they must be made at all, to the men. Stung by his words, Doris answered sharply that she thought it silly in an American citizen to be talking about "spheres" and "place." In this country a man's place was where he placed himself. As for leaving the work of helping others to the men, if they were all like him, of what use would it be to wait? She even challenged him to tell what "helping hand" he had ever held out to Garrett Randall. Whereupon he told her promptly of several kindly acts of which she had never before heard. This mollified her greatly, and made room for the thought which was already crowding upon her that she was being unjust to Richard, and did not always understand him. He made good use of this rift in her dignity, and they parted on the usual terms of comradeship.

But Doris thought long after she was alone. The subject of her thought was: how much heed ought she to give to Richard's evident aversion to her helping, in any simple, wholesome ways that she could, young men who stood in need of friends? It seemed to her that her work for others lay much in that direction. Girls, she did not understand very well, did not get on with beyond a certain point. But boys had always seemed to her to have about them elements of comradeship. Richard himself was a case in point. There had been many girls in her circle of acquaintances when she chose him for her friend.

It was clear, too, that this particular boy, Garrett Randall, was especially obnoxious to Richard, while Doris confessed herself specially drawn to him. There was something wholesomely frank and sincere in his nature, and his ideas of life were based on true principles. In some respects he was superior to the young men who laughed at his awkwardness, and made merry over his slips in etiquette.

With this thought came the memory of the first conversation she had ever held with Garrett Randall; it had been that which had contributed to her unrest. She had noticed him standing alone near the college entrance. He was gazing apparently at the clouds, and there was about him an air of irresoluteness and loneliness. Throngs of well-dressed young men and women, most of them in groups of two or three, and gaily chatting, were passing him constantly, without even a nod. He was very new to all this life. Doris wondered if he felt the newness oppressive. She had hesitated, and finally turned back to speak to him.

Chapter 7

"Choose the things that please me."

She had asked the most commonplace of questions: "Is it going to rain, do you think, Mr. Randall? I noticed you were studying the clouds."

He had looked at her like one dazed for a moment, and then laughed.

"Are there clouds?" he asked. "I didn't notice them, though I guess I was gazing right up at them. Fact is, I was having a debating society."

"Oh, are you on the debate?" Doris had asked, surprised.

"No," he said quickly, "this is a debate of my own; I've got the affirmative and negative both on my hands, and the worst of it is I have got to be the judge, after the thing is argued."

Then Doris had laughed, and been interested. He felt her quick appreciation; the lonesome fellow was hungry for friendly talk, and without urging had stated his problem.

"Why, you see it is this way. I've had a streak of luck, and streaks of luck always did play the mischief with me, somehow. A fellow can plod along the old way, you know, without anything to bother him; it has all been settled, and he has just to tackle it and go ahead; but let a lucky streak in on him, and along with it come a thousand questions, standing around waiting to be answered. I've had a present of a ticket to Dr. Henderson's Friday night lectures; they're exactly on the subject that I'm tugging with, and it's a pretty tough tug, too. I haven't had the drill that most of the boys have, to make it easy. There would be no end of help to be got from the lectures, but they come on Friday nights, and there we are."

Doris had not been able to follow his argument, and had questioned.

"Why, I've given Friday evenings to that night school down on Water Street. You know about it, don't you? It has been going for five or six years, but teachers are scarce, and I've got a lot of boys down there, trying to do something for them. Now you see the question, don't you, and the mix that the argument is in? Affirmative says: 'Take the lectures, you need them.' Negative says, 'Take Water Street, it needs you.' For that matter, I need it; maybe I need it worse than I do the lectures; I don't know."

Doris's interest had grown.

"In what sense can you need Water Street, Mr. Randall?" she had asked. His merry eyes, which seemed usually to have a laugh in them, had grown grave, and he had hesitated as though the question had not been expected.

"Well, let me see if I know how to explain. Water Street helps to keep me plumb, I guess. Keeps my vocation straight. I guess I was in danger of mixing my vocation and my avocation." The gray eyes were merry again. "I'm airing my knowledge now," he said, in response to Doris's bewildered look. "We had a talk in class this morning about words; I found I was awfully mixed as to the meanings of some of them. You'll think I'm a dunce, and you'll think about right—I am; but I didn't know there was any difference in the meaning of those two words, 'vocation' and 'avocation.' If I had been going to use them at all, I should have taken the one I happened to think of first, and believed myself all right. I haven't got over my astonishment yet at finding how different they are. But you see what I'm getting at in my argument, don't you?"

"Only in part," Doris had replied. "How do either of them apply to the Water Street problem?"

"Well, it's this way." He was grave again. "My vocation, I take it, is to serve God; that's what I have set out to do. 'With all your heart, and soul, and mind,' my directions are; and the other things are secondary, when it comes to a question between them. Even the education that I am bound to get, is an *avocation,* according to the dictionary, and not a vocation. I think I've been mixing them up, and I've kind of slanted over to one side; but I want to keep plumb, and Water Street has a way of helping me."

Someone had called Doris at that moment, and she had gone away without hearing the verdict; but that word "vocation," seen in the light of Garrett Randall's words, had stayed with her and contributed to her unrest.

She recalled the talk, phrase by phrase, and remembered that she had met Garrett Randall on the Friday evening before, evidently on his way to Water Street; the judge must have given his decision against the lectures. The thought, for some reason which she did not stop to define, made her the more anxious to help him. But Richard was opposed to it. How far ought she to be governed by his ideas? Richard was absurd. Why couldn't he understand that she was merely carrying out his own suggestions and giving the young man a chance to use his eyes and ears?

She left the question of her next effort unsettled, however, and circumstances settled it for her in a way that had not occurred to her.

Again it was a chance encounter that led to results. Garrett Randall overtook her within a square or two of her own home. He commented again on the weight of the books she carried, and told her she ought to use a wheel-barrow, or employ him. The chances were that he might be coming in her direction every day.

"I'm on my way now to plan for just that," he said gaily. "I'm going down to the Simpson place; they live on that street just back of your house, you know. Do you know those folks? I don't suppose you do, I guess they aren't your kind. They are in search of help, though, and I may perhaps get in."

"What sort of help do they need, Mr. Randall?" Doris asked, perplexed.

"Oh, any sort they can get, I guess. It's housework, you see, and such help is scarce; but I'm up on that kind of thing. I've helped mother ever since I was big enough to trot around after her. I believe I could run a boarding-house, if I had a chance; and if I couldn't run it better than that one where I used to get my dinners, I'd go drown myself for very shame."

"Was that at Wheeler's?" asked Doris, laughing. "I thought you were there still. Where do you board now?"

"That's a question my appetite has been asking me for a good while," he said, joining in her laugh.

"I left the Wheelers two weeks ago; since which time I have been 'ateing mesilf,' as an Irish chap in our neighborhood used to say. 'Will ye ate me?' he would ask, when he was talking about a job, 'or will I have to ate mesilf?' So it's mesilf that I've been 'ateing for two weeks, and mighty poor feed do I find it, so I'm going to try the Simpsons."

"But, Mr. Randall, I don't understand. Are you going to give up study?"

"Not if I know myself, and I think I do. It hasn't come to that yet, by a good deal. It may have to be done; but I should awfully hate to, on mother's account, leaving myself out of the question entirely. I've got a tip-top mother, Doris. There isn't anything she isn't ready to do, or do without, for the sake of giving me a lift. When my courage gets away down to my boots, I have to remember that I mustn't go back on her, even if I could on myself. You see what I mean, don't you?"

"I think so," said Doris, slowly. "But I don't know what you mean by looking for work."

"Why, I'm planning to work for my board, you know. Don't you know that's done in this town a good deal? I know two or three boys who are working their way through, and some of them say it does first-rate. One fellow told me that it meant a good deal of work and very little eating; but I thought I'd try it. It couldn't be worse than—well, than some other things I know of."

Doris thought swiftly. She recalled the eagerness with which this young man had swallowed his food at her mother's table—an eagerness that Richard had called disgusting. Perhaps here was one of his temptations; he was a gourmand who could not be satisfied without the hearty food and many dishes that he had been used to in the country. His mother was, by his own showing, one of those who sacrificed herself to her son; she might have spent her life ministering to his appetite. Could she not use this chance to give him a hint of the very secondary place that eating ought to hold in the mind of one who meant to be more than a mere animal?

"Wouldn't that be much more disagreeable than boarding yourself?" she made haste to say. "You said you knew how to cook some things; why don't you resolve to be content with just those plain dishes that you know how to prepare, and make less of the mere matter of eating?"

She had more to say, but stopped abruptly because her audience was laughing immoderately, even uproariously for the street.

"You must excuse me," he said at last, a dim sense of discourtesy dawning upon him. "I'm not laughing at you, you know, but just at my own fancies. I saw myself setting out to make less of this matter of eating, and walking about, after a while, a fellow in bones, without any flesh on them; it seemed to me I could see the figure I'd cut, and see the folks stare, and it was too much for my silly head. I always did laugh too easy. The fact is, you see, I've reduced that thing to its lowest terms already; there isn't the ghost of a chance for anything but a ghost doing better than I have in that line. It isn't the cooking of things that troubles me, it is the getting them to cook, or to eat raw, for that matter."

"Is it really so bad as that?" Doris's voice expressed more than sympathy, there was a note of dismay. The young man detected it, and was at once on his guard.

"Oh, it is nothing very dreadful; I've been hungry before, and I dare say I shall be again, a good many times. I don't know what made me tell all this to you; I don't go around parading my housekeeping trials, I don't honestly. But somehow you have a way of making a fellow tell you what he would tell his sister, I guess, if he had one. I never had anybody but mother, and you know there are lots of things that a fellow can't tell his mother, because they'd worry her. Still, he needn't be a gump and talk about them at all. I don't mean to. I'm as chirk as can be, and don't you go to wasting sympathy on me.

"Oh, no, I'm not going to your house to dinner, not I! I wasn't fishing for a dinner"—this with a genial laugh. "I'm going down to Simpsons' to hire out. If they know when they are well off, they will hire me at once; I'm the best sweeper and dish-washer in the country, my mother says so. Good night. I'm awfully sorry I gave you the notion that I am having a tough time; I live in clover the year round; and if I didn't, I could afford to live on dried corn-stalks for the sake of the chances I'm having here."

He would not be persuaded, though Doris urged the hospitality of her home upon him and went into the house with a cloud on her face because of him. She could not get away from the feeling that the young fellow was a sort of protégée of hers, for whose well-being she was somehow responsible. The very freedom with which he used her given name—a freedom that moved Richard's indignation as often as he heard it—showed her in what light Garrett Randall viewed her. To him she was a comrade, who was, as a matter of course, interested in a friendly way in all that concerned a fellow-student. He would need to learn that Richard's use of the familiar name, "Doris," dated back to their childhood, and stood for a degree of intimacy attained by the very few; but this was only one of the many little things that he would learn in time; and while it meant nothing but ignorance and confidence in her friendship, it was not possible for her to resent it, as Richard thought she should. Instead, it increased the feeling that she ought to be of use to him.

It was an unusually quiet dinner table. Doris, occupied with her puzzling thoughts, had little or nothing to say about the events of the day; and her mother and sister, who depended much upon her for their outside interests, had fallen into the habit of awaiting her moods. It was plain to them that she was troubled, as in truth she was. In imagination she was following young Randall on his errand to the Simpson household, an errand that she did not like. The Simpsons were what Athalie called "around the corner people"; they kept what Doris believed was a second, perhaps even a third, rate boarding-house; and the young people of the family were loud-voiced on the street, and common in all their ways. How was Garrett Randall to learn in such a place any of the lessons which, according to Richard, must come through his eyes and ears?

Suddenly there appeared before her a plan so simple and reasonable that the wonder was she had not thought of it before. Just as Athalie, tried by her silence, was asking if she had brought nothing but her body home with her, she brought forth her thought, or at least made ready the way for it to be presented.

"Mother, with all our plannings to make less work for you, I wonder we have not thought of student help. There are always students here who are looking for places where they can work for their board. Why wouldn't that be a good way for us to help ourselves and other people at the same time?"

"Perhaps it would," said Mrs. Farrand, with the quick interest which she always showed in any scheme of her children. She made haste, however, to add that while it might be a good way to help the students, she should suppose that the work done by those whose minds were absorbed with their studies would be of doubtful value both in quantity and quality.

"Still," said Athalie, "it must give fair satisfaction, or people wouldn't employ them as much as they do; the world isn't given over to pure benevolence. Mother, don't you know that Mrs. Howell, who called yesterday, was telling how many steps her student help saved her? If we could find a real nice girl among the students, I should like to try it. What suggested it to you, Doris? Have you anyone in mind? "

"Yes," said Doris, firmly; "I have Mr. Randall in mind. He is out tonight looking for a place where he can work for his board."

"A boy!" said Mrs. Farrand in dismay. "My dear child, what have we that a boy or a young man could do?"

"Hosts of things," said Athalie, promptly. "Furnace, kindlings, kitchen fires, porches, sidewalks! Dear me, mother, I could keep him busy sixteen hours out of the twenty-four. How many hours do they give, Doris? But is the poor fellow really reduced to such straits? I wonder what Richard would say to your plan. Still, I don't know but he would approve. He would heartily, if the young man could be persuaded to give up his ambitions, and turn servant outright. Richard is a born aristocrat; I don't know how he is going to manage in the ministry, with such ideas as he is nursing now."

Doris ignored her sister, and gave attention entirely to her mother.

Chapter 8

"He that followeth after righteousness and kindness, findeth life,
righteousness, and honor."

"Don't you think he could make himself useful, mother? Enough
so to pay for his board? I am really afraid he is going hungry. He
has been boarding himself, it seems, and, according to his account,
he has reached the Mother Hubbard stage. He made merry over it,
though, and was troubled lest I should think he was complaining.
He has gone around to the Simpsons' in search of work."

Athalie uttered an exclamation.

"The poor fellow will be in need of pity, if he gets there," she
said. "I never in my life saw a noisier or worse acting set than they
have in that house. I closed the back window this morning to get
away from the sound of their tongues. Doris, I hope you advised
against his going there. It isn't the place for a young man like him,
for more reasons than one."

"I didn't offer advice," said Doris; "I wasn't asked for any. But
I think Mr. Randall would rather work for mother, if she will let
him. He says he can sweep, and wash dishes, and do all kinds of
housework. He has helped his mother with her work ever since he
was big enough to walk. I tried to have him come in to dinner, so
you could talk things over with him afterward, if you chose. But he
was so much afraid I would think he had been what he calls
'fishing for a dinner,' that he wouldn't come. There wasn't the
least hint of that about him; but I am sure he is very hard pressed; I
wish we could help him."

"Poor fellow!" said Mrs. Farrand, with a far-away look in her eyes. "It is dreary work—this boarding one's self; your father did it for two years."

"Father!" exclaimed both girls in incredulous tones.

"Yes, for nearly two years, while he was in the theological seminary. He used to write me some very funny letters, giving his experiences in cooking. I must go over those letters and let you read bits from them. They will give you a hint of what some young men were willing to do for the sake of getting ready for the ministry. I have thought that there were no such young men in these days. Not that your father was ever abjectly poor, as some of his classmates were. The seminary was only twenty miles away from his father's farm, and his mother saw to it that doughnuts and mince pies, and all sorts of dainties, as well as good bread and butter, traveled over the road to him pretty regularly. But money was scarce, and he saved a good deal by boarding himself. He used to share his goodies with boys who, he said, were hard put to it to live. Your father used to grow quite indignant over it, years afterward, and say it was a shame for the church to allow such sacrifices as some of them made. But I don't know; it helped to make men of them, perhaps. Very few of them were of the cringing kind. Still, living in that way has its serious drawbacks. I remember your father used to say that he almost dreaded to come and see me during that time; it seemed to him that he had forgotten how to act at a civilized table."

"One cannot imagine father as ever being anything but a very model of propriety," said Athalie.

"No," said her mother, quickly. "Your father's fears were quite unfounded; but it is different with this young Randall; he hasn't had early advantages."

"And he will take on uncouthness at the Simpsons'," said Athalie, "instead of having some of it rubbed off. I hope they have no place for him; there is a new, slatternly-looking girl banging

60

around there today. I vote for this new idea of Doris's, mother, notwithstanding the two lines of frowns there will be on Richard's forehead when he hears of it. Rich doesn't have to plan our household matters for us, does he, Doris?"

"I did not know that he wanted to," said Doris, trying to have her smile come free. Athalie could not know how it tried her sister to be unable to count upon Richard as a helpful factor in any kindly plans for others, especially for the students. It is true she had settled it once more, for the twentieth time, that Richard was not to blame for his lack of interest. One could hardly have grown up with a mother like his without growing unconsciously selfish. She was sure that continual association with people of less narrowed interests, and a growing knowledge of the world's needs, would give him in time that touch of helpful friendliness for those outside his immediate circle that he now lacked. Meantime, she must be resolute to do her part, even to overdo it, almost, to make up for his lack.

She made it her first business the next morning to have a few words with Garrett Randall. He had failed at the Simpsons"; was too late by twenty-four hours, and wouldn't have stood any chance, anyway, he told Doris, with a merry laugh. Mrs. Simpson had been frankness itself, and had told him that "goodness knew she didn't want a *boy* anyway. The house was full now of fellows who couldn't earn the salt for their potatoes."

He was in no wise depressed by his failure, nor swerved from his purpose. He had with him a list of names, and assured Doris that he should start out presently and stop at every house until he found the right one.

"The 'right one' isn't on that list," said Doris, joining in his genial laugh. "Put my mother's name at the head of it, Mr. Randall, and call on her this morning, if you have time. If you and she can agree as to hours, etc., I don't think you will need the other names."

"What!" said Garrett Randall, his eyes alight with pleasure. "You don't mean it! Your mother? Well, now! 'I'm bound for glory,' as old Pomp sings all the while he is sweeping our class room. But I didn't expect to reach paradise this term. If there is anything in this world that can be done for your mother, I'm the fellow who wants to try to do it."

Doris went away smiling. As the young man had in his own, odd way expressed his gratitude for little kindnesses that her mother had shown him, all his soul was in his face, and he looked every inch a gentleman.

The advent of Garrett Randall into the Farrand household was productive of certain perplexities which necessitated family conferences. Mrs. Farrand opened one by thinking her thoughts aloud: "I don't know how to plan for this kind of help. I wonder if he is supposed to sit with us at table."

Doris, who had brought her books to the sitting room in search of sunshine, looked up from them with a startled air, and Athalie laughed, to the infinite peril of the pins in her mouth. She was laying a hem for Doris, and making use of her mouth as a pincushion.

"Dear me!" she said, laying down the pins, "we don't want to pose before a table waiter, just we three, especially when the waiter has been a guest at our table. And it would seem equally absurd to have him sitting around in the kitchen, waiting for us to finish; there would be nothing he could do at that time but wait."

"It would be quite unnecessary, of course," said Mrs. Farrand; "but then, when we have company, won't it be awkward?"

"Richard, for instance," said Athalie. "Fancy Richard sitting at table, on terms of equality with a person who presently rises to remove the plates and bring in a second course. I think I see his face the first time he discovers it. It was almost as much as Rich could manage to have a daughter of the house so demean herself;

if it had been Doris, I don't think he could have borne it."

Doris's eyes had gone back to her books, and she was to all appearances giving them her thoughts.

"There are embarrassments connected with it, whichever way one turns, I am afraid." Mrs. Farrand sighed as she spoke. She wanted to be helpful to others, poor lady, but she wanted the way made plain and easy for her. Embarrassments she hated.

Athalie did not like to hear her mother sigh. "Never mind," she said soothingly, "there are points to be adjusted, of course; but there are very delightful features about it, I am sure. Think of me, for instance, seated at my sewing, instead of wrestling with that cook stove, as I should have been at this moment. There will be a better fire, too, than I should have had. It was taken hold of with the air of a master. Doris, perhaps the young fellow should be helped to a position as fireman on the railroad. I wonder if Rich is right, and he should be discouraged in his effort for a college education. I don't believe it. I believe the boy will succeed. What do you say to mother's problem?"

"If we are to be of help to him in the little refinements of family life," began Doris, slowly, "I don't see how much will be accomplished if—" She hesitated, searching for just the words she wanted, and Athalie came to her aid.

"If he stays in the kitchen and continues to swoop up his soup with accompaniments, and use the same spoon for apple sauce and beans, for instance? I don't, either. Why not give him the advantages of our table 'with all the benefits that flow therefrom'?" The quotation from the catechism, which had been the bane of Athalie's childhood, was made with a mischievous glance at her mother. Then she continued:

"But I tell you, Doris, Richard is in the way of this helpful plan of yours. I don't believe any of the other students you bring to our table would have the least objection to meeting on a social equality one who was helping to earn his way by serving it; and, of course, Mr. Holmes wouldn't; but Richard is different. You wouldn't like to make our table an unpleasant place for him, would you?"

"You take Richard too seriously, Athalie," said her sister. "His surface talk about a great many things does not show what he really feels. I don't think he will furnish any obstacle to mother's doing as she pleases." And then Doris gathered up her books and departed to her recitation. Athalie had replied to her only by lifted eyebrows; but as the door closed after her, she said:

"That means, Mother, that Mr. Richard Shipley, if he has any more dinners here, will have to take them in company with Garrett Randall. My little sister has asserted herself. I like to see her do it; if she had had the bringing up of Richard, without any interference from his mother, she would have made a man of him."

Said Mrs. Farrand, "I don't see that either of you have made the way very plain for me." But it came to pass that Garrett Randall was the one who made the way plain.

"Suppose we have a fair and square understanding about this thing," he said, the first time he was invited, and, finally, earnestly pressed to sit with them at table. "I'm not blind and deaf, although about some things you might have supposed I was. The first time I was here to dinner I saw there was a lot of things that I needed to learn; I mean things that I never supposed had to be learned: I thought they came of themselves, but I guess they don't. Lots of forks, I mean, and spoons—which is t'other, and when the which comes, you know," and he laughed genially. "That was one thing which made me strike for housework, instead of a stable or a garden. I thought I'd look on, and learn—at the Simpsons', you know," with a merry glance for Athalie, who was enjoying every word.

"But I meant to do the looking on while I was waiting on table. I didn't expect to sit down, with the folks. I knew that the boys who were doing this sort of thing didn't. But you are different

64

from most folks; I knew that the first time I set eyes on you; and if you mean it, honor bright, as I know you do, why I'll tell you what I should like. When there are just you three, I should like awfully well to sit down with you and eat; and I'd make a big effort to keep somewhere within sight of the proper way of doing it. But when you have company, then, says I, I walk out and turn into a first-class waiter. I watched Miss Farrand the three nights that I was here to dinner, and I believe I could do it shipshape, after a while. Yes, I should like that way a great deal better than the other; I should, honestly. I'm not an out-and-out gump, Mrs. Farrand, and I know you are doing the unusual thing by me all the time, anyhow; I just want to make it so that you won't have reason to be sorry for it, if I can, and I guess I can."

He had his way; and as the days passed, and he grew more accustomed to his work, it became increasingly apparent that his ways, in general, were for the comfort of the family.

The first time that Mrs. Farrand watched the young man through the perils of dish-washing, she dropped afterward into a chair in the dining room with a sigh of relief, and said to Athalie:

"He really knows how; his mother taught him, he says, and he goes about it all in the nicest way. I am so glad; I don't believe I *could* have taught a man how to do it."

He knew how to do other things, many of them. He was quick-motioned, and neat, and the personification of good humor. Moreover, he had a keen sense of gratitude for what he was pleased to consider very special kindnesses shown him by this family, and was always on the alert to discover ways of saving Mrs. Farrand's strength. This, added to his innate sense of respect—not to say reverence—for all womankind, made him an especially valuable and enjoyable helper.

Perhaps no one looked with more satisfied eyes upon the new arrangement than did Richard Shipley. To sit at table with Garrett

Randall, and watch him rest his elbows on it as he ate, was one thing, and to have him at his elbow, swift and skillful in supplying his wants, was quite another. A white-aproned table waiter, and a man waiter at that, were steps upward socially in Richard's eyes, and his approval was hearty.

"Your scheme works remarkably well, Mrs. Farrand," he said cordially. "I have not been in favor, heretofore, of student service, but I am not sure but you will convert me to it. Randall certainly serves very well indeed; it looks as though he had reached his level; and it gives the poor fellow a chance to have plenty to eat, which I understand was not the case before he came here."

The satisfaction that it was to him to see Garrett Randall standing respectfully behind Doris's chair, waiting to serve her, instead of sitting opposite to her as a guest, Richard said nothing about; but Athalie, the observant, understood it perfectly, and smiled mischievously over what he would say or feel on discovering that when the family were alone, Garrett's place was opposite Doris.

Chapter 9

"The law of kindness is on her tongue."

In one respect Richard Shipley proved himself correct in judgment. The most that young Randall needed was a chance to use his eyes and ears. The speed with which he assimilated quietness and refinement of speech and manner with regard to all table observances was a daily source of satisfaction to those who were trying to aid him,

But it was Athalie who proved to be his most efficient helper. Instead of Doris, it was she who gave him hints in directions where he seemed most to need. It came about quite naturally: had she been asked to render him such service, she would probably have shrunk back and declared that she never could, she was not fitted for it. It simply happened that her household duties brought her to the work room while Randall was there, and the habit of chatting together grew upon them, and came to be almost equally interesting to both. Then Athalie was by nature outspoken, and she had a nature to deal with that understood outspokenness, so they got on well together. His education in trifles went on somewhat after this fashion: "Ain't it pretty near time there was a fire made up for that bread, Miss Farrand?"

"Not quite. Did you study grammar, or language, or whatever they called it, in the school where you prepared for college?"

"We did that!" with great animation. "Your humble servant on those occasions arose to the height of his genius: stood at the head of his class, and carried off the gold medal prize for having all the rules in the book at his tongue's end. Hurrah for Randall the champion!" and he flourished a baking spoon over his head.

"Then will you have the goodness to tell me in what conjugation of the verb 'to be' you find that word 'ain't,' of which you are so fond?"

The spoon was dropped, and the young man looked at his questioner and laughed.

"It's like lots of other rules, Miss Farrand; I know them, but I don't apply them—not in everyday life. I keep them for what old Aunt Betsey used to call 'company manners.' I don't write my favorite 'ain't'; or, yes, I do, to mother—force of habit, you see. I was brought up in a neighborhood where everybody used such words, and I do it with the rest, without thinking anything about it."

"I understand; but why do you allow yourself to do so? Isn't the application to everyday life of the things we have learned what makes at least the surface difference between the uncultured and those whom we call cultured? And ought not a young man who is making sacrifices, and accepting his mother's sacrifices for the sake of getting an education, to apply what he learns as fast as he conveniently can?"

"That's as true as preaching," said Randall, after a moment's silence. "In fact, it is preaching, isn't it?" with one of his merry smiles. "And the application is plain, which cannot be said of all sermons. Thank you, Miss Farrand. Honestly, I never thought about such words; that is, I never studied out the difference between my talk and—Doris's, for instance. Though of course I knew they were miles apart; I don't mean now that I've found out the whole difference between us, only one out of the million, you know."

He had taken her sermon so well that Athalie determined on another effort.

"I understand. Since I have turned preacher, may I venture a sermon on calling your young women acquaintances by their first names? Is that, also, one of the rules you have learned and not applied?"

"No," he said frankly; but a flush of red was spreading all over his brown face. "Do you mean that it is rude in me to say 'Doris'? I'm awfully sorry. It is the last thing I ever meant to be. I wouldn't be rude to any lady, certainly not to *her!* And I'll own that I don't understand you. I say 'Miss Farrand' to you; but she—well, we are schoolmates, in a sense, and she has been kind and friendly to me, and I thought—Why, I have heard others do it. Shipley brings her name in with every other word."

"My sister and Mr. Shipley were children together, Mr. Randall, and have been intimate friends all their lives. If you notice, you will see that he is the only one who takes such liberties, though most of the other young men you meet here are her college friends. But it isn't a serious matter. No harm has been done, nor will be, if you continue to call her 'Doris' as long as you live. It is simply one of those little things about which we were talking, that help to indicate culture. I shouldn't have mentioned such a trifle to most young men, especially in connection with my sister, who is not disturbed by it; but I judged you to be sincere in what you said when you first came to us, and offered it as one of my little hints."

She had not made a mistake. Young Randall was rubbing the carving-knife with an energy that its condition did not call for, and his face was grave; but he presently gave her one of his heartiest smiles, as he said:

"I shall not get mad at a friend for trying to help me, you may be sure of that. There's a lot of things that I know I need to learn, and I think I'm man enough to be thankful for the chance. I hope you understand that I'd chop off my hand with this carving-knife sooner than I would be disrespectful to any woman; I think too much of my mother for that. But I'm just what Shipley calls me, 'a back-country booby.' The more I see of you folks, the more sure I am that Shipley has put it about right. But I'm sure of another thing, too; that is, if I know myself, and I think I do, I'll—well, I'm not good at explanations; but if you can stand me around here for a while, I guess I can show you what I mean."

The knives were finished by that time, and he had rinsed and dried his hands. Athalie turned to him with an answering smile, and held out her hand.

"Then it is a compact, is it? You and I are comrades. I will give you what little hints I can about trifles that have escaped your notice, and you shall give me lessons in true nobility of character. I think it quite probable that I should have been angry if anyone had talked to me as plainly as I have to you."

From that time Garrett Randall became an especially interesting study to Athalie. "My pupil," she called him, when speaking to her mother, and daily boasted of her pride in his improvement. He was certainly an apt scholar; not once again, after her hint, did she hear that obnoxious word "ain't" from his lips; and the very distinct manner in which he said "Miss Farrand" when speaking to Doris brought satisfaction to the eyes of his mentor.

Nor was Athalie's first venture by any means her last. She had been moved to speak frankly about her sister's name, chiefly to save the young man himself from possible discomfiture, because Richard had more than once hinted that the "fellow ought to be taught his place"; having done that, she felt that she might safely advance any other help that Garrett Randall needed.

"Say, Miss Farrand," he began one morning with great eagerness, "I believe the thing to do with that stove is to let me—" but Athalie interrupted him.

"What is it I am to say, Mr. Randall? I think that is the fourth remark of yours since I came out this morning which has begun with 'say'. Isn't it time for you to tell me what is to be said?"

He laughed, and reddened.

"That's another of my fool words," he said. "I noticed it myself last night, if you'll believe it. About everything I said to your sister began either with 'say' or 'well,' and neither word had a thing to do with the sentence. I resolved then to break myself of it. But it is like pulling teeth to get rid of a bad habit."

Athalie was tempted to remind him that his simile, like many that he used, was more striking than elegant, but she checked herself. "One dose at a time is enough, perhaps," she reflected, then laughed softly at her own expense. How much better was her mental simile than Randall's spoken one? After all, there were more important slips to correct than his vivid word illustrations.

It came to pass that there were really two sides to the compact between Athalie and Garrett Randall. He came to the sitting room one evening with an armful of wood, and after adjusting a gnarled little stump in exactly the right manner to cause delight to lovers of open grate fires, lingered a moment to admire the bright-colored wools spread out on Athalie's lap. There was such a singular look, meanwhile, of something very like wistfulness on his face that it caught and puzzled Athalie. Could this boy's mother at any time in her hard life have worked at bright-colored wools, and made them hold forever a wistful memory for him?

"Is this work that you burn to do?" she asked, holding up her long bright strip, and making gay reference to a recent talk she had had with him.

"I can't say that I hanker after it for myself," he answered, smiling; "I was thinking of our girls."

"Our girls!" Athalie mentally repeated the phrase after him with dismay in her thoughts, while she gave him a swift, searching glance. He had no sisters, and no cousins who were almost sisters—was he getting entangled already in some foolish friendship, so far advanced that the words "our girls" came naturally to his lips?

"I did not know that 'we' had any girls," she said dryly.

He laughed again. "We have," he said, "lots of 'em. I wish you knew some of them, Miss Farrand; they are starved, a great many of them, in more senses than one. The girl I was thinking of just now has raveled out an old gray stocking and is trying to make a mat of some sort from it for her mother's Christmas; but she can't shape the thing very well. She wants a bit of red, too, for a border, but is afraid that it will be beyond her. I was wondering what she would think of all those colors on your lap. You don't know much about that kind of poverty, do you, Miss Farrand?"

"What girls are you talking about?"

"Why, the scholars down at the Friday night school, you know. They are very poor, all of them, and work hard all day for just bare necessities. I didn't know anything about such people until I came here, although I thought I knew all about being poor. But a raveled-out gray stocking is more than the most of these girls can manage, for pleasure. But they like pretty things just as well as though they were used to them, and they are always trying to make things. This girl asked me the other night if I couldn't crochet, and wanted to know what a college was worth if it couldn't teach people how to do something pretty."

"Poor child!" said Athalie. "Take a seat, Mr. Randall, and tell me more about that school. Why don't they have a class in crocheting and fancy knitting, and teach the girls how to make pretty things? Wools of the common sort are not very expensive, and it would be a good way to get the scholars interested in learning things of more importance."

"It is teachers that are expensive," said Garrett Randall, with the first touch of bitterness that Athalie had ever heard in his voice. "They can't get teachers, Miss Farrand. Not enough to teach reading and arithmetic and things of that kind, to say nothing of knitting. People haven't time for it, women haven't. I never knew before that the young women in cities were so busy. Our superintendent told me that he spent two whole days last week going from house to house, where possible helpers lived, and being refused. We have to count the pennies very carefully down there; but we could get the tools to work with a great deal easier than we can the teachers—we can't buy them, you see."

"Sit down," said Athalie, peremptorily, "and begin at the beginning and tell me all about it. What are they trying to do? Who is it that is doing? What kind of help do they need?"

"All kinds," he said, his face kindling, and he launched forth on what had become to him an absorbing theme. He had not sacrificed the lecture tickets and his Friday evenings for nothing. Heart and energy were absorbed in the work he had undertaken. Athalie listened with flattering attention.

"You tell the story well," she said, when he reached a period. "Why doesn't the superintendent send you out to canvass for helpers? Or why don't you do a little on your own account? For instance, you might ask me, one would suppose, to go down there occasionally and show some of your girls how to knit. I never posed as a teacher, but I presume I might teach that; and I'm sure I could supply the red wools for the border."

She laughed at the light which flashed into his face. "Would you, Miss Farrand?" he asked. "Would you *really?*" His voice trembled with eagerness. How thoroughly he had espoused the cause of the strugglers!

In this way began a new outlook for Athalie Farrand. None of her friends realized it—there was a sense in which she did not realize it herself—that her life was in some respects disappointing. She had been always sacrificing in small ways for others. So small, some of them, and others of them so obscure that they were not recognized as sacrifices. In young girlhood it had been Doris who had gone on little outings with the mother, because it was rarely convenient for both girls to go, and Doris was the younger, and not very strong; and it was generally Athalie who first spoke of it as settled that Doris was to go, as a matter of course. In school, Athalie had been a fair scholar, but Doris was a brilliant one. When, after the father's death, circumstances made it necessary that one of the girls should leave school for a time to be with the mother, it was the older daughter who made the sacrifice. This seemed reasonable from all points of view.

It would be a pity, the friends said, to interrupt Doris, who was by far the best scholar in her class, and of course Athalie, being older, could be more helpful to her mother.

When the two finally graduated from high school, Doris, nearly four years the younger, had become her sister's classmate.

Athalie would have enjoyed continuing her studies; but Doris had a consuming passion for study, and her friends all felt as though she must go on. A higher education for both was so far out of the question that it was not even mentioned, and again it was Athalie who pushed with resolute will and cheerful courage the plans for her sister's advancement. It is true that by that time Doris was old enough to realize the situation and make vigorous protest in her sister's favor, but she was one against many, and was accustomed to defer, not only to her mother, but to Athalie. What it cost the older sister to carry out her will was kept so utterly to herself that it was not even suspected.

She was, and continued to be, glad in her sacrifice. Yet, as the months passed, the sense of there being a dividing line between Doris's world and hers grew upon her. She coined a word with which to express, quite to herself, the state of things.

"There is a kind of left-out-ness in my life, and it will grow upon me. Doris and Richard have college plans and college friends, and when they graduate it will be college interests still; while I—oh, well—never mind. I will be it nice, wholesome old maid, and sit in their coziest chimney corner, and patch for them while they read Latin together, and write books and sermons."

Chapter 10

"Seest thou a man wise in his own conceit?"

The Friday evening school was good for Athalie, although it was true, as she had told Garrett Randall, that she had never "posed as a teacher." She had dropped out of Sunday-school of necessity for a time after her father's death, and afterwards no one had thought to enlist her as a Bible teacher.

Yet it appeared that she could teach. Not crocheting, nor needlework alone—though she was skilful with her needle—but other, and in one sense more important, things as well. Before the winter was over, there was in active operation a large class which had been christened by the somewhat pretentious name of "English Club."

"There is nothing like being well named," said Athalie, laughing. "We are learning to write business letters, and friendly social letters, and letters requiring tact and sound judgment and a general sense of propriety; we are even learning to write polite society notes of invitation and acceptance and regret. Why not? Who can tell, in this splendid country of ours, just what my boys and girls will need to use, later in life? We are trying to write excellent English, and we give the most careful attention to spelling and punctuation and all the matter-of-course proprieties."

"They are not all of them so 'matter-of-course' as one might think or wish," said Doris, pushing a note of invitation toward her sister with a significant smile.

"The writer of that note is a senior; isn't it a pity that she cannot join your English Club? Really, Athalie, I think you are doing a grand work; I can hardly keep from envying you the opportunity."

Others fully agreed with this estimate. The officers of the Mission looked on with keenest interest and pride at the sweep of this new movement. No division in all the busy school was more popular than Miss Farrand's; though the teacher was rigid in her requirements and almost stern as to discipline. Only those who were regular in attendance and conscientious in doing the work assigned were continued as members. In due time it became not only an honor, but a matter of social prestige, to be quoted as a member of the English Club.

Garrett Randall made merry over it in the family circle. He had now been long enough a resident of the city to understand some of its idiosyncrasies, and he wove them into his account of the English Club.

"You may live on the north side of Grand Avenue, Mrs. Farrand, instead of the south, and you may even live on the east side of the river instead of the west, and be countenanced as a respectable sort of creature, after all; but if you are not a member of the English Club, there is no hope for you."

Doris, looking on with eager interest, ready with her questions and suggestions, grew to be almost as familiar with the histories of the girls as was Athalie herself. The undisguised wistfulness of some of her words moved Athalie to sympathy, and Richard to laughter.

"I believe she actually envies you your Friday night sacrifice!" he said. "She longs to be in the thick of it and gather admiring hosts about her as you have evidently done, and be the center of all their eyes."

"She may well," said Athalie. "It is fascinating work. I had no idea that there were so many people in the world eager to be taught what I could teach them—people grateful for the merest scraps of whatever may help them toward that broader life of which you are always talking, Richard. I wonder that you do not want to embark in some work of the kind yourself. Wouldn't you like to help broaden other people, instead of keeping all the broadness for yourself?"

"I should like it very much indeed," said Doris, before Richard could reply. "I can't think of any work more delightful than to help give some of those starved lives a little brightness and beauty. That girl Athalie tells of, whose nerves fairly quiver at the sound of music and who longs for a chance just to touch the keys of a piano, appeals to me keenly. How I would like to teach her to play! Think of creating a new world for her! I have been trying all day to plan a way to give her just one hour a week. I could do it if she were free at the hours which I can command."

Richard lifted up his hands in horror. "Don't mention it, Doris! I have been afraid of something of the sort. Mrs. Farrand, I trust to your good judgment as a mother to put an emphatic veto on all such fanaticism. Doris is working beyond her strength now; and an hour in such an atmosphere as that would be simply suicide for her."

This brought Athalie to the front. "Richard, the idea! You show that you don't know what you are talking about. There is nothing objectionable at that end of the town, nothing but great factories that are deserted at night; and we have a very large room with plenty of windows. I don't want Dorrie to undertake any work there, much as I know she would enjoy it, because I don't think she has time to spare; but you mustn't slander our atmosphere."

"My dear friend," said Richard, in his most patronizing tone, "I was speaking of the aesthetic atmosphere, if you will allow the term. Doris is more susceptible to such influences than some are. I hope you don't misunderstand me. I am behind no one in giving all praise to those who are willing to sacrifice themselves to such work; but when it comes to enjoyment, why then I confess I must be counted out."

Doris, as usual, was tried by this conversation, or rather by the impression which she felt that Richard's words must have made on the others. She continued the subject when they were alone, beginning with some warmth.

"Richard, I cannot understand why you want to appear so out of sympathy with Christian work of any kind. I know you are not. Why should you care to lead people to think that you are aristocratic and cold-hearted?"

"My dear Doris!" said Richard, in his injured tone, "what have I done now? Either I am growing obtuse, or you are becoming supersensitive. Did I not express myself as having great admiration for those who sacrifice themselves?"

"You have done just what you seem lately to delight in doing. You shrugged your shoulders, and spoke with almost a sneer of those girls, quite as though they belonged to another world than ours."

"Oh, that is granted at once, so far as the other world is concerned. I certainly did not sneer, and if my shoulders said too much, they must bear the blame, not I. Be reasonable, Doris. I am sure I commended Athalie's work, as I have countless times. Nothing could be kinder or more helpful than what she is doing; I admire her for it with all my heart. But to *do* and to *enjoy,* you will surely grant, are different matters. I can conceive of a fellow like Randall going down to that night school and being able to teach them some things out of books, and having a thoroughly good time with them. He is not so very far removed from their world; but you and Athalie and, if you will allow me to include your humble servant, I myself, certainly belong to quite a different sphere. Ought I to be blamed for seeing what is so evident?"

Doris was not to be easily appeased.

"You and I have talked about 'spheres' before," she said. "I remember always that people who seem to be below me may entirely outstrip me in the end; and it is not worthwhile to plume myself upon any early advantages that I may have had, which they have missed."

The speaking shoulders were used again, as Richard confessed that, for himself, he preferred to wait until all such growing intellects reached somewhere near his own level. Then he attempted to turn to pleasanter themes, but Doris persisted.

"Seriously, Richard, I wish you would not be always seeming what you are not. Even mother and Athalie, well acquainted as they are with you, are often deceived by your talk. Athalie, especially, is beginning to credit you with views which I know you do not hold. I don't think you realize how careless you are growing. Why, for instance, need you have said what you did to Dr. Bannister the other day? He did not understand you. How could he, when he doesn't know your random way of talking? I think he went away believing that you take even the Bible in installments, and reject the parts which you don't happen to fancy."

"I don't remember in the least what I said in his august presence," said Richard, airily. "We were discussing theology, I believe, and I presume I tried to modify some of his statements and bring them to a level with the facts. If, in doing so, I infringed on some of the statements in the Bible, that would be so much the worse for the Bible, wouldn't it? Not for me."

"Richard, I cannot understand why you should talk in this way to me. I am not talking simply to amuse myself. Surely you and I ought to be able to say something besides nonsense to each other."

Richard laughed immoderately.

"I beg a thousand pardons," he said, when he could speak. "But how is a man to maintain his gravity in the face of such an absurd charge? Fancy anyone listening to us and imagining for a moment that we were talking nonsense! Haven't you been arraigning me in your most dignified manner for the last fifteen minutes? Finding fault with what I have and haven't said in cruel style. If I were not the most long-suffering and good-natured fellow in the world, I should get offended, because, positively, there is no pleasing you nowadays."

He spoke in a whimsical tone and evidently expected Doris to answer with a laugh. But she would not smile and would not be turned from her thought.

"Will you tell me what you mean?" she asked. "If you are not speaking nonsense, and yet are not speaking lightly of the Bible, I am sure that I do not understand you. There are often times when I do not understand how you can reconcile your words with your professions, on any other basis than that of frivolous talk."

He was growing restive under the pressure.

"That is because you are permitting others to crowd in between us," he said coldly. "Since you will insist upon my speaking according to the books, when I am bent simply on a little relaxation from the grind of the day, I will remind you that there is such a thing as modern scholarship which touches even the Bible, with its higher criticism, and that some of us young men have risen superior to certain old-fashioned notions. Why, your man Holmes said a great deal more than I did the other night. Why don't you attack him?"

"There is a sense in which it is not especially important to me, Richard, what Mr. Holmes does or does not think. It is difficult to think of him as one who has grown to manhood; at least he is very young in most of his talk. I knew that Dr. Bannister was more than equal to a dozen young men of his shallowness; but I confess that I did not like to see you posing as one of the dozen, and I gave you the credit of thinking that you were only talking at random, as you like to talk sometimes, without regard to sense, or to the impression you are making."

Richard's face flushed. Doris had touched a sore point. His

ardent ambition was to be considered not only broad, but deep; and "shallowness" was the worst word he could think of, as applied to himself.

"You are quite mistaken," he said with dignity. "I was saying what I thought, and so was Holmes. The truth is, Doris, that Dr. Bannister, with all his admirable qualities, is a back number. He hasn't kept himself in touch with modern thought, but is content, as he has been all his life, in delving among the musty tomes of a forgotten past. Why, Holmes has books in his small library that Dr. Bannister doesn't even know by name!"

And then Doris laughed outright. "It is of no use," she said. "You are determined to frivol tonight. It is foolish in me to try to get you to be sensible. With your mind in such state that you can, with apparent seriousness, compare Dr. Bannister and that poor little Mr. Holmes, the case is hopeless. One would suppose that you really did not know the position that Dr. Bannister holds in the church, and for that matter, in the world. Wasn't he quoted only last month, in the list of the great Hebrew scholars of this country? Isn't his library considered the finest one in the state? Are not his opinions sought after and quoted, and his scholarship deferred to by thinking men of all denominations? Could anything be more absurd than for a man in his senses to call such an one a 'back number'? I think there can be, and that you have attained to it when you try to compare him with poor little Mr. Holmes."

"It is a pity," said Richard, "that you are a member of Holmes's church, since you have so poor an opinion of him."

Doris turned from him coldly. "Yes," she said, "it is; it is one of my mistakes."

His words contained a thrust that was hard for her.

When the family had come to the city as strangers, and the choice of a church home had been under discussion, Richard had been eloquent in favor of the church on Grand Avenue, which he had attended more often than any other. It was the most aristocratic church in the city, he told them. In that society they would have opportunity to associate with the most exclusive social circle to be found.

"And to wear our one good dress apiece wherever we went until we were each known by it!" commented Athalie, when Richard had gone.

The decision had been delayed for weeks, and the discussions had been many. When choice was finally made of a small, and in every way unpretentious, church within three squares of their home, it was to Richard's intense dissatisfaction.

"It is almost a mission church," he told them. "And they have a wheezy abomination of a cabinet organ to lead such singing as they can muster. Now at Grand Avenue Doris would have a chance to hear classical music every Sunday, and that is what she needs."

But the Farrands were obstinate, each for a different reason. Mrs. Farrand thought of car-fare and pew-rent, and shook her head. Athalie looked at her last winter's coat and her furs that had done duty for years, and said:

"Let us go where we shall not be tempted to compare ourselves all the time with our surroundings, to the great discomfiture of ourselves."

As for Doris, she was in the midst of one of her spasms of unrest, and saw in the plain little church, even in the wheezy cabinet organ, a possible chance to quiet her mind by being of use. From her childhood it had been one of this girl's ambitions to do for others; her father had rejoiced in the trait, and had he lived, it would have been developed. Doris thought of him when she gave her vote very firmly in favor of the little church on an unimportant street.

When it was settled, even to the giving in of the church letters, and Richard, still grumbling, had joined them, compelled to do so, he said, because he couldn't very well go off and "flock by himself," then they learned two things which, had they known them before, would have made a difference.

Chapter 11

"Riches certainly make themselves wings."

Their first discovery in connection with the plain little church was that its pastor was posing as a martyr, in a small way. He had tastes and ambitions that the down-town church on a side street did not satisfy. He assured his special friends that he was only staying there in order to do some graduate work at the university; he could not be contented to settle down as a fixture in such a cramped atmosphere. He was modern and advanced and broad; he skimmed the highest of higher criticism, he dabbled in the new philosophy, he borrowed their phrases for his conversation, and quoted their vague utterances in his sermons, until most of the plain people of which his congregation was formed were in doubt as to what he was talking about; and a few, like Athalie Farrand, boldly asserted that he did not know himself.

In short, Mr. Holmes was a disappointment to the new family.

Richard, however, declared himself happily disappointed, and became forthwith Mr. Holmes's intimate friend and general admirer. He lent him books, and suggested quotations for his sermons, and upheld his views as belonging to "advanced thought." Doris, poor girl, believed in her secret heart that Mr. Holmes's influence was injurious to Richard.

Their other disappointment grew out of the discovery that Dr. Bannister's church was within walking distance of their home, and that Dr. Bannister was a delightful man, personally, and had known Dr. Farrand somewhat intimately. Why Richard had been silent with regard to the location and merits of this church, which was quite the wealthiest if not the most aristocratic one in town, was a bewilderment to Athalie; but Doris knew that Dr. Bannister had views which were not in accord with Richard's advanced ideas.

"We might have gone to Dr. Bannister's church," Mrs. Farrand said mournfully, one day, after he had walked the length of a square with her, and talked about her husband. "They do not sell pews in his church; he told me that the offerings were voluntary. It would be a great pleasure to hear a man preach every Sunday whom your father admired so much."

"Never mind, mother," Athalie said cheerfully. "The solemn question of being properly clothed is quite as important in that church as it is in Grand Avenue. It is true that in Dr. Bannister's church there are circles and *circles*. We could probably have sat somewhere and looked complacently on the grades below us, the back gallery grades, for instance; but, alas! The circles above us would have destroyed our comfort. Besides, what would Richard have done? He wants the Grand Avenue church, where there is but one circle, and he fancies he is in it. I tremble to think what that boy will do when he gets into the ministry and has to fellowship, perhaps, with his laundry woman!"

Words like these she was learning to avoid when Doris was present, but she could not help occasionally giving them to her mother.

Yet, despite their lack of hearty interest in the church of their choice, the winter seemed to pass more swiftly to the entire family than any winter of theirs had done in a long time. They were all so fully absorbed in their daily living, involving as it did new and pleasant interests, that there was little time for that heart-weariness which wears the deepest furrows, and is the outcome of either sorrow or loneliness.

Doris, who loved study merely for study's sake, had long been able to absorb herself in it, but Mrs. Farrand and Athalie had had their lonely hours.

Now, however, Athalie's English Club and the interests which grew out of it absorbed not only all her leisure time, but much of her mother's.

Athalie's skill with her needle came to be understood and much appreciated in the Club. By degrees, though always by special invitation—they were proud, those working girls, and never begged favors—one and another brought her hat to the pleasant sitting room on Willow Street to get advice about the trimming, or her coat to be told how to remodel the sleeves, or her dress to be shown how to set a bit of trimming so skillfully as to cover darn or stain. If they were proud, they were also grateful and discerning. They came to understand and fully appreciate the hearty interest which Athalie had in them as individuals, and learned to meet her advances halfway.

The habit of running in on any evening to ask a question upon some matter vital to them grew upon half a dozen of the more winsome, and in this way Mrs. Farrand made their acquaintance, and gradually began to add not only advice, but the skill of her swift-moving fingers, to the wondering delight of the girls.

Nor was it questions of dress alone that interested them and that they gradually brought, at first only to Athalie, then, after a time, a few very personal and troublesome ones, to the mother. There were those among them who had never in their lives been mothered, and they did not know how to approach the older woman, but there were a few who hungered after mother interest and solicitude.

Mrs. Farrand had believed that she could never again enter with hearty interest into the affairs of young people, as she used to do in the days when she was the wife of a beloved pastor. It was a matter of tender surprise to her that the interest roused again, and that she had not forgotten how to help the girls.

Not girls alone. There were boys in the English Club, and while they did not have important questions of sewing and trimming and general refurbishing to interest them and open the way for other intimacies, still they came to understand that the little house where the English Club woman lived was a veritable Bureau of Information for anything that they needed to know. Not only that, but it was growing to be a refuge for people with burdens or anxieties.

Along with the English Club boys came from time to time two or three of Garrett Randall's boys, who were not supposed to be sufficiently advanced for "higher English." At first they came shyly, to ask a question *too* important to be held over until Friday evening, but they gained in courage and opened the way for others.

It was Doris who thought of giving Garrett the use of the dining room whenever one of his boys wanted to see him alone. Athalie seized upon the suggestion and developed it, aided and abetted by her mother, until at last Garrett Randall announced in his characteristic way that he had an "Evening at Home" of his very own, with the best mother and sister to help him entertain that could be found in the United States.

"I tell my mother all about it," he said, watching Mrs. Farrand get out the plates that five boys were to use for their taffy. "I describe all the jolly Monday evenings, and the games and the music, and how you 'mother' all the boys, so that they tell even their state secrets to you. She enters into the whole thing and enjoys it with all her heart. She knows the boys by name, and sends them messages. Mother would be a royal helper in such work if she only had a chance and knew how. She hasn't had any chances, has had to grind away at work, all her life, you may say— all my life, anyhow."

There was always a tender wistfulness in his tones when he talked of his mother. Athalie had come to the kitchen in time to hear his last sentence, and replied to the wistfulness:

"Your mother seems to have known how to help one boy in a great many wise ways; I presume she could do it for other boys, if opportunity offered."

He flashed one of his grateful glances at her out of singularly expressive eyes, as he said:

"Thank you, Miss Farrand. I don't want you to think for a minute that I'm going back on my mother. She suits me better than any other mother could in all the world. And you're right, too, about what she could do. She has done things for other boys now and then, when the chance came. There are one or two who will have good reason to remember her all their lives. I should like to have you people in this house know my mother; but I don't know anything less probable than that you ever will."

"Don't waste your breath on probabilities," said Athalie, gaily. "Remember we live in a world in which the improbable is happening all the time. Think of mother and me running a dressmaking, millinery, yes, and tailoring establishment in connection with an English Club!"

Richard Shipley looked on at the doings in sewing and dining room with pleasant interest. He commended Athalie's work heartily, and found no fault with her frequent descents into lower spheres. He told Doris that he thought it was probably an excellent thing both for Athalie and her mother that they had interested themselves in work of this sort. Since they were neither of them deeply interested either in study or society, it broadened their lives to reach out into the world even in this way.

Doris laughed at the bringing in of his favorite word, and said that, whether or not it "broadened" her mother and Athalie's life, it certainly had a very broadening effect on some of those whom they were reaching, and was fascinating work.

No argument resulted, because Richard was really not deeply

interested in those "lower spheres" in any way, so long as they did not touch Doris. He was well pleased to note that Doris was giving herself so completely to study that she had no time to do other than admire what was going on in her own home.

Her recreations were, almost of necessity, so entirely within college circles and under Richard's sway that she was gradually and unconsciously withdrawing herself from family life and home interests.

It is true she was often telling herself that next week or next month, when she would have more time, she would help the home plans a little in ways that suggested themselves to her. She did not realize, as the weeks flew by, that the "more time" to which she had looked forward did not appear, and that every minute was absorbed in her own interests.

Nothing could have satisfied Richard Shipley better. The indications of narrowness which he had observed in Doris had almost entirely disappeared. His influence over her seemed to be supreme, which in his judgment was as it should be. The thought helped him to be on pleasant terms with all the world. He was even complacent toward Garrett Randall. That young man, who was growing skilful in measuring degrees of friendliness, took care not to cross his path any more in offensive ways; and Richard, who meant to be friendly and helpful whenever to be so crossed neither his pleasures nor his prejudices, grew tolerant even of the effort to secure a higher education. He commended Garrett Randall's improved appearance, and several times reported to Athalie that her protégé was doing fairly well in his classes. "Garrett is my protégé entirely. Do you know that, mother?" Athalie said, with mischief in her eyes. "Richard likes him better so; he would have tolerated Garrett with a reasonable degree of equanimity all the while, if Doris had hated him a little. Isn't it fun to watch a man make himself miserable over nothing?"

Said Mrs. Farrand: "I don't see but Richard is right so far as your work is concerned; it is undoubtedly you who are helping Garrett. Doris is too busy in these days to think of him or other people." And then the mother sighed a little.

The ten o'clock postman was the one for whom the Farrands always watched. Athalie said that there seemed to be very little need for the other four deliveries of the day, the first one always brought the important things. She was parceling out the mail as she spoke. "You have the most formidable-looking document," she told her mother, "but I suppose it is nothing but a dividend letter." Then she absorbed herself in her letter. Neither she nor Doris noticed the effect which the "dividend letter" had upon their mother. There proved to be no dividend enclosed; the business letter was brief, so brief that Mrs. Farrand had time to read it slowly three times and take in its full meaning, then drop it suddenly as though it hurt her, and sit looking into space, before Doris interrupted.

"Mother, I have a long letter from Ethel Wynne; she thinks she can come for commencement week, after all. Won't that be delightful? Now if Estelle could only come at the same time, my joy would be complete. I wonder if—Why, mother dear! What is the matter? Did you have unpleasant news? What has happened?"

She came swiftly toward her as she spoke, and Athalie, looking up quickly at Doris's words, dropped her papers and came also. "What is it, mother? You haven't bad news from Aunt Mary, surely!"

"No," said Mrs. Farrand, trying to speak in her natural tone. "It is nothing so bad as that. It is only money matters, children; and when we have one another, and all our dear ones are well and happy, we ought not to be greatly disturbed about anything, ought we? I did not mean to frighten you. The news took me by surprise, that is all."

"But what is it?" asked Athalie, who was always the impatient one. Doris stooped and kissed her mother, and took a slightly wrinkled, trembling hand in her own firm, cool one. Mrs. Farrand tried to smile her thanks, as she said:

"It is the man who had our five thousand dollars; he has failed."

"Not Mr. Ramsey!" exclaimed both girls at once.

"Yes, Mr. Ramsey; your father thought he was as good as the government. It is something connected with the bank, too. I don't understand the details, yet, but Mr. Aiken thinks the money is hopelessly gone; that part is plain enough."

"But, mother," said Athalie, "didn't we have security?"

"It seems not," said Mrs. Farrand, wearily. "That is, it seems that the property which was supposed to secure us has depreciated terribly in value, on account of the railroad coming there, or not coming; I don't really know which. Read the letter; you will both understand it better than I do, probably. Your father used to say that I was not designed for a business woman, and it is too true. All I could do was to trust."

The facts seemed, as Mrs. Farrand had said, to be plain enough. The girls realized both them and the probable effect on themselves, even before they stated the case to Richard Shipley, who appeared just then, and heard him tell what ought to have been done that was not. Nor did any of them feel the happier for his assurance that the business had all been managed in a most unbusinesslike way, and that Mrs. Farrand's advisers must have been singularly ill chosen.

Chapter 12

"If thou faint in the day of adversity, thy strength is small."

It was Doris who came first to the front, with a flash in her eyes for Richard, such as he had not seen of late.

"Never mind all that," she said resolutely. "What has been done has been done, and cannot be undone by regrets. My mother's advisers, Richard, were the best business men in the town—men whom my father and everybody else trusted implicitly. They could not accomplish the impossible, I suppose; and men of excellent business capacity have failed, before now. The thought which concerns us is just what we would better do in view of our share in the loss. I know one thing at the outset—I can give up my college course."

Both Mrs. Farrand and Richard uttered a dismayed exclamation. It was Athalie who spoke.

"I should like to know why you should! How would that help matters, in the end?"

"I can get a position as teacher," said Doris, firmly. "I am not in the least afraid but that I can earn my own living, and help the others."

"Neither am I. But you can earn a much better living after you have completed your college course. After that, I shall be quite willing to sit and fold my hands and let you support mother and me; but until then, there are other ways."

Athalie was so composed, and the dry humor of her speech and manner were so entirely like herself, that they all began to feel less tragic. Mrs. Farrand even smiled; and her elder daughter continued:

"We can take a few boarders, three, as well as not. Garrett is such a capital helper and manager that I don't have enough to do nowadays. I know he would approve of such a scheme. He said the other day that our family was too small for the best economy, that there was always enough left for another person."

If she had not been so much in earnest, she would have thought of and enjoyed the look on Richard's face. His voice compelled her attention.

"Don't speak of it, Athalie! Of all horrible ways of economizing I consider that the worst and the most imbecile. My mother tried it years ago, and made a disastrous failure. I was always glad that she did. The thing is unutterably offensive to me. Think what it would be to your mother to have people, outsiders, always at her table, whether she felt like it or not, actually finding fault, perhaps, with her arrangements! If you haven't a sensitive nature yourself, Athalie, so that you shrink from such depths, you surely ought to be able to think of your mother."

"I am thinking of her," said Athalie, coolly. "I am planning to help support her. We shall not make a disastrous failure of it; mother and I know how to do it; and what we don't know Garrett Randall does; there was never a better helper or friend, either, than he. I know he will approve of my plan."

This was too much for Richard. "Oh," he said, in strong irritation; "if he is to be taken into the family, undoubtedly his opinion should be asked. I beg your pardon, I am sure. I supposed he was employed to serve, not to plan and direct."

The flush on Doris's face brought Athalie at once to a better mind.

"Don't be disagreeable, Richard, if you can help it," she said, in her usual good-humored tone. "We all seem to feel rather crisp this morning, except poor mother. We shall try not to do anything rash, or horrible, and whatever we do, Doris must not sacrifice her college course; that is a foregone conclusion, isn't it, mother?"

But Mrs. Farrand had slipped from the room. This gave Athalie a chance to speak plainly.

"We may as well face facts, Richard. Of course, since we have five thousand dollars less to depend on, something will have to be done to help along. What we want to do is the most reasonable and least revolutionizing thing; and I believe that to be the taking of a few boarders. It is something we could do without changing our present ways of living, or giving up anything to which we are accustomed. I spoke prematurely, perhaps, but this is not by any means the first time I have thought of it as a means toward a certain end."

"Whatever the end may be," said Richard, "the means are horrible. Five thousand dollars isn't an overwhelming sum. Why couldn't you—" But Athalie could not wait for his question.

"No, it isn't," she said. "Our entire income is not overwhelming. Our father was a minister, you remember, and we had no wealthy uncle. Doris and I know that it has required careful management to live on what we had; and to have five thousand dollars cut off will make a difference."

She was vexed with herself for having produced her thought in Richard's presence, and so brought upon them his opposition. This was but the first of many discussions. Richard continued to vigorously oppose the plan of taking a few boarders. Athalie accused him of being the more vehement because he learned incidentally that Garrett Randall had caught at the thought with enthusiasm, and demonstrated with pencil and paper just how it could be made to contribute to the income.

This idea she kept, as usual, for her mother; and Mrs. Farrand, much tried in many ways, said what she had never before so much as hinted:

"Sometimes, Athalie, I am sorry that Doris and Richard ever came together again after their girl and boy friendship was interrupted. There are times when, with all his talk of broadness, he seems to me too narrow for my girl, not fitted to make her happy. For one thing, he is so obstinate, not only about things which do not rightly belong to him to settle, but about very trivial matters. Your father used to say that that was a mark of a narrow mind. I am not sure, after all, but that Garrett has the better mind of the two."

"Why!" said Athalie, startled, "you mustn't be hard on Rich, mother. I sputter about him to you because I think he belongs to us, and we have a right to criticize him; but I confess I shouldn't like to have anybody else do it. Oh, Richard is one of the family, of course. I look upon that as a foregone conclusion; and I am just as fond of him as ever, in spite of all his follies. When I am inclined to be too hard on him, I think of his mother and am mollified. You don't know what a horrible creature I should have been if I had had Mrs. Shipley for a mother."

But, after that, Athalie guarded her speech even from her mother. It would not do, she thought, to have the mother get seriously out with Richard; that would make unhappiness for them all.

She carried her point, however. She was not in the least like Doris in yielding to Richard's whims. She waited, as she had promised that she would, and weighed carefully several other suggestions of her own and others.

One of hers was that she should open a very select millinery establishment, utilizing their sitting room for the purpose. When Richard heard of this, he had no words with which to express his horror; and it had the effect of almost reconciling him to the project of keeping boarders. Teaching was the only occupation which he himself suggested for Athalie. That, he assured her, was an employment with which even the most fastidious could not find fault.

"Indeed they can," she said gaily. "I am one of them, and I bristle with fault-findings. That is, so far as my becoming a teacher is concerned. I wasn't trained for it, Richard. My work would have to be very elementary and not strictly honorable. I do not understand modern methods, and I won't pose as one who does. My good girls at the factory, for whom there are no 'methods,' I am willing and glad to teach what I can; but I will never teach for money."

He grumbled at this, called her over-scrupulous, and reminded her that she had not been trained to millinery.

"That is very different," she said good-humoredly. "There is such a thing as native talent, you know. Milliners, like poets, are 'born, not made.' You, being only a man, and being compelled always to wear ugly hats of the prescribed style, cannot be expected to understand; but I know I can make hats and bonnets for which people would be willing to pay money. However, I shall not open a millinery this spring, so you need not frown."

The only point on which the two agreed fully and unwaveringly was that Doris must by no means be allowed to drop out of her class, and begin her work at once as a teacher. Here Athalie was as vehement as Richard, and the two succeeded in so bracing the mother that she was able to withstand all Doris's arguments and entreaties, and forbid the heroic sacrifice the girl was bent on making.

There came an evening in their history when Richard was sullen, Doris silently resigned, Mrs. Farrand a trifle nervous, and Athalie and Garrett Randall were in a highly satisfied state of leisure and expectation. For the house, from attic to basement, was ready for the four boarders whom they had finally decided that they could receive, and the morning papers were to have modest announcements to that effect.

There had been talk of securing students, without general advertising, but both Athalie and Richard disapproved.

"Students cannot be expected to pay the price which we intend to charge for our superior accommodations and service," Athalie said loftily. "Besides, we cannot wait until fall for students, and most of them will be flitting for the summer."

Richard disposed of them briefly and surlily, without argument.

"You don't want students here."

During the trying days of preparation for the new order of things, Athalie had been a tower of strength to her mother. If she understood how sorely that mother shrank from having the quiet of their home invaded in this way, she neither by word nor sign let it be known; but treated the whole matter as though it were a scheme gotten up for the sole purpose of making certain persons, compelled to board, comfortable for the first time in their lives.

Doris, in the privacy of their own room, commented on this state of things.

"Athalie, I think you are wonderful! It was you, you know, who always used to groan over our poverty, and wish for a thousand things that we had to do without. I used to be sorry for you because you cared so much. Yet when the real loss comes, you take it much better than I do."

Athalie laughed, and kissed her.

"I haven't seen you in hysterics over the loss," she said brightly. "I'm going to admit to you in strict secrecy that I whistle a good deal in order to keep my courage up. But then, the whistling is good for me; there are times when I succeed in persuading myself that I am glad the five thousand are gone, and I am compelled to rouse myself and do something for the world."

"As if you were not doing wonderful things before!" said Doris, reproachfully. "Do you suppose you will have to give up your Club? Wouldn't that be dreadful, when you are making such a difference in the lives of those girls! And yet, I don't see how you are to continue it, with all this added work and care upon you. That is where poverty hurts, Athalie; it spoils our plans for others."

Athalie only half heard her. She had gone off into a reverie. "We have never been poor, have we?" she said meditatively. "I thought we were; I groaned over it a good deal, as you say. But I have been learning, this winter, that poverty is a relative term. 'We are not poor,' that little Katie Welch said to me, and she drew herself up with the air of a princess. 'Mother and Jennie and I make a nice living. We have two rooms, and a fire all day, and meat once a week, and Jennie goes to school, afternoons.' What is her standard of wealth, do you suppose? You should have seen the light on her face when she told of their prosperous state as compared with the poor around them. And here are we with our twelve rooms and a fire all day in all of them, complaining of poverty because we have lost five thousand dollars! It is entirely a relative term, you see. I wonder if riches are the same. How much money would we need to have, for instance, in order to call ourselves rich? I am almost certain that little Katie would think herself an heiress if somebody should give her a thousand dollars."

"The probability is," said Doris, "that we shall never have a chance to discover how we should feel. It is singular, isn't it, that for generations back our family has represented the ministry?"

"And is likely to continue in that same good way, having 'neither poverty nor riches,'" said Athalie. At which Doris smiled.

So the evening had arrived in which they sat together enjoying, or trying to enjoy, what Richard solemnly called their "last comfortable time together."

"And even that is to be invaded," said Athalie, as she arose to answer a ring at the front door. "I hope it isn't callers; I am in no mood for any unless they want to look at rooms, and even then I would quite as soon they would wait until morning."

"It is a stranger," she said, coming back to them, "a solemn-looking man of great dignity. He wants to see Miss Doris Farrand: But first he asked if 'Mrs. Doris Farrand' lived here. Mother, how do you suppose he learned your first name? He is rather a formidable-looking person, Doris; I hope you haven't been doing anything dreadful that he has been sent to investigate. If I had a guilty conscience, I think I should be afraid of him. Mother, perhaps you would better go with her."

"I think as much!" said Richard. "What right has a man who is a perfect stranger to call for a young lady? You would better let me go and ask him what he wants."

Doris laughed at them both, and went her way. The people she left could not get away from their wonderment. Entire strangers were so unusual to their quiet life that the man's possible errand interested them.

"Do you suppose he can have heard that we are going to open our house to boarders, and has come for the first choice of rooms?" Athalie asked. "But in that case he would have asked for 'Mrs. Doris Farrand' instead of 'Miss,' always supposing that he knew the name of either. It really was very queer that he should have asked for mother in that way. For the moment I could not remember whether she was 'Doris' or not? You don't think he can be merely in search of board, do you?"

"I should hope not!" said Richard, fiercely. "I see no reason for any person mixing Doris's name with that charming occupation."

And then Doris's step was heard in the hall. She opened the door and spoke quickly, "Mother, will you come here, right away, please?"

Chapter 13

"Riches and honor are with me."

"This is beginning to be exciting," said Richard, as the astonished mother promptly answered her daughter's call, and he and Athalie were left behind.

"I suppose it is all right," he added. "I confess I did not fancy her being left alone so long with an utter stranger; but now that your mother has gone . . ." He did not finish his sentence, and rising from his seat began a restless walk up and down the room.

Athalie laughed. "Aren't you growing 'narrow' in your ideas as to the liberty of woman?" she asked. "Why shouldn't Doris be left alone with an utter stranger as long as she chooses to stay? She is no child; on the contrary, she is a young woman gifted with an extra amount of common sense. I presume she is being interviewed by an enterprising agent who has the finest cosmetic on the market, and has chosen a unique way of introducing himself to households. I have heard of their asking for the lady of the house in such a way as to suggest to servants that they were expected guests; perhaps this one has taken a brilliant step in advance and learned how to ask for the young ladies."

"The idea!" said Richard, savagely. "If I thought he was an agent, I would go in and shoot him."

The interview in the parlor seemed to those in the sitting room to be unaccountably prolonged.

"His wares must fascinate them," murmured Athalie, continuing to carry out her conceit of an agent. "They have had time enough to buy him out, I should think. Why do you suppose they don't call us in to share their pleasures? He can't have many goods with him; he had only a small bag in his hand. To be sure, they might be diamonds! But in that case I shouldn't suppose that mother and Doris need stop long over them; one can't feed boarders on diamonds."

Richard had an engagement of importance at nine o'clock, and he kept looking at his watch every few minutes and murmuring his annoyance. He could not get his own consent to leaving the ladies with a strange man in the house, despite Athalie's assurance that there was no need whatever for his staying.

"Of course Randall must be out the first time in his life that he was wanted in," he muttered savagely, watch in hand. "At last!" he added, as there was a movement in the front room.

"I must go in two minutes," he said reproachfully to Doris; "Keller will be waiting for me as it is. I couldn't feel willing to leave you at the mercy of an entire stranger, though if one may judge by the length of time you allowed him, he must have been very agreeable."

"What is the matter?" asked Athalie. "You both look—not exactly as though you had seen a ghost, for your cheeks are red, and ghosts always make people pale, don't they? What did the man want? And how did he know that mother's name was Doris? Don't keep us in suspense any longer. I thought I should have to send out for some sort of a sedative for Richard."

"It is a very strange story," said Mrs. Farrand, at last. "I hardly know how to tell it. Perhaps you can do it better, daughter."

"It is news from an old friend of mother's," said Doris. "One from whom she hasn't heard since she was a girl. And it is very strange news; so strange that I don't know what to think of it, nor how to tell it. It doesn't seem as though it could be real."

She stopped and laughed, though evidently in strong excitement.

"What an exasperating couple!" said Athalie, concealing her

impatience under a serio-comic air. "Why didn't you call Richard and me to listen, instead of leaving us here to imagine all sorts of terrors? I could have told the exciting part in one word, I am sure. Try it, Doris. 'Earthquake! cyclone! smallpox! shipwreck!' though what any of those would have to do with 'Mrs. and Miss Doris Farrand' I confess I don't know. Was that man your friend, mother? He was rather severe looking, I thought."

Mrs. Farrand shook her head. "No," she said. "I never saw this man before. He is a lawyer. My old friend is dead, and in his will he left something to Doris."

Richard put up his watch.

"This grows too interesting!" he said gaily. "Keller may fume if he wants to; I can't go until I have heard the sequel. What did he leave you, Doris? Athalie made a wild guess that there were diamonds in the man's bag. If you really get a diamond after all, before I—" He stopped suddenly, laughing and flushing.

"It is more than a diamond," said Doris, whose face was grave, though her eyes shone with an appreciation of Richard's unfinished sentence. "Oh, mother, how can I tell them? It seems so strange, so impossible. I feel as though I were in a dream."

"I know it," said Mrs. Farrand. "It is very strange; but we must tell them what he said. My old acquaintance was a rich man; he died a year ago; he has left his fortune to Doris; stocks and bonds—everything!"

She spoke in the terse phrases of one under the influence of strong excitement, giving what might be called the head-lines of her story, without regard to the exclamations of her amazed audience.

Richard was the first to recover himself. "My dear Mrs. Farrand, isn't this an extraordinary tale? Are you quite sure that you haven't been made the victim of a lunatic? Did he give you any clue as to the reasons for such a will? Moreover, you say that it is a year since the man died; if everything is straight, why has a year been allowed to pass without your hearing of it?"

The instincts of a profession which Richard at times still affirmed ought to have been his, were strong upon him. He asked his questions with the air of a lawyer examining a witness, growing more judicial every minute.

Mrs. Farrand's face began to take on the air of weariness and perplexity which always beset her when there were business matters for her to consider.

"I don't understand much about it, Richard," she said. "Perhaps it would have been better if we had called you to talk to him." Richard magnanimously refrained from saying that he thought it would. "Still, there are reasons why it looks less strange to me than it does to you."

She stopped, as if in doubt how to put what must be said next, and a slow red crept up again into cheeks that had faded. Athalie regarded her curiously and thought that she might have been a girl of twenty. She began again, turning from Richard and addressing her children.

"I knew this man years before I met your father; he was an intimate friend; in fact, we were engaged to be married."

Exclamations from both daughters deepened the flush on her face and quickened her speech. "It was before I had ever even seen your father. I was quite young. The engagement lasted for three months, then we quarreled and separated. There was good cause for it; he was not what I had thought him; my mother had never approved of the friendship. He went away—very far away—and I never heard any more of him. I had ceased even to respect him, and of course it was natural that I should forget him after a while. I have known nothing about his life, until this man told us tonight something of his story."

"It is very extraordinary," Richard said for the third time. "Still, it begins to sound a little more probable. Evidently the man never forgot you; and the name—" He wheeled toward Doris as he spoke. "It was the name that brought you good fortune, wasn't it? This is a romance in real life! I have often wondered how it would seem to live a novel."

They were in such a state of unnatural excitement that any interruption was to be welcomed as a relief, even though it came in the shape of a peremptory summons for Richard. Keller was to take the nine-thirty train, and sent word that unless Richard came at once he must go without seeing him. Richard went away grumbling that he wished Keller and his schemes were in Jericho, notwithstanding the fact that the schemes were chiefly for his own benefit, but the little family were not sorry to be left quite to themselves for a while.

Richard, too, as he walked rapidly toward the railway station, had time to calm his excitement and smile at it as extreme.

It was more than probable, he decided, even on the supposition that the strange tale of the strange man had a foundation of truth, that the "fortune" as Mrs. Farrand had called it, was a small affair. To people accustomed all their lives to small means, a few thousands meant a fortune. The gift, if it was money at all, might be a matter of four or five thousand dollars. Still, it must be a little more than five. If it had been the exact sum so recently lost, they would naturally have mentioned it at once. It was possible that the amount was nine or ten thousand. His pulses quickened a little again over such a possibility. Ten thousand dollars in judicious hands could be made to accomplish a great deal, as he knew from experience; and this would belong to Doris alone. He had often thought that if he had a few thousand dollars to manage as he pleased, it would be strange if he could not double it in a few years; at least he should like the pleasure of trying.

Before morning Richard Shipley's fertile brain had developed several interesting and absolutely sure ways of increasing capital, and he chafed at the extra duties which kept him from rushing at once to the Farrands to learn the details of the new situation. The day was filled with vexations, and by night he was in an irritable and unbelieving mood. He felt almost certain that the whole thing was a fraud. What could be more improbable than that a man away off in the wilds of a western country, unheard from for almost half a century, should be romantic enough to remember a girl to whom in his boyhood he had been engaged for three months, and leave his money to her daughter! That would do for a third-rate, three-volumed novel, but it wasn't common sense. They had all been foolish to credit it for an hour. It was well that Doris cared so little for money that the discovery of humbug would not seriously affect her. If it were her sister who was the supposed heiress, he told himself savagely, it would make a different state of things.

Despite his decision that they were victims of a fraud or a huge joke, he was tried by the delays that kept him from investigating, almost as much as Doris was by his absence.

Athalie wondered openly: "I am amazed at Richard. What can have become of him? I thought he would be here to breakfast without fail, and now it is dinner time. Have you seen him today, Doris?"

Doris shook her head, and then explained that this was Richard's day to be at the other building, a mile away from her class rooms.

"But I don't understand how he could go on just as usual," said Athalie, "nor for that matter, you either. You seem to have gone through exactly the regular routine, while I haven't been good for anything all day. I burned the cake, and set the cream in the oven instead of the refrigerator, and did a hundred other silly things. If it hadn't been for Garrett, there wouldn't be a dish in the house tonight fit to eat."

It was the evening for the mid-week prayer meeting, and Mrs. Farrand and Athalie went; to "calm their minds," the latter said, and try to get themselves down to common levels again. Doris stayed at home; ostensibly because she had work which the excitements of the day had delayed, but really because Richard must surely come in the evening; which he did.

"Thank heaven I am here at last!" was his exclamation, as Doris, recognizing his step, opened the sitting-room door. "And that you are, also. I did not remember that it was Thursday evening until I turned the corner and saw the church lighted. If you had been away, it would have been the drop too much in this exasperating day. There never was such a day, Doris! I have tried, ever since it began, to get into your neighborhood, either here or at college, for fifteen minutes. I made a dash for the library this afternoon and just missed you. It seems to me that I have just missed, all day, the things I most wanted. How have you been? I imagined all sorts of things. Sometimes I half made myself believe that last night's experience was a dream or a hallucination. Once, today, I got up a theory that it was the scheme of a sharper to inveigle your whole family into some trouble; though just what the trouble could be, or why anyone should go about it in such an absurd manner, my common sense refused to say. How has the day served you? Begin at the beginning and tell me everything."

He had drawn a chair close to hers, and as he glanced at the open books on the table, he said: "Are you really working away, just as usual?"

"Only trying to," said Doris, smiling. "It has been a strange sort of a day for us all. That lawyer was here all the morning, going over as much of the business as he could make us understand, and answering mother's questions. Everything seems straight, though of course we do not understand about it very well; he says there are forms of law to be gone through with. Mother thinks we ought, perhaps, to have a lawyer of our own to attend to it all. I told her I would ask your advice as soon as you came."

ISABELLA ALDEN

"I wish I had been here to see the man," said Richard, restlessly. "I could tell in five minutes whether or not he is a fraud."

"Oh, he isn't a fraud, Richard! What object could he have?"

"Why was there that year's delay that you mentioned last night? Couldn't he get trace of your family?"

"Of our family? Yes, he had no trouble. Grandfather Farrand was very well known indeed, you remember; it was easy to trace the name. He says he has known for nine months just where we were living and all about us. But there was some one else whom they couldn't find. A boy, or a young man I suppose he is, a stepson of the man who left the property; he had been lost track of for years, and was to be hunted for. If, at the end of a year, no trace of him had been found, the property was to go to whichever of mother's daughters had her name. It seems he knew there was one who had. Mr. Malcolm says if the earth had opened and swallowed that boy he couldn't be more surely lost to the world. Not a suggestion of his possible whereabouts led to anything, and there have been hundreds of supposed clues. He is simply gone."

"Nice boy!" said Richard, approvingly.

"I don't know," said Doris, joining in his laugh. "I only half think so. I don't like money that belongs to somebody else and is only mine because he couldn't be found."

"It doesn't belong to somebody else now," said Richard. "Isn't the year of probation gone?"

"Yes, but there is more to it. The will says that if that boy is found at any time within five years, half of the property is to become his. Think of having to be always on the lookout for one to whom half that you have belongs! Would you like that?"

"What a *fool* will!" said Richard. "But it is not at all likely that he will be found. What those sharp lawyers and detectives cannot accomplish in a year's time, is generally never accomplished. What is the precious youth's name? A stepson did he say? The

108

mother is dead, of course?"

"Of course. She was his first wife; the second one died a few years ago. The lawyers never saw or heard of this boy until the will was drawn. It was an episode, Mr. Malcolm says, in the early life of the man. The boy's name was Smith. George Smith."

"He couldn't have hidden himself better than under that name," said Richard, cheerfully. "It's romantic, isn't it? So George Smith, whoever he is, comes in for his share if he appears within five years, does he? Are you supposed to carefully divide and set apart his portion to solemnly wait for him?"

"Oh, no; he is to share whatever the property is worth at the end of five years."

"Oh, that's an easy problem. Use it all up at once. When am I to know how much this remarkable gift represents? Don't you feel cruel keeping me in suspense all this time?"

Chapter 14

"Labor not to be rich; cease from thine own wisdom."

The girl flashed a brilliant glance at him and laughed.

"You don't know, do you?" she said, a note of satisfaction in her voice that he could not have understood. Athalie, in one of her careless moments, had remarked that Richard would probably find out before he slept just what the legacy was. "How much do you think it is?"

"Well, I have vacillated between that diamond ring which I did not want him to give you, and—other things. When your mother talked of stocks and bonds, it sounded like money. There are times when I have been very generous with you and made it the full five thousand that recently slipped away. But most of the time I have been far more modest than that."

"Richard, it is at least a hundred and fifty thousand dollars."

"What!" said Richard, and he sprang to his feet. "Doris, what did you say? What do you mean?"

Doris also arose and stood before him.

"It is fully that sum, Richard—at least, so Mr. Malcolm says. He has put it in round numbers, he says, and valued the real estate at a low figure. The man had mining interests, and they developed wonderfully, and are still producing. There is a great deal about it all that I do not understand, but Mr. Malcolm repeated several times that he was giving us figures quite below the facts."

"Why, Doris!" said Richard again, his voice indicating strong excitement. "Why, darling, you are—" He stopped abruptly and looked down at her, and laughed. "I ought to beg a thousand pardons," he said, "but some way I can't. Isn't it time for this farce between us to reach its end? Don't you know, and haven't you known, for I cannot tell how long, that you are my darling, and must ever be, no matter what happens? I assuredly did not mean to tell you so tonight; that word came to the surface spontaneously under excitement. It has been in my heart so long that it was only natural it should. Don't I know, darling, that you belong to me? Haven't I rights that might as well be recognized?"

His arm had gone about her waist, and he drew her close to him and kissed her for the first time since he was a boy of twelve, when he had dared to kiss her for a forfeit, at a children's party. Her face had turned as red at that time as the crimson gown she wore, and she had told him indignantly that if he ever wanted her to speak to him again, he was never to do that as long as he lived. The childish memory swept back upon them, relieving the strain of the moment.

"You told me never to do it," Richard said, kissing her again and again, "but you know now that I cannot obey you. I have done well, done nobly. Even now my stern self-control has been surprised out of me. I did not mean to claim you yet, darling; certainly not tonight! It did itself. Can I help it?"

"What did Richard say?" Athalie asked the question of her sister that night in the privacy of their own room. Doris hesitated, giving a little embarrassed laugh.

"You heard several things that he said, I am sure," she replied at last. Richard had stayed until midnight, looking into the papers that the lawyer had left with them, reading and re-reading portions of the correspondence connected with the business, bringing his judicial mind to bear upon it all, in a way that filled the Farrand family with admiration.

It was Athalie who said, after he had gone, "I half believe that Richard is right in thinking that he ought to have been a lawyer; he certainly has a clear head for business."

"Brains are useful in the ministry," Doris had replied, and there had been a ring in her voice that was new. Was there also a new light in her eyes? Athalie had looked and wondered. Was Doris's rare good fortune already working its subtle change upon her?

"I know," she said, in response to her sister's words. "But I mean, what did he say when he first heard the news? Had he heard before he came this evening?"

"Not a syllable. He thought it might be a diamond ring, and didn't like it." There was that happy little laugh again, with a new note in it. Doris was certainly different. Her sister waited, while Doris's abundant brown hair was brushed with quick, nervous fingers. Suddenly she dropped the brush and came over to where Athalie sat, engaged in the commonplace work of unbuttoning her shoes. There was a hassock near at hand, and Doris pushed it into place with her foot and sat down, with her hands clasped over Athalie's lap, after a fashion of her younger days when she had anything special to talk about.

"You have taken it for granted for so long," she said, "that I don't know as my bit of news will impress you much, but I want you to know that Richard and I are engaged."

"So soon!" exclaimed Athalie.

"Soon!" There was an injured note in Doris's voice. "Why, Athalie, it was only last week I heard you reminding mother that I had been as good as engaged to Richard for years."

"I know, dear; I am used to the 'as good as,' but I didn't expect the actual fact to occur so soon. It is all right, of course, only— Richard is so eccentric! He never does things like other people. A less absorbed man would not have wanted the engagement to press so hard upon your having inherited a fortune."

A red glow overspread Doris's face, reaching even to her temples. "Athalie," she said, "if I thought that you associated the two for a moment—"

"I don't," interrupted Athalie; bending forward to kiss her sister. "I was only thinking about what other people will say."

"Never mind other people," said Doris, with lofty scorn. "We understand each other. Richard never thought of it at all—of speaking, I mean, just now. He has felt all along that it would be more honorable for him to wait until he was through with his studies; but tonight—it just said itself." She laughed softly over some memory, and then tried to explain.

"He used a name for me, Athalie, in his first moment of astonishment, that needed apology or explanation—that was the way it came about; utterly unplanned. Have you nothing but critical questions for me tonight?"

Thus reminded, Athalie took her sister in her arms and kissed her with a tenderness that was almost motherly.

"You will not expect many words from me, darling," she said. "You know I never speak out my inside thoughts, only the surface ones. But you know without my telling you what I want for you, and how dear—" She stopped abruptly; she never allowed herself to speak when her voice would insist upon having a tremble in it.

Life took on an utterly new aspect in the Farrand household after that first day. Richard proved himself a faithful and indefatigable adviser and helper. Athalie's only spoken complaint of him was that he rushed things. To her secret self she made others. The subtle change she had noticed in Doris was by no means subtle in him. He unhesitatingly assumed authority. Not in an ungentlemanly or offensive way, but with the matter-of-course air that the male head of a household naturally has.

"He couldn't manage more completely if they were already

married!" This was what Athalie said to the only safe confidante she now had. As she said it, a new thought dawned upon her. When those two were married, it would be "Doris and Richard" in very truth; and the money was all Doris's, and therefore Richard's! The oneness of their family tie, thus far, was emphasized in the fact that she had never before thought of this. She dropped the duster she was using, and sat down to consider the new, strange condition of things: Doris with money, plenty of it, and she and the mother straitened, having to go perhaps to Richard for help.

"I never will!" she said, setting her chin in firm lines, "not if I am on the verge of starvation; I will not be beholden to Richard Shipley."

"Why not, Athalie Farrand?" Her common sense asked the question, but she put it away with impatient gesture, refusing answer. Yet the problem haunted her, declining to be permanently put away.

A phase of it found expression unawares before Doris, and that young woman turned back just as she was leaving the room to express her dismay.

"Is it possible, Athalie, that you think it will make any difference with our affairs because the money happens to be in my name? It is mother's money, if it belongs to any of us; sometimes it seems to me as though, by right, it didn't. That stepson ought to be found. As soon as Richard is through with the commencement whirl, he is going to plan ways of making further search. But meantime, do you know how you hurt when you throw out such hints as you did just now? Don't you trust me any more?"

"I did not mean to hint," said Athalie, guiltily. "I did not think beforehand how what I said would sound. Of course I trust you, dear, but we might as well take a common-sense view of things. The money is legally yours and no one's else, and you will be a married woman one of these days. That will necessarily make a difference."

"I am to be married to no one but Richard, remember; and you certainly know him well enough to be sure that there will be no difference."

Then Athalie closed her lips and assured herself that she would not say another word that might trouble Doris.

But she had set Doris to thinking, and the result was expressed later to Richard.

"There is one thing, Richard, that I am anxious to have attended to as soon as everything about this business is fully settled. I want to have part of the money given legally to mother and Athalie, so that they will be entirely independent. Don't you think that will be a nice way to do?"

Richard was prompt with his reply. "My dear Doris, what a singular idea! Why should your mother and sister be considered apart from you for the first time in your life?"

"Well," said Doris, reflectively, "for the first time our lives are different. Can't you feel the reasons? It was natural enough for me to be always beholden to mother, but when the relations are changed, it will not be quite so natural for her to look to me, or, at least, it will not be for Athalie. Sisters need to be more on an equality. I want Athalie to feel an independence that I am afraid she could not if—Besides," she broke off to say, "something might happen to my part of the money, and by the law of happenings— which I always thought was an absurd way to talk, as if anything ever simply 'happened'!—the same experience would not be likely to befall us all at the same time. Don't you see the reasonableness of it?"

"I shall have to confess that your brilliant logic doesn't convince me," Richard said, trying to laugh. "On the contrary I think you would be working against the best interests of all three. A hundred and fifty thousand dollars isn't an immense fortune, Doris; it will need to be managed with care in order that it may increase instead of diminish. To cut it into pieces and put portions of it beyond your control would be most unbusinesslike. I cannot imagine any sane legal adviser consenting to such a plan. There is no reason why a judicious use of your capital should not, one of these days, put you in circumstances to do whatever you choose for your mother and sister. But it must be managed, not wasted. Moreover, shall I confess to a little personal feeling in the matter? Doesn't this suggestion look as though you could not trust your future husband to care for the interests of your mother and sister?"

She flashed a look at him, out of bright eyes, that ought to have quickened his pulses with pleasure, as she said:

"That remark about 'trusting' doesn't deserve any answer; you know what I think. But I am putting sentiment entirely out of the question and being a business woman. You see, Richard, the money isn't really mine; it is mother's. If there is any reason for our having it, it is because somebody cared for her and remembered her all through the years, and settling it upon her is simply giving her back her own. What I should like best would be for mother to have it all, and give to us what she pleased; but I know she would never consent to that. Then there is Athalie; if she had not sacrificed herself for me, I should not be in college now; it would not have been possible for me to go on with my studies if she had been like other girls. You don't half know her, Richard."

Clearly, Doris was not in a mood to be argued with from a business standpoint, business woman though she considered herself. Richard resisted the temptation to tell her that her ideas were pure sentiment without any business about them, and spoke lightly.

"Darling, you are mistaken; I know that your sister is an angel in disguise. I have always known it; in fact you have almost occasion to be jealous because of my high estimate of Athalie. We will both prove to her, in the years to come, what we think of her."

"I know you will," said Doris, gratefully. "And you will aid and abet me in this scheme, will you not? I was sure that you would understand."

"Your motive, beloved, is as clear as sunlight, however much one may differ from your judgment. What sum are you proposing to settle upon your mother, or haven't you reached details yet?"

Contrary to his hopes, she was ready for his question. This was not, then, a passing fancy out of which he might hope to argue her, but a matter that had been carefully planned.

"Yes, indeed; I have thought about it a great deal. At first I planned to have the estate divided into three equal parts; but when I remembered, I mean realized that—that there would be four of us, some day," this last, accompanied by a conscious little laugh and a vivid increase of color, "then I decided that that would not be the way. So then I settled it that the money should be halved, and that half of it must be divided again for mother and Athalie. I want that dear sister of mine to have money of her very own to do with as she chooses; she will always choose the best things. The other half must, for appearances' sake, remain mine for the present, but—Oh, Richard, you understand."

He understood a great deal, and it was hard for him to feel entirely patient with this visionary girl who wanted to toss money about as she would roses, and could not be made to understand that her mother's and sister's best interests would be conserved by judicious management of the property, instead of by divisions. Seventy-five thousand dollars practically thrown away! For neither Mrs. Farrand nor Athalie knew how to take care of money. For their sakes, if not for Doris's, this scheme ought to be thwarted. But how to thwart it was the question. He told himself that he knew by past experience the futility of trying to argue with Doris—women could not argue; and Doris seemed to use other people's opinions for the purpose of entrenching herself more firmly in her own. The utmost that he could hope to do would be to delay this absurd division, perhaps until he should have the right to do more than merely advise. When once Doris was his wife, it would be strange if he could not find some way to protect not only her interests, but those of his mother and sister-in-law. Doris was all heart; he could not find fault with her for that, but it was another reason why he should guard her from mistakes with jealous care.

Chapter 15

"Her clothing is silk and purple."

As a family the Farrands were all but breathless over changes present and prospective; and the whir of important questions awaiting decision seemed to be constantly in their ears.

The first tangible effect of their altered circumstances was that their house was not opened to boarders. They had Richard's foresight and promptness to thank in connection with that. Among other matters to which he gave attention on that first bewildering evening, after seeing Keller off on the train, was the visiting of the leading newspaper offices to suppress that modest little announcement which was to have appeared in the morning papers.

"I knew," he explained to Athalie, "that whatever the outcome of this affair might be, you certainly would not want to give your attention just now to boarders."

They were all grateful to him, and commented on his thoughtfulness, Athalie holding herself firmly from saying that it was his pride and not his thoughtfulness that was to be praised this time.

"Still," she said to Garrett Randall, the "still" referring to unspoken thoughts, "it is a great relief to be rid of those boarders who never came. I hated them in prospective so thoroughly that there is no knowing what I might have done had they been here in the flesh."

Garrett regarded her admiringly.

"Did you, really, Miss Farrand? You made so many plans for

their comfort and were so jolly over it all the time that I honestly thought you rather welcomed it as a pleasant change."

Athalie laughed. "I believe in welcoming what has to be, and at least pretending that it is just what should be," she said. "When I was a schoolgirl there was a line set for my copy which read: 'When what you *will,* is not, then *will* that which *is.*' It made an impression on me and I have always tried to live up to it. That is good philosophy, isn't it?"

"It is better than philosophy," Garrett said cheerfully. "It's poetry and Christianity. 'My times are in thy hand;' that is the way the old Hebrew poet put it, you know. When one feels that, then one wants it to be as it is, doesn't he?"

"I don't know," said Athalie, with an accession of respect for the young man who while he talked was drying the glasses with such care that they shone, and felt like velvet to the touch. "I don't think I consciously put any religion into my thought. That is an article to be laid away in tissue paper and looked at once in a while on leisure days, is it not?"

"If it were," said Garrett, whose replies were never in accordance with her expectations, "what would poor fellows like me do, who never have any leisure?"

Athalie laughed and acknowledged herself worsted. She generally failed in shocking this young man. He seemed to know just how much, or rather how little, she meant by her flights into recklessness.

"There is something in that," she said, and turned away, thinking, as she had thought a hundred times before, that here was one who put his religion into daily use.

The next marked result of their changed fortunes was having money enough to make ready without anxieties for the functions connected with commencement week.

Mr. Malcolm, the business manager of the fortune which had come to Doris, explained that although there were legal technicalities to be observed before the property could be formally placed in the hands of her guardian, there were certain accumulations of the past year's interest on which she was at liberty to draw at any time; and fairly dazzled her by mentioning the sum.

"It is simply intoxicating," said Athalie, "to have your new gown made of white silk instead of muslin, and to be able to use as many yards of lace on it as one pleases. In my wildest flights of imagination I did not use real lace, Doris."

"There is no sense in using it now," laughed Doris. "The imitation would answer every purpose, and not one in fifty who looks at it will know the difference."

Still, she liked the real lace and the soft creamy silk and expensive gloves instead of the cheaper ones she had expected to wear. It was all delightful, and so sudden—almost as though she had gone to sleep in a prosaic world whose hours were filled with cares and responsibilities and boarders and bills, and awakened in a silk-covered, lace-trimmed, rose-perfumed one, where all that was beautiful was real, and where all that was pleasant to the eye and to be desired could be had for the plucking. Wherever she turned, the delights of this new world met her in small and charming ways. Not her dress alone, but her mother's and Athalie's were of special interest at this time. Both ladies were bidden with Doris, to the President's reception given to the graduates and their friends. This reception was a time-honored custom and the social event of the season in college circles. Mrs. Farrand's gray silk was still handsome, and Athalie went into society so little that her "one good dress," as she called it, was still in order. It had long been settled that these two, with a little furbishing, would be ready for the occasion, but that Doris's dress must be quite new.

Not one of them understood what a delight it was to Doris to attend herself to the refurbishing of the other gowns; to buy just the width and shade of ribbon that she knew Athalie would like best without regard to the fact that there was a narrower and cheaper grade that might answer. To buy unhesitatingly the lovely creations in lace and chiffon that would set off both dresses. To order the best gloves for each, and to add expensive fans and handkerchiefs, without having a family council over each separate expenditure.

"I never liked shopping before," she said gleefully to Richard, who was attending her. "It is the first time that I haven't had to walk squares in search of something cheaper that could be made to answer, and work mathematical problems at lightning speed to discover just how much could be saved by skimping an eighth of a yard here, and two inches there. It is great fun not to have to skimp."

Still, she was constantly forgetting her privileges and being prompted by Richard. "I hope it won't rain tonight," she said, on the afternoon of the eventful evening, and she looked anxiously at the doubtful sky. "The street cars are always crowded on rainy evenings, and one gets dreadfully mashed, done up in rainy-day wraps."

"Street cars!" echoed Richard. "I hope you are not going to patronize them tonight, whether it rains or not!"

"But it is too far for mother to walk, and none of us would enjoy it in the rain."

"Of course not. Walking is not to be thought of in any case. Why wouldn't you order a carriage as a matter of course? "

Doris laughed softly.

"Do you know, Richard," she said, "I forgot! In our family, carriages have so long been counted out as extravagant luxuries, that the force of habit asserted itself. We will have a carriage. Isn't it delightful that I can really take care of my mother in the way that she ought to be cared for?"

But there were drawbacks to Doris's comfort, and one of them grew out of that very carriage.

"I shall not be able to go up with you this evening," Richard said, as, all details being settled, he was about to take his departure. "That decoration business will claim me until the last minute, and I shall stay up there to dinner. But I can meet you at the door; and I shall claim the spare seat in the carriage for return, if I may."

"Very well," said Doris. "Then Mr. Randall can ride out with us. It arranges itself nicely, for he is to stay at the campus all night."

"Randall!" said Richard, turning back in surprise. "Is he to be at the reception?"

"Why, certainly; you remember that he is one of the honor men."

"I knew that the prize he won entitled him to an invitation, but I had no idea he would accept it. I didn't suppose he had anything suitable to wear. I thought he would probably stay away."

"He isn't going to stay away," interposed Athalie. "He has been shaping his work all day with a view to a leisure evening; he looks very well in his Sunday suit, Richard."

Richard's hand was on the door-knob.

"Oh, it's all right," he said lightly. "If he cares to distinguish himself by appearing at a function of this sort, the only one in the crowd not in evening dress, it is nobody's business but his own; still, it might be friendly to give him a hint of the embarrassment. And it might be just as well, Doris, to avoid including him in your party. One never knows what to do in such places with a chap of that kind; at least I don't. I'll watch for your carriage and meet you at the door." And Richard was gone.

Doris's face was shadowed, and she went away at once, making no comment. She did not want anybody else to understand what a trial it was to her to have Richard so unsympathetic with the needs and limitations of others, especially of other young men.

An hour passed before she was seen again. Then she went straight to the kitchen, where Garrett Randall was hurrying the preparations for dinner, and said:

"Mr. Randall, my mother and sister and I are going to have a carriage for the evening, and there will be room for you, if you like, to ride to the campus."

She did not wait for his eager thanks, but turned at once to her mother with some question of detail. Athalie, in the pantry, cutting bread, flourished her bread knife in air and thus addressed it:

"You may be glad you belong to a family that is represented by such a girl as that! Not one in fifty would have done it after what he said. Richard Shipley is a good manager, but he will have to study law for a century before he will learn to manage my sister Doris." All of which the knife, probably, did not understand.

That evening the college President's home was fair to see. The large, plain rooms had been made to glow and blossom. All that light and color and the breath of flowers could do to transform commonplace prose into the poetry of living had been done. Richard Shipley, as chairman of the decorating committee, had accomplished wonders and fairly earned his right to distinction in still another line of work. Exclamations of delight over the artistic effects were heard on every side.

Nor was it draperies and flowers and vines alone that made the vision of color. Every room glowed and sparkled with young bright life. Every color of the rainbow and all the exquisite tints which blend into it were represented in the human tide that flowed through the rooms. The President's annual reception was an opportunity which those favored ones who were admitted to its delights could not afford to slight in any way, and the fashionable world there represented was dressed in its best.

Conspicuous amid all this brilliancy of light and color, even painfully conspicuous in the eyes of any who cared for him, was Garrett Randall. It is true he was not quite the only one who was not in evening dress—half a dozen other young men in plain everyday attire could be counted among the throngs; but he was one, somehow, whom it seemed natural to single out. Athalie's gay remark that Garrett Randall would always be conspicuous for something, had a foundation of truth. He was rather unusually tall and his form was well developed. Also, he had a well-shaped head and a pair of changeful gray eyes that mirrored every shade of feeling. If his clothes had been of the regulation style and had fitted well, he would have been singled out as a fine-looking young man. Even as it was, there were a few who glanced his way and looked again, and thought of something besides his business suit.

There was an air of aloofness about him as though he did not belong to the gay scene. The others who were in everyday dress were apparently much at home; they seemed to be acquainted with everybody, and moved at ease among the throngs with the air of those who had relegated the matter of dress to the secondary place where it belonged, and were having a thoroughly good time. But Garrett Randall stood apart, as one left out.

Conspicuously lovely amid the throngs of loveliness that evening, moved Doris Farrand. More eyes than her mother's followed the girl wherever she went, and remarked, aloud or to themselves upon her beauty and grace. That Doris Farrand was a very pretty girl had been a definitely settled matter with her acquaintances for years. On this evening she was more than pretty—she was charming.

"Doris isn't a mere girl anymore; she is a woman!" said Mrs. Farrand, softly, to herself, with a little catching of her breath, and a strange feeling at her heart. It is an event to be remembered when one first realizes that one's little girl has passed the gateway of childhood, and is moving swiftly forward.

There were commonplace reasons why Doris's beauty was more in evidence that evening than usual. We may talk in a superior way about the secondary place that matters of dress occupy, and mean it, too; yet most women know that there are times when it insists unreasonably upon claiming a place of undue importance.

Nor are these the times when one is consciously well dressed. On the contrary, most women of sense, whether young or older, being reasonably sure of that fact, can dismiss the subject from their thoughts. It is when a girl is painfully conscious that her skirts have not quite the required slope and rustle; that her sleeves are too wide at the shoulder and too narrow at the wrist—or the reverse of this, according as the mode dictates; that her gloves are not perfectly fresh and of just the right shade of color; and her trimmings have a "cheap" look, that she finds it well-nigh impossible to get away from herself in continual comparison with others better gowned than she, and look and act what she really is.

For almost the first time in her life, Doris Farrand, in her soft, creamy tinted, exquisitely appropriate gown, knew that from the crown of her shapely head to the sole of her well-shod foot she was not only in order, but in the prevailing mode. There was not a touch on her garments which could be described by that expressive word "cheap," in the sense that those mean who make much use of it. She probably knew, also, that her taste in such matters was faultless and left nothing for people to criticize. The effect of it all was to make her feel more than usually at ease, and at leisure from herself. There was a sense that was new and pleasant to her, in which she had been able to dismiss Doris Farrand from her thoughts as soon as the last pin was settled in its place.

Richard Shipley, the fastidious, studying her with critical eyes, comparing her with well-dressed throngs about him, decided once more—what, to do him full justice he had often decided before—

that she was peerless; and this was as it should be, for did she not belong to him?

He had just settled it that he had sacrificed himself to the society of others sufficiently for one evening, and might safely enjoy a little of Doris's company without making them the subject of remark, when she crossed the room and went directly to the corner where Garrett Randall stood beside a table, going drearily through a portfolio of photographs for the second time.

Chapter 16

"The King's daughter"

"What have you found to interest you?" she asked.

"Nothing in life," he replied promptly, pushing the pictures from him as he spoke. "I'm only trying to pretend that I'm interested, because I don't know what else to do with myself."

"And you are not good at pretending, I think I once heard you say?"

"I'm not; I never learned how. It is a great pity, too; in places like these I can see how very useful it would be."

"Why not decide to become interested in something, and leave yourself no occasion for pretence?"

"How could I do it? Suppose a fellow doesn't fit in anywhere, how is he to help it? This thing, you see, is not in my line. I have never been to a dozen of what might be called social functions in my life. Not even to church sociables and affairs of that kind. There were reasons why mother couldn't go, and I didn't care to leave her alone and go off by myself. I did it a very few times, but it was to please her, not me; and I don't know anything about such places. I ought to learn; I realize that it is part of the education I am trying to get, to know a little about society. That's why I am here. I made myself come tonight, when the other part of me wanted to stay away, just for the sake of seeing how it was all done, so far as my eyes could tell me."

"That was sensible. Are your eyes serving you well, so that you are getting from it what you wanted?"

"Only in part," he said, turning them on her full of merriment, yet with a background of earnestness that she did not fail to see. "There is too much Garrett Randall here; I can't get away from the fellow. He knows that he hasn't the regulation rig on, and that his feet are too big for the rooms, and that his elbows are forever around in the way, and he keeps poking such facts at me all the time. I ought to have left him at home, and yet I couldn't, somehow. I wonder if you can understand anything about such a plight as that?"

It would have amazed the young man to know how well the fair and faultless creature before him understood. It seemed to her that she had lived through just such experiences; not because of her feet or elbows, but because something about her outer covering was not quite as it should be, and persisted in robbing her of ease.

"I understand perfectly," she said, and her tone was sympathetic. "The Garrett Randall of whom you are complaining is reaping the result of having made a social hermit of himself. He needn't be greatly troubled, however; such matters right themselves, with a little care. Haven't you acquaintances here, Mr. Randall?"

"Very few, almost none; the fellows I know the best didn't have a chance to come; there are none of my class here, you know."

"Of course, I had forgotten that this was one of your rewards for being an 'honor man.'"

He laughed genially; her tone told him that she appreciated how he regarded the reward.

"I shall live through it," he said, "and I shall know several things that I did not before."

"But you must do more than live through it; you must insist upon enjoying it. That is part of your duty. Don't you always try to do your duty, Mr. Randall? That is the impression I have of you. Have you had refreshments yet?"

"No; I'm going to dodge the refreshments. I don't know a soul to take out, and I am sure she would be too much for me anyhow. They don't go alone; you see I have learned so much. Eating is the last thing I need nowadays, Miss Farrand."

"Nevertheless, you are to eat; that is part of the reward. Take me out, please; I'll try not to be too much for you. I am thirsty if not hungry, and an ice will be refreshing."

"Do you mean it?" he asked, looking eagerly down on her from his greater height, his eyes expressing merriment, and some other feeling. "Do you mean that you will undertake to pilot me through? Remember, I don't know the ropes."

"Certainly, I mean that you are to serve me to an ice and a salad, and anything else that I fancy."

"I believe you do," he said, without a trace of merriment in his voice. "It is just like you, and I might have known that it was."

Doris laughed. "Why should it not be like me to want a share of some of the choicest delicacies of the season?" she said, lightly. "There are seats in the dining room now, Mr. Randall; if you watch your chance, you will be able to secure two near together."

Without more ado they joined the streams of life that were perpetually setting in that direction, and made their way down the length of the refreshment room. The young man's manner of accomplishing this somewhat difficult feat showed Doris that he had been using his eyes to good purpose. Nor had she occasion to blush for her escort during the ordeal that followed. She gave him suggestions in the frankest manner as to the selection of dainties and the mode of serving them, and he did her bidding implicitly, without visible sign of awkwardness. She introduced him to certain friends of hers who chanced to be near them, and in the merry talk that followed he held his own extremely well; so much so that while he was gone for coffee, Edith Draper, one of society's favorites, leaned forward to say to Doris:

"How quick he is in repartee, isn't he? Did you say he was a student?"

"There!" said Garrett Randall, as they made their way successfully through the throngs back to the point from which they had started, he perfectly conscious the while that he was escorting the lady who was the observed of all discerning eyes. "We still live, and I have not stepped on a train nor tipped over a dish since I started with you, and I shall not forget it."

Doris laughed genially.

"I wouldn't if I were you," she said. "Let the memory of it assure you that social functions are by no means such frightful affairs as you have imagined, and that you are entirely capable of making your way through them with credit. You will not dread society so much after this, I think."

"Not so much, thanks to you; but I don't think I shall see a great deal more of it in the future than I have in the past."

"Why not? Didn't you tell me that you recognized social functions as part of your education?"

"To be used once in a while, yes. At least, I suppose a man who is to live in this world ought to know how to act; and that necessitates a certain amount of doing the thing, doesn't it? I'm not sure just where the line should be drawn, only I'm sure that it should be drawn, and that much of this sort of thing is not for me. It doesn't *belong.*"

"To a student's life, do you mean? Of course, while one is in college, one cannot give a great deal of time to society. But a little recreation is necessary, surely."

He was too honest to let the inference pass.

"I wasn't thinking of study," he said gravely, "nor of expense, though both must keep me pretty close for the present. But I was looking away ahead, and thinking that I shouldn't ever have much use for what is called society. It doesn't fit in with my vocation. I don't suppose you remember that tussle I had with 'vocations' and 'avocations'?"

His eyes were as merry as possible, but Doris's were grave and almost troubled.

"I remember very well what you told me about it," she said. "But I do not understand you now. What has society in general to do with that argument? You surely do not think that religion means asceticism?"

"Not a bit of it; it means anything but that. What I mean is that the thing we call society doesn't match my directions so far as I can see. I don't know much about it, and I may grow wiser; but at present I do not know how I could manage it. 'Whether ye eat or drink, do it for God's glory,' are my orders, and I am unable to see how such as this is going to honor him."

"But if you help to make other lives more cheery, contribute to their good times, or help them through a lonely hour by some social effort, wouldn't that honor God?"

"Perhaps it would," he said, his eyes shining. "Of course it would. I can see how other people could do it—you, for instance. How you have done it tonight, for that matter. I believe you have given me some new thoughts. Shall I tell you of whom you remind me tonight? I said it over as soon as I saw you in that shimmering dress."

This was too outspoken for an ordinary compliment, and this young man did not know how to compliment, although there was evident admiration in his gaze. Doris found herself wishing to know just how she impressed him. It was rather surprising that he should have an acquaintance of whom she reminded him.

"You rouse my curiosity," she said, smiling. "Tell me, by all means. Is it someone whom I have seen, so that I can weigh your judgment?"

"I never saw her before; I have only thought about her—the description, you know. 'The King's daughter within the palace is all glorious.' That is the way it should read. Dr. Bannister talked on it one evening to our girls down at the school."

Nothing more simply sincere and dignified than his tone and manner could be imagined. Here were no empty words put forth in an effort after a flattering personality. Doris was strangely moved. She had known all the evening that she looked well; she had read unmistakable admiration in many eyes, she had been the recipient of certain compliments too broadly pointed to be quite agreeable; but this was unique.

"But that applies to the inner life," she said, while he was still looking down on her shimmering robes as one might look at a picture.

"Yes," he said, "yes, of course; and yet, there is no harm in their—their matching, is there? The Bible has a good deal to say about, white robes, you know. It seems as though they were meant to match. Anyhow, I thought of it when I saw you. Thank you for your revelation to me that even that bugbear, society, could be used and glorified because of the purpose behind it. I see possibilities from it for even our girls down there on Water Street. I always think of our girls, you know."

He laughed apologetically; and Doris smiled her appreciation of his thought as she moved away almost reluctantly. It would have been pleasant to have talked longer and discovered just how he thought society and Water Street could be united. This man certainly did not grow like other people in his thoughts.

The remainder of Garrett Randall's evening was fairly pleasant. Some of the people to whom Doris had introduced him chanced his way and were genial and friendly. He smiled afterward to himself over the thought that whether or not he should ever succeed in making social functions helpful to others, more than one person had certainly done so for him.

What Richard would think of her effort at helpfulness was a question that had crossed Doris's mind more than once while she was talking with Garrett Randall.

But Richard was in amiable mood. He had watched the entire scene, and had been filled with admiration at the way in which Doris managed herself and her companion. He told himself that he couldn't do that sort of thing, and that there were very few who could. Doris was unique. Moreover, despite his objection to Garrett Randall's attending the reception, he was conscious of a growing interest in that young man. He could not help a sort of admiration for the persistent energy of character that would not allow itself to be turned from its purpose, no matter how adverse the conditions. Also, it was increasingly evident that Randall would succeed in his effort to secure at least a fair education. That he was gaining in the eyes of his classmates, and winning the respect of his professors, was every day more apparent. In short, Richard had some time before this decided that Garrett Randall was probably an exception to the usual rule that people who had not had early advantages would better be content without higher education. In addition to all this, the uncouthness which had sorely annoyed the carefully trained Richard was steadily wearing off; it was no longer a trial to his sensibilities to be greeted by Randall as an acquaintance. He could even have tolerated a degree of familiarity but Garrett had learned that lesson with the others and never obtruded himself any more.

The two young men were so utterly unlike in all their views and feelings that under the most favorable circumstances they would probably never become warm friends, but there had certainly been great advance toward friendship on the part of one of them.

For reasons which he had never stopped to define, Richard Shipley's friendly feeling for Randall had made a distinct advance as soon as matters between Doris and himself were definitely settled. With no reasonable excuse for the feeling, he found that he had resented Doris's interest in the young man, and been fiercely opposed to her helping him in any way. He was personally relieved to find that this state of mind was passing away, and that he could even admire Doris's skill in doing the unusual thing, and putting the country-bred youth at his ease.

He was in the best possible spirits during the drive home, and did not hesitate to speak his thought.

"That was a gracious deed of yours tonight, Doris. You have no idea how my heart thumped with pride as I saw you piloting that poor fellow successfully through the shoals and breakers of the dining room. Did you see it, Athalie? I doubt if another person there could have done what she did for him. And he did you credit, I must say. How well he got through with the ordeal! I trembled for him over the coffee; those cups were made with a special view to the ease with which they can be tipped over. I didn't draw a free breath until yours was safely in your hands; but he did it nicely. Still, I am not sure but it is your mother instead of you who deserves the credit. His training in your dining room has done wonders for him."

Doris was silent and distrait. Not even Richard's hearty commendation of Garrett Randall drew other than a wan smile to her face. So marked was her silence that her mother inquired tenderly as to her state of health, and said she was glad that commencement week was now quite over; late hours and all sorts of excitements had been too much for Doris.

Richard was all sympathy and solicitude.

"Poor girl!" he said, stealing an arm around her under cover of the darkness. "It has been a hard week, and a hard month, for that matter. Cheer up, Doris, I shall never graduate from college again, and when you get through with your own commencement week two years from now, we shall have all that part of our life done."

Doris tried to laugh, and made a heroic effort to throw off her weariness, if weariness it was, and appear like herself.

She allowed Athalie to help her with the process of disrobing, much as if she had been a child, and was tucked between the sheets and kissed for the night in a surprisingly short time after reaching home. But sleep did not soon come to her. She lay very still, and allowed Athalie, who tiptoed about and made all speed with her own preparations, to think that she was sleeping. But long after the lights were out and the house was in absolute quiet, she lay with wide staring eyes, looking into the darkness, unable to get herself away from two sentences that probed and troubled her. These were: "Walk worthy of the vocation wherewith ye are called," and "The King's daughter within the palace is all glorious."

Chapter 17

"Wealth maketh many friends"

The summer that followed Richard Shipley's graduation from college was a busy and in some respects a distracting one to the Farrand family. The formalities connected with the bequest had all been observed at last, and an old friend of her father had been appointed as Doris's guardian. This was regarded by all concerned as a mere matter of form, since Doris would soon be of age and able to control her own property. The man she had chosen was one who stood ready to consent at once to whatever she and her mother might propose.

That division of property about which Doris had been so anxious, it had been discovered must wait until she was legally at liberty to do what she would with her own. That was a trial to Doris, and she chafed under the restriction which Richard assured her was eminently wise.

Both were fully agreed, however, that a home of their own, to be secured at once, was desirable. The Farrands had known for some time that in the summer they must move, as the house they rented was wanted by the owner. Athalie had in imagination borne all the fatigue and expense of the moving, several times, and groaned over them; but to move into a house owned by Doris would be quite another matter, having about it all the charm of novelty, and the two girls looked forward to it with enjoyment.

Mrs. Farrand was the one to object and argue.

"Dear child, why should you buy a house here? There is no

reasonable probability of Richard's settling here. You will have to leave your new home so soon for another, that it does not seem worth while. We have been very comfortable all these years in rented houses."

"Does it seem 'soon' to you, mother?" was Doris's smiling reply. "I haven't got beyond the age when three years seem a little eternity. I like the thought of a home of our very own right away. It isn't being foolish, mother dear. Richard says a house here will be a good investment for that money which is now lying idle."

Richard pushed the investment with an energy and skill that won golden opinions from them all, and made others, besides Athalie, remark upon his qualities as a man of business.

The home that was at last found and bought and moved into, was delightful beyond Doris's wildest childish dreams when her ambition had been to "buy a nice house for mother."

The final decision had not been made without a good deal of earnest argument between Doris and Richard, Athalie listening, amused over the skillful tongues of both.

Doris, having been brought up on economical lines, could not get away from her early lessons, and was forever contending for less fashionable localities and less outlay of money. While Richard, who had been trained to think much of appearances, had all the arguments ready to prove conclusively why such and such streets would not answer, no matter how charming the house. He prevailed, generally, though Doris in her secret heart believed some of his arguments to be trivial.

The place finally settled upon may be said to have been of Richard's choosing, and its appearance certainly justified his taste.

Then began an experience new to the family; that of securing a train of efficient servants who should be able to manage this choice establishment. One maid at a time, and she rather young and untrained when she came to them, had been the extent of Mrs. Farrand's experience. Most of the time since Dr. Farrand's death the little family had been without hired help. To interview a company of so-called trained servants, with their alarming prices and advanced ideas, and discover the things which they would and would *not* do, grew increasingly formidable as the days passed.

Mrs. Farrand learned by trying experiences that a maid's estimate of herself was not always to be relied upon; and that some of the carelessly worded testimonials presented were of not much greater value.

Athalie, who was of course her mother's aid and confidante, expressed her opinion of the ordeal in characteristic fashion.

"If there is a well-regulated lunatic asylum anywhere about here, I think some of us would better be securing a place in it for mother. I don't believe she will endure this strain a great while longer. The last cook who interviewed her was a sort of climax; she declined to wash even her own baking dishes!"

"Your mother is too much afraid of them," remarked Richard. "She lets them talk too much, and explain their ways of doing things, instead of laying down the law to them about her ways. She doesn't help them to know their place. It takes my mother to manage servants! I doubt if the most impudent of them could get the upper hand with her."

"Mother would rather have service from people who know their place, without being trained to it by her," said Athalie, coldly, who was always unreasonably annoyed whenever Richard compared her mother with his. "She has been used to some who were able to fill whatever place they had to occupy for the time being; and those are the best."

It was a slow process, and far more painful than those not actually engaged in adjusting matters could be made to understand. In truth, the adjusting was never fully accomplished, as it rarely is in these days. Before that first summer was over, not Athalie alone, but her mother, were converts to the belief that domestic service, in such perfection as it was once known, is a thing of the past. Not only that, but it was a sort of service that in the nature of things could not be hoped for again. When Doris; who was looking over a new magazine, read to them in triumph the deliverance of an eminent student of sociology who proved that a people who had advanced in all other directions were trying in the matter of household service to cling to a relic which did not fit in with present-day surroundings, Athalie lifted up her voice in triumph, and declared that, without the aid of a college course, she had reached by experience the same conclusion.

"If it is nothing but a relic," said Mrs. Farrand, that evening, dropping wearily into a chair, "I wish we could lose it and begin all over again. There is no let-up to my trials. Cook says she will not stay another week if I am going to keep Hannah; she has 'stood all the impudence from her that she means to.' And Thomas will leave if I discharge Hannah, so what am I to do? Think what an ungrateful wretch I am when I cannot help sighing for one of the nice little dinners that you and Garrett used to get up. I am almost afraid we have had all the cozy, comfortable times we shall ever enjoy."

"No, we haven't," said Athalie, cheerfully. "When Doris and Richard are married, they can run this big house, and you and I will live in a cunning little flat, with Garrett to help us; and invite them to our little home dinners, and make them green with envy. Think of our making such speeches as these, when we are almost smothered under magnificence! I am glad Doris can't hear us. Let me wrestle with Cook; she has quite worn you out, and I am fresh from a victory over Thomas, who was bent on sweeping the piazza with the parlor broom, and who told me that he was not used to ladies who dictated what broom he should use!"

As a rule, all such perplexities, and indeed friction of whatever sort, were kept from Doris. There was an unspoken feeling that she had planned the new home chiefly with a view to the comfort and pleasure of her mother and sister, and that her joy in doing so must not be shadowed by their trials.

They had no difficulty in keeping their own councils, for Doris was absorbed in another sort of life. After the fashion of the town in which she lived, her engagement had been formally announced, and not only congratulations but invitations poured in upon her. Indeed, the new neighborhood into which they had moved opened for them all a new world, as Richard had hinted that it would. Social functions were numerous.

There was a constant succession of calls, and invitations including the whole family, to informal luncheons, afternoon teas, receptions, formal dinners, even to breakfasts, were frequent.

Garrett Randall, looking on in wonder at the energy of the gay world in planning and executing its gayeties, asked Athalie if she supposed they kept a business manager who took charge of the dates, and when a new invitation came, puzzled out for them whether or not they had a spare hour.

"I should think he would have to sit up nights to figure it out," he said. "Train dispatching must be play, compared to it."

Garrett Randall, by the way, had a new office. Much discussion had arisen as to his future position in the reconstructed family. Richard was emphatically of the belief that Randall would have to go.

"You can't very well make a regular servant of him; if you could, you would find that he would not fit in with the others."

"I should never think of undertaking it," Mrs. Farrand said, with unusual firmness. "Garrett is as truly a gentleman as any man we ever had in our family and shall be treated accordingly."

"Very well," said Richard, quite willing to take that view of the matter. "Then that ought to settle the question of retaining him in your employ. As society is at present constituted, one doesn't expect to meet one's friends in the capacity of table waiters. Not that I find any fault with such an arrangement; I am only trying to remind you that what could be carried out successfully on Willow Street, will, on St. Mark's Square, subject you to endless embarrassments."

Mrs. Farrand was much disturbed, and confided to Athalie that she had moments of wishing with all her heart that they were back on Willow Street. The truth was, Garrett Randall had made himself almost necessary to the good woman's comfort. It did not seem to her that she could keep house without him.

"See what a tower of strength he has been through all this terrible ordeal of moving," she complained to the sympathetic Athalie. "It is all very well to talk about professional movers and trained servants, but when it comes to genuine care-taking, and forethought, and after-thought for that matter, I would rather have an hour of such help as Garrett's than any that a houseful of trained servants could give me."

The trouble was too real to be kept from Doris's eyes and ears, and it was she who finally came to the rescue.

"Mother, why wouldn't it be a good idea to put all those bills you were looking over, and the accounts generally, into Mr. Randall's hands, and let him be responsible for them? Figures are his specialty, you know. I cannot think of anything that would relieve you and Athalie more than to get rid of all that kind of thing. The gas bill, and the water tax, and laundry bills, and servants' wages, and everything. Pay him a regular salary, and let him take the entire responsibility."

"I don't know but that is a good idea," said Mrs. Farrand, looking instantly relieved. "Garrett knows just how to manage all such things, and to look after supplies, too. He is splendid at that, and could save his salary by his management. He never gets into a muddle with figures, and never buys over-supplies of things, to be wasted. I believe I will speak to him about it this very day. What a woman of business you would make, my dear!"

Richard arrived in time to hear that last sentence, and respond to it.

"It is a great relief, Mrs. Farrand, to know that you think so. Doris will have heavy business on her hands when she undertakes to keep me in order, you know."

Athalie wondered whether or not the smile with which her sister greeted this remark was a trifle constrained. Was it her imagination, or was Doris troubled about something? And had the "something" to do with Richard in any way?

Doris's idea was promptly carried into execution.

In the reconstructed household Garrett Randall was duly installed as family secretary—at least that was his nominal office, and the letters he wrote, not only the more strictly business ones, but acceptances and regrets as well, made the name appropriate; but as a matter of fact, his duties, many of them self-imposed, were multiform. Put into brief language, they consisted in watching out for the interests of the entire family, whether in the line of supplies, and the minute details of comfort, or the seeing to it that young Thomas was faithful to the work supposed to fall to his share. It is doubtful if even Athalie, who generally understood what was going on, realized the full force of the service rendered them, until she learned it with the rest, by missing him.

That they were all rather gay, much gayer at least than they had ever been before, was evident. Even Mrs. Farrand was being coaxed out of the seclusion of years—not altogether to her pleasure, it must be confessed. She told Athalie that she wished she knew just how much Doris's pleasure was involved in having her mother recognized again in society; that for herself, their quiet home life before society found them, suited better; but she could not have the child disappointed in her plans for making life brighter for them all.

Richard stopped in one morning to make final arrangements for a trip to the larger city close at hand, which was planned for the following evening.

"Oh, by the way," he said, having arranged to his satisfaction the part that immediately interested him, "Keller can't come down, after all; I have a note from him saying that his plans have been upset. That leaves an extra ticket on my hands. Is there anyone to whom you care to give it?"

"Why not give it to Mr. Randall?" asked Doris. "He doesn't get much recreation. I don't think he has been to a paid entertainment since he has been with us; and he works very hard at his books every spare moment. I think a little change would do him good."

"You mean, have him join our party? Very well, I have no objection. Your mother and Athalie would probably enjoy his society quite as well as they would Keller's; he never knows what to say to ladies. I'll leave the ticket with you, then, and you can make the necessary explanations. I'm in a rush this morning; two men are waiting for me at the library."

Doris was out among the flowers, and Garrett Randall was attending her with scissors and basket, when she gave her invitation.

"Do you know, Mr. Randall, that we have designs on you for tomorrow evening? Mr. Shipley's friend cannot come, so there is an extra ticket for the play. We would like to have you join us, if you will. My mother and sister are going."

To Mrs. Farrand and Athalie, young Randall had become simply "Garrett," but Doris adhered strictly to the formal address.

The young man walked the length of the rose arbor before replying, and handled the thorny roses with unusual vigor. He seemed at a loss for words, which was not common with him. At last he said:

"It is very good of you to think of me. I should like to be able to show in some way how much I appreciate it—"

Doris interrupted the flow of words:

"There is no occasion for any depth of gratitude, Mr. Randall. It is a very commonplace matter. There is simply an extra ticket unexpectedly on Mr. Shipley's hands, to which you are welcome if you care to use it."

Chapter 18

"To the wise the way of life goeth upward."

"Oh, I understand your part perfectly," said Garrett Randall. "But it is a little difficult to make my side understood; at least I don't know how to do it. Straight truth has always served me the best, though, and I'm going to try it now. I don't see my way clear to attending a theatre, and so, of course, I stay away; and at the same time I'm ever so grateful for the invitation."

"That seems plain," said Doris, lightly. "But still I am tempted to pry into your affairs a little and ask why you should not go, occasionally, in the way of recreation. You are not giving yourself any amusement nowadays, are you? Of course we all appreciate your motive in saving time and money, and honor you for doing so; but once in a while, when the way happens to be made clear—I don't know whether you understood that the railway ticket is included?"

He was visibly embarrassed.

"It isn't that," he said hurriedly. "The plain truth is that I leave the theatre out all the time because I can't make it fit in; but I don't consider it part of my duty to force my notions upon others."

"You are not doing that," Doris spoke very gently. Her present aim was to try to enlighten a narrow-minded youth. "I asked for your reasons, remember. Now I am going to ask how you reached your conclusions. Indiscriminate theatre-going, I think, we should all agree about. To give much time to even the best, is what those of us who live busy lives cannot think of doing. But an occasional play, carefully chosen and rendered by rare talent—isn't that worthwhile? The artist who is the attraction of this play has an international reputation, you know."

"I know it," said Garrett Randall. "She's great! They say she has been deserted thirty-five hundred times, and stolen I don't know how many; and yet she lives to tell the tales!"

There was a gleam of fun in the gray eyes, but Doris looked dismayed.

"Where do you get such figures, Mr. Randall? What has set you to thinking in that direction?"

"I got them out of a book." His face was grave again. "It was the book that set me to thinking. It isn't any clap-trap writing, Miss Farrand. I've taken pains to find that out. Dr. Bannister knows the man who wrote it, and he says no one stands higher for 'sane living and strong thinking'; I'm quoting his very words. He said if any human guides were to be trusted, one couldn't find a better than that man. So I bought his little book and studied it; it has helped me out along several lines, and theatre-going was one of them."

"But don't you make any exceptions?"

"I don't know how I can. At least I don't see my way clear to it just now; I may change my mind, of course. I want to hold myself open to conviction. If, for instance, I get hold of a person who can blow away the arguments of that book as chaff, why then I shall reconsider."

"Tell me some of the arguments. Or, first, tell me this: Suppose this famous artist has been abducted on the stage hundreds of times, how will that affect you and me? The play we are to have tomorrow evening has certainly no such plot."

"Isn't it our duty, sometimes at least, to consider how such a thing is affecting her? Don't you believe that if I should spend my life in trying to look and talk and act like one who is deliberately planning sin, that it would become second nature with me, after a

147

while? That isn't my thought, I got it out of the little book, where it is enlarged upon; but I can't get away from its logic. 'True acting,' the book said, 'consists in entering into the spirit of the act performed'; and I know that is so. In order to halfway do anything, you have simply got to enter into the spirit of it."

"But, Mr. Randall, you surely know that there are, and have been all through the years, men and women on the stage who live true and honorable lives."

"I suppose there are; in fact, as you say, I know there are. But people who have studied into this business think they are rather the exceptions, don't they? I am told that those very persons frankly admit that it is a life of peril. And people think they are true men and women in spite of their profession, not because they have been helped by it, don't they? What I can't get around is that the evil passions of men and women are the chief subjects of the theatre."

"Oh, I don't think that is so!" Doris said earnestly. "You forget the beautiful stories that have been staged."

"No, I don't, and I don't pretend to know very much about it at first hand; but I'll tell you where I got that notion. It was from reading a quotation from Palmer, the great theatre manager, you know. He said in plain words that the chief themes of the theatre today are just what they have always been—jealousy, terrible anger, murder, and so on, down the long list of sins. It seemed to me that he ought to know, if anybody did, and that his testimony could be trusted. But I have looked into it a little for myself since, and I don't think there is any getting around the facts, in spite of the exceptions to the general rule."

Doris was not prepared to argue, neither was she disposed to be convinced.

"Oh, well," she said, speaking lightly, "if one is going to condemn wholesale, the portrayal of all evil doing, there is a long list of standard books in prose and poetry, some of which you and I are studying with interest, that would have to be tabooed. I am afraid you will find it very troublesome work if you try to be consistent."

"I'm not trying to be anything," he said eagerly, "except a follower of Jesus Christ, and I want to do that just as well as I know how. But do you think that about the books is quite fair? Isn't there a difference? There are people who think so. I quote a good deal from that one little book, but it is partly because I have found it, so far, true to facts; and it puts into better English than I can a good many thoughts that have come to me through looking on at life. That book says that a man may describe evil, for a purpose, in prose or poetry, or music, even, without putting himself into it in the sense that the actor must. That to be a true artist on the stage, he must not only think and act, but literally feel, as though he were the sinner. I believe that. I have seen enough of some things in this world to make me pretty sure of its truth. Now, believing that, and leaving the influence on my own life out of the question entirely, ought I to help sustain a man in his deliberate attempt to live sin?"

Said Doris: "Don't cut any more roses; we have enough. Carry them in, please. And don't feel yourself compelled to go to the play in order to gratify us. I should not have thought of asking you if I had imagined your state of mind on the subject."

There was a look of perplexed distress on Garrett Randall's face. Doris's manner, as well as her words, told him plainly that he had offended, yet he had but tried to answer her questions. He hesitated, even opened his mouth to ask why, then thought better of it, and without a word strode off toward the house with his roses. If he had been misunderstood, he could not hope by any words of his to make things better.

As for Doris, she left the roses to fade if they would, and went straight to her room in a conflict of emotions, of which indignation was the uppermost. What right had this untrained youth to sit in judgment upon those who were infinitely better prepared than he to weigh such questions, and who had evidently reached very different conclusions? It was of no use for her saner feeling to tell her that Randall had done nothing of the kind, had simply answered as best he could the questions she had forced upon him. She would not listen to reason; she was beyond measure disturbed. It would be very humiliating to have to tell Richard this story, and let him see that his estimate of Garrett Randall was the correct one, just as, for the first time in his life he was joining affably in a social function with him. How would he feel to have his courtesy thrown back upon him, as it were?

Doris fretted over it all, until she was astonished at herself, and realized that she was giving undue importance to the affair. She resolved that she would not think about it any more, and took up the first book on which her hand rested, to aid her in fixing her thoughts elsewhere. It chanced to be a little volume of quotations from great minds, and among those which met her eyes was this, from Phillips Brooks:

"The trouble with the theatre is its dreadful indiscriminateness. The same house which gives good Mrs. Vincent her benefit today, may have almost anything tomorrow. What can one do with an institution like that?"

Doris dropped the book as though it had burned her, and uttered an exclamation expressive of intense annoyance. Had even inanimate objects conspired with that fanatic downstairs to help her feel uncomfortable? In truth, the girl did not understand herself.

She dimly realized that her mood was most unusual. Was not she the person who but a short time before had argued with Athalie against the influence of the theatre? Had she not been brought up all her life, at least until quite recently, under the direct influence of such ideas? Why should she act now as though Garrett Randall had advanced some new thought? Was it she who had changed?

She had to go down in response to a call from Richard before her disturbed mind was settled. But Richard was simply amused over what she had to tell.

"The fellow is going to develop into a prig, is he? That is worse, in some respects, than being merely a country blunderer. Never mind, by all means let him deny himself, if that is the way he gets his enjoyment. I'll tell you what we will do with that ticket; we'll let Holmes have it. I wonder I had not thought of it before. His ridiculous salary doesn't give him a chance to indulge his tastes in that line very often."

"Mr. Holmes!" said Doris, startled. "He would not go, would he?"

Richard was hunting among the bookshelves for a volume he wanted; he faced about at this point and regarded Doris with an amused smile.

"Why not, dear? Has Randall converted you already? Why shouldn't poor Holmes enjoy an occasional treat of the kind? He lives a starved enough life as a rule."

Doris said not another word on the subject. She was startled, and, in a sense, bewildered. There came to her a memory of the day in which she had challenged Richard for holding Mr. Holmes to a plane of conduct which he had apparently thrown off for himself. Was not this what she was doing now? Had she advanced since that time?

With the closing days of summer came two unexpected events. Richard, who was supposed to be making ready to enter a theological seminary situated in a neighboring city, astonished the Farrands one evening by his reference to certain lectures to be given under the auspices of the college.

"It will be a fine course," he said. "I am glad to be able to take it just at this time."

"Why, you won't be here to take it!" exclaimed Athalie the

outspoken. Richard looked from her to Doris and laughed.

"My little secret is out!" he said. "That is just like me; I can never keep a surprise until it is ripe—not even for my own pleasure. I always contrived to find out, weeks before-hand, just what my Christmas presents were to be.

"The truth is, Doris, I have decided to postpone the seminary course for a year. There is some graduate work I want to undertake, and there are several other reasons why it seems better to delay a little. So you are to be burdened with my presence all winter. Do you think you can endure the infliction? I meant to keep my secret until all my plans were definitely made; but of course it popped out, as usual, before I was ready."

He had certainly surprised them. Doris, at least, had never for a moment thought of any other possibility than his going away. She did not understand it now. How could Richard be willing to put one more year between him and his life-work? Besides, there was his mother, who had been long separated from him, and who was looking forward to keeping a little home for him during his seminary course. It was of her that Doris finally spoke.

"What does your mother think of this sudden change of plan? Isn't it sudden? She must be disappointed."

"Oh, mother is all right," he said lightly. "She will think whatever I do. I haven't told her yet, but I have no anxieties on her account. It will be a fine opportunity for me, Doris. Danforth is to be here this year, you know; I have hoped for years to be able to manage a course under him, somehow."

"I thought Professor Danforth belonged to the law department," said Athalie. "You are not going to turn lawyer, after all, are you?"

"Not just at present, my keen-eyed sister. I am not ready to turn anything until after a few more years of study. But I am going to attend some of his lectures. Every well-educated man, no matter what his profession, needs to know something about legal matters; especially if he has reason to suppose that he will have more or less business to look after. I have always meant, however, to spend a little time in that way, as soon as I could manage it, and now that an opening has come unexpectedly, of course I could not afford to lose it. Let me tell you how curiously it has all seemed to arrange itself."

He drew his chair nearer to Doris's, and presently his voice dropped lower, excluding Athalie, who took up a book, and then slipped away unheeded, while the murmur of voices went steadily on. Doris's face, the sister could not help noting as she went, was shadowed by a troubled look. Evidently the surprise was not all pleasure to her.

Athalie went to her mother with the news, and the two talked it over upstairs, as the others were doing below.

"How will Doris take it?" the mother asked.

"She will be talked over to it by the time Richard has sugar-coated it for her," said Athalie, laughing. "Doris is growing like his mother; she thinks what he thinks, more than she used to. That is a good thing, I suppose. But she is disappointed just now; I saw it in her face. The poor child has set her heart on seeing Richard in the pulpit, and she never will, I believe. He will preach, without any doubt, but his audience will be confined to two or three."

"Why, daughter," said Mrs. Farrand, "what a strange idea! That has been settled ever since Richard was a boy of twelve."

"I can't help it; you mark my words and see if I don't prove to be a prophet. I don't believe Richard Shipley will ever preach from a pulpit; and I don't believe he intends it himself, now. He did once; but since the money came and he felt that he could give up the ten thousand, he has changed his mind."

"You must have little faith in him!" said Mrs. Farrand, looking hurt in Doris's stead.

"Oh, I have great faith. I think he thinks it is the wisest course to take, and I am not sure but I agree with him. Richard wasn't designed for the ministry."

The other unexpected event followed in the wake of this one.

Chapter 19

"They were turned aside."

"Don't let us hurry," Athalie said, as the family were at the breakfast table. "This is our last day of sanity for months to come. Tomorrow will begin again the rush of college life; and here is Richard, whom I had expected to see employed in a more dignified manner—they are more dignified in a theological seminary, aren't they?—in the thick of it once more."

Richard had now become a recognized member of the family circle, being the only "boarder" they had cared to receive.

"I am not very familiar with theological seminaries," he said lightly, "but I haven't been deeply impressed with the dignity of many of the specimens from those regions. Do you think Holmes, for instance, is over-stocked with it?"

"One never thinks of Mr. Holmes in connection with a theological seminary, someway," said Mrs. Farrand. "Nor, for that matter, with the pulpit. If I had met him socially before knowing who he was, I think I should have mistaken him for a commercial traveler, or something of that sort."

"Which is a compliment to Holmes," said Richard with decision. "If I ever should be a clergyman, I trust I shall be one of that kind. The clerical atmosphere which some ministers succeed in carrying about with them is always offensive to me—a kind of ministerial cant, I call it."

"I don't know," said Mrs. Farrand, doubtfully. "One doesn't like 'cant,' of course, anywhere; but there is, as you say, a kind of atmosphere about some ministers; it isn't unpleasant to me—at least, the kind that I mean isn't. Do you remember, Athalie, how often when we were traveling, entire strangers in dealing with your father would say, 'You are a clergyman, are you not?'"

"I remember it," said Doris. "One of my girlish admirations, who was three or four years older than I, told me once that she would know my father was a minister, if she had never heard of him nor heard him speak a word, just by looking at him.

"'How would you?' I asked.

"'Oh, I don't know,' she said. 'He carries heaven about with him, someway, as a minister ought.' She admired father very much."

"Everybody did," said Athalie, "strangers as well as acquaintances; and he was as far removed from anything like cant as possible. There is a vast stretch of country between a sanctimonious clerical air and a manner that says, 'I am a clergyman on Sunday, it is true, but I am properly ashamed of it; pray forget it during the week as much as possible.' Garrett, why don't you express your views on this important question? I know you have some. Has the thought of college work beginning taken away your breath?"

Garrett Randall, who had been promoted to a permanent seat at table, answered her question with a merry smile before he said:

"I'll own to a preoccupied mind. I have some great news, at least it is great to me. I should like the advice of all of you, if I may have it."

Then they heard for the first time that, through the influence of a former professor who had accepted a higher position, Garrett Randall had been offered a scholarship in the college to which he had gone. The offer had been delayed, awaiting the decision of another man, who at a late hour had determined not to accept it, and Randall could have the opening if he wished.

This item of news created an entire diversion, and the family lingered long discussing the situation. The result left Mrs. Farrand in a state of depression.

"Of course he ought to go," she said to Athalie, when the others had scattered. "I felt that at once; such an opportunity is not to be lost. That it has been offered, shows what others think of him. I hope Richard is discovering that there is sense in his trying for a higher education. But I cannot help wondering what we are to do without him. It seems strange that we have so soon got into the habit of leaning on him; but I feel as though this great house, and Cook, and Thomas, and all the rest of them, were too much for me without him."

The verdict was general that Garrett Randall should go, and no obstacles were placed in his way, notwithstanding his earnest explanation to Mrs. Farrand that if she would but say the word, the scholarship and all the chances which it represented should go. He had let her plan her new home with a view to his help throughout his college course, and if he really could help her better than a stranger could, he should be glad to stay. He felt under lasting obligations to her, and all of them, and felt that they had the best right to his work; and his mother agreed with him.

This was the touch which Mrs. Farrand needed to make her hearty and strenuous in her approval of his going.

In three days more he was gone, and the household proceeded to rearrange itself without him. The vacant places were so conspicuous that not an hour in the day passed without their being uncomfortably reminded of his absence.

But if they missed him in the home life, what shall be said of the loss to Water Street?

"There is one prolonged howl over it," Athalie said, the first time she went without him. "The boys simply can't get over their disappointment. Poor fellows, I am sorry for them! It is the same there that it is in this house: no one knew how much Garrett was doing until he left. Mr. Ansdell says any other four of the workers might have gone, without being missed as he is."

It was Doris who asked how his place was to be filled, and her sister replied at length:

"That is more than any of us know. They have the hardest work to find teachers; it is a wonder that Mr. Ansdell doesn't give up in despair. It seems strange that in a city full of intelligent people, many of them seeming to have not much to take their time, more cannot be found who are willing to help in a work so well started, and which already shows the results of a little effort.

"I wonder if Richard wouldn't help some this winter. He isn't a regular student. Couldn't he manage a couple of hours, or even a single hour, on Friday evenings? It would be good for him to get acquainted with life down on Water Street; if he is going to be a city pastor, he will have to come in contact with just such districts, or ought to. Couldn't you coax him into the work?"

"I don't know," said Doris, doubtfully. "You say he isn't a regular student, but in some respects it is almost worse than if he were. He has undertaken very heavy work in the law department. Still, perhaps he might arrange for one hour a week; I will talk with him about it."

When she did, he was almost offended with her for imagining such a thing as possible. He had undertaken to do two years' work in one, he told her, in order to save time. Perhaps she could imagine why he was anxious to save all the time he could. The last was spoken in a reproachful tone, and he added with dignity that justice to his body demanded of him not to take any additional mental strain.

When Doris heard in detail what he had mapped out to accomplish that winter, she quite agreed with him; but the result of the effort dismayed him even more than the first proposition had done, for Doris herself undertook Garrett Randall's interrupted work. Not by any means all the work he had done for the boys; but the Friday-night class, lasting an hour and a half, she assumed.

"A great deal can be accomplished in an hour and a half a week," she said, well pleased when it was finally settled. Richard had been hard to manage.

"If you persist in this thing, you will seriously hurt me," he had said in his most injured tone. "Think what you are doing: working harder in college than any member of your class, and then using the only evening left for recreation to teach a class of rough boys who ought to have a man over them if they are ever to be taught anything. I did not think that you would care to go contrary to my expressed wishes, Doris."

She was winsome and charming. She placed a soft hand over his eloquent lips and spoke in the most coaxing of tones:

"Ah, now, don't be hurt and positive and cross and bad. It isn't anything dreadful that I want to do; it isn't even a cross to me; I like it. I have always wanted to try to teach somebody. It is only for an hour or so, early on Friday evenings. There will always be evening enough left after the class for anything we may want to do. As for the 'rough boys,' they are all under Mr. Ansdell's control, you know, and he is at the other end of the same room all the time. Besides, they were never rough when Garrett Randall was there, and I don't mean they shall be with me. Do you mean to insinuate that I cannot have as much influence over boys as a great big man would? Do please be good, Richard"—certain tender little pats designed to be irresistible accompanied this sentence—"and let me enjoy my one little venture into another sort of world. I have been very good to you, sir. Don't you know that I gave up Miss Mayburn's Bible class and broke her heart, just to please you? And I didn't take the class of little boys in the Sunday-school for the same reason, though even Mr. Holmes thought I ought. I think it is time I was rewarded.

"Besides, you know you are to be busy with Professor Steene

on Fridays after this. Why shouldn't I be on Water Street during the hour that you give to him? Really, Richard, I look upon it as a rest; it will be such a complete change from all my other work."

Of course she prevailed; she had meant to when she began. Water Street, had it known, would have blessed the hour when she conquered Richard's prejudices and appeared there.

It proved true, as Richard had foretold, that she gave much more than the hour and a half to her new and fascinating work; still he had no real cause of complaint. The hours given to Water Street were invariably those in which he was himself busy, and for his leisure Doris seemed to be always ready. She entered into his plans with a zest that went far toward proving the truth of her assertion, that Water Street rested instead of wearying her. Richard was so genuinely busy that the gay world could not claim very much of his time; yet it is surprising how much leisure can be found for entertainment pure and simple, even by busy people, when they are bent on finding it.

In the course of that winter another change took place, the announcement of which surprised most of the members of the Farrand family. Richard made it known one evening at the dinner table.

"Holmes is going to give up."

"Give up what?" Mrs. Farrand and Doris asked the question at the same moment.

"The pulpit, and the magnificent salary, and everything. In other words, he isn't going to preach any more."

Exclamations from Mrs. Farrand, a disturbed look on Doris's face, and sagacious nods from Athalie.

"What an extraordinary proceeding for a man as young as he!" It was Mrs. Farrand who spoke. "What is he going to do? Small as his salary is, it is surely better than nothing. I suppose he has the student craze; but how is he going to live while he is studying?"

Richard gave attention to a single phrase of hers.

"The 'student craze,' did you say? Isn't that a curious word from your lips? You don't really think that to be enamored of study is a disease, or evil spell, do you? "

"Sometimes it seems a little like that, in these days," she said, smiling on him. "I am old-fashioned, you know. Of course a genuine student is always eager for study. Your father," with a bend of her head toward her daughters, "was a student all his life, and said he should remain so, he was sure, if he lived to be a hundred. But after he was graduated and had begun his life-work, he did not give it the chief place anymore. And he didn't do much studying outside of the line of his profession, either. He could have been an authority on geology, people said, if he had kept at work; he was very fond of that study, but he always said he couldn't spare time for it from more important things."

Mrs. Farrand was not trying to rebuke her promised son-in-law; she had all but forgotten him, and was speaking to her daughters of their father.

Athalie, however, was waiting to express her opinion of Mr. Holmes.

"Nevertheless, mother, I'm glad to hear Richard's piece of news. I think when a man is evidently not fitted for a profession, as soon as he finds it out he would better drop it, whatever the consequences."

"But, child, he has been set apart to the ministry, and been ordained, and taken solemn vows upon himself."

"I can't help that. When the vows set as lightly as they do on Mr. Holmes, it can't hurt much to break them. The veriest child can see that in the ministry he is out of his sphere."

"It seems a pity, though, that a man of average sense cannot learn for what he is fitted, and to what he has been called, before taking solemn vows upon himself merely to break them."

It was Doris who spoke.

"That is true," said Athalie, quickly. "But people get into the wrong place sometimes through outside pressure, when, if left to themselves, they would have chosen otherwise."

Richard gave her an approving smile. "That is splendid common sense, Athalie; you ought to be a lawyer, you would settle half the disputes in the world for people without bringing them into court.

"Well, whether wise or otherwise, Holmes has called a halt. It seems he has always wanted to study medicine, and medicine he is now to study. A friend has made an opening for him, somehow; I haven't heard the details, and his resignation is to be presented next Sunday. I made haste to tell it as a piece of good news; you have all been so down on poor Holmes as a pastor that I thought it would rejoice your hearts."

The talk continued, waxing warm at times. Mrs. Farrand admitted that she should like Mr. Holmes much better as a physician than as a clergyman, but still could not believe that solemn vows ought to be lightly laid aside. She believed, on the contrary, that a call to the ministry was from God; was peculiar and definite; was as plainly understood at the time as if actual words were spoken. How could a man draw back from an experience like that?

"If you are right, Mrs. Farrand," Richard said gloomily, "then some of us have never been called to the ministry; that is all I can say."

Immediately afterward he asked to be excused, and departed. Doris remained noticeably silent.

Chapter 20

"A word in due season, how good is it!"

Before the family seemed to have fairly adjusted itself for the new year of work, the mid-year vacation was upon them. They were very gay indeed. Social gatherings of one form or other filled each evening. For three weeks in succession Friday evenings had to be given entirely to society. Invitations were so special, and followed one another so closely, Water Street interests were crowded out. It was not until the season of Lent approached that the social world called a halt. It was, therefore, after an interval of several weeks that Doris went to Water Street to discover that her class had scattered, only one member being present.

"They thought you wasn't coming any more," he explained. "Ted said you wasn't; he said you had got sick of us, and that you wasn't the kind, anyhow. Ted said you was the dancing kind; his brother was a waiter at one of the big doings down on the avenue, and Ted got in to help one night, when the regular boy was sick, and he see you dancing like a top, he says; and he says them ain't the kind that ever stick to such doings as we have here."

This was plain speaking. Doris laughed, though she felt her cheeks glow; she made haste to try to check the voluble tongue.

"Ted is very wise, isn't he? He would have been wiser if he had come this evening and helped to gather the class again. I have been detained for several weeks, but I expect to be here regularly after this."

"Ted could have got 'em," said the boy, who was known as

Billy. "He's our leader, Ted is; a lot of 'em do just what he does and think what he thinks; and when he made out you was gone for good, and didn't care much about us anyhow, why, they up and swallowed it. They said they wasn't coming no more, they was sick of changing around. But I guess I could get 'em back if they knew you was here. Shall I go out and try it?"

Doris felt that it was a pity to lose the entire evening; the other teachers were at work, as usual, and there seemed to be nothing for her to do, so she agreed to the novel proposition that the stray students should be hunted after through the streets.

Billy made a dash for his cap and departed noisily on his errand, while Doris sat alone and looked about her. Half a dozen boys were seated not far from her at a reading table. Each had a book and seemed to be absorbed in its study. She recognized one of them as belonging to Athalie's English Club. He looked up, presently, and challenged her help. He had come in his study to a legal phrase which he did not understand. Doris's attempted explanation awakened a series of questions which soon took her beyond her depth.

"You must remember that I am not a lawyer," she said, smiling. "If you will write out your questions, I will refer them to a friend who will be here soon, and he will answer them for you." It pleased her to think how readily Richard could help this inquiring mind.

Before the boy's questions were written, his next neighbor had asked one upon a different theme. The conversation that followed reached a point where it called for a better knowledge of physics than Doris possessed. Here, too, Richard could help; she suggested another series of questions, and went away smiling. Richard would be compelled to help the Water Street scholars in spite of himself. In doing so she felt sure he would become interested in them.

At that moment the veritable Ted himself lounged in, and glanced listlessly over to his accustomed corner. His eyes lighted when he saw Doris, and he came to her at once.

"So you're here!" he said, marked surprise mingling with the pleasure in his tones.

"Of course I am; but you were not."

"No, I didn't expect you. I thought it would be another new one, and then another, and another, for a spell, and then nobody for a spell. That is the way we was before that last man came here, and I got sick of it."

"There isn't to be 'another one'; I expect to be here through the season, though I may have to be absent occasionally. I thought you could trust me to that extent. Where are the boys? It is a great disappointment not to see them here. Billy thought you could bring them back."

"Has Billy gone for them? He'll get 'em. I don't know tonight where a last one of 'em is; I've been thinkin' about something else. But Billy does, mostly; he'll bring 'em.

"Say"—glancing about him quickly to see if anyone else was within hearing and lowering his voice— "before they come back I want you to tell me something. That man we had, you know him, don't you? His name was Randall."

"Yes," said Doris, "I know who you mean."

"Well, he told us fellows a lot of queer things. He said that if a fellow wanted to do a mean thing the worst kind, couldn't hardly keep himself from it, you know, that if he belonged to Jesus Christ he'd help him *every time*—kind of keep him in spite of himself, somehow."

He looked searchingly at Doris's face to see if he were speaking a language that she understood, and seeming satisfied with what he saw, went on eagerly:

"And he said that kind of livin' was satisfying—that's the very word he used; that a fellow got so after a while that he didn't hanker after them other things no more; he got all made over inside, you know?" The questioning look again.

"And he said that the Bible, if a fellow read it regular, and thought about it, and tried to do as it said, would keep helpin' of him right along. And he said you could learn to talk to Jesus Christ—anybody could, you know, that wanted to—and he'd listen, and let you know he was listening. Now what I want to ask is: Do you believe them things? I mean do you believe them *for me?* I can see how they might be true of a splendid man like that Mr. Randall; but I'm nothin' but Ted Mullins, drunken Pete Mullins's boy, that looks just like his father, and is like him, and is goin' his road as fast as he can."

"Of course I believe them." There was a ring of gladness in Doris's voice. "Every word is true. Jesus Christ is just as ready to hear and help Ted Mullins as he is to hear Mr. Randall. I am as sure of it as I am that you and I sit here talking."

"Well, and that about the Bible; reading it, and doing of it as fast as you get on in it—do you do that?"

The vivid crimson glowed on Doris's cheeks.

"I read it, Ted," she said, and she tried to think when she had last given other than a hurried glance at it.

"And you keep doing all it says?" His keen eyes were searching her face. "There's things in it that seem awful hard; and it doesn't seem as if folks was doing of them, not many folks; *he* is, I guess, but he ain't like other folks in lots of ways. He give me one of his verses and told me what he thought it meant. 'Do all to the glory of God'—them were the words, and he said it meant eating and drinking and talking and everything; that they was all to be done so as to honor God. That seems awful hard! I've been watching a good deal, and it doesn't seem to me as though hardly anybody was a-doing of it; and yet they pretend to belong to Jesus Christ. What's the use of pretending if you don't do it? And then again, how could you do it? A fellow like me, anyhow? Do you do that?"

What was Doris to answer? His searching eyes seemed to look

into her very soul. She opened her lips to reply. "I—" she said, and stopped. She had meant to say, "I try to." An instinct of honesty stopped her. Was she even trying?

He was quick-witted, this boy whose chief education was of the street. The shadow of a smile flitted over his dark face. He seemed to feel that, as he would have expressed it, he had put this young woman in a corner. A wisdom more than her own helped Doris at last. "Ted, what difference do you suppose it will really make to you whether I, or anybody else in this world, believe and obey God? Do you know about a great day that is to come, when people are to meet God face to face and give in their account?"

"Heard of it," said Ted, gravely.

"Well, when Ted Mullins's account is called for, will it help him any to be able to say, 'I knew what you wanted, but Miss Farrand and a crowd of others didn't do it, so I didn't'? How would such an excuse serve in the police court?"

"It wouldn't go down," said Ted, still speaking gravely.

Doris waited for a full minute for another word from him, then she said:

"You see how it is: while it will make a solemn difference to each of us what account of our life we bring, it will make no difference to Ted Mullins what other people say. If all the world goes wrong and you alone go right, it is you alone who will win."

There was another silence; then Ted drew a long, heavy sigh, as he said:

"It might help us fellows along, though, if we saw the others at it; but the long and short of it is, I've got to do something. There ain't no living much longer in the way I be now. I'm gnawed at and jawed at inside and out all the time to do the things I promised him I wouldn't do no more, and to give up the things I told him I'd stick to; and I've got to have some kind of help mighty soon, or go under. He wrote me a letter! "

The sudden change of tone was startling. He spoke as commonplace people would in saying, "He sent me a thousand dollars!"

"Do you want to see it?"

Without waiting for reply, he drew from his pocket a carefully wrapped package and spread before her, with the air of a miser showing his gold, a letter from Garrett Randall. It was a wholesome, manly letter, just such as she could imagine Garrett Randall would write; not long, not in the least "preachy," and full of the heartiest interest in the present and future of this Water Street boy.

"Ain't that fine?" said Ted, as the letter was returned. "It would be hard on him if I should give the thing up; I guess he'd care *awful!* I should hate to disappoint him, and I won't, either." His chin settled into firmness with those last words. Then he looked at Doris with the air of one who had reached a decision.

"So what I want you to tell me now is, How do you do it? You've done it, haven't you? So you'll know. He tried to tell me, but I wasn't ready for it then; I hadn't made up my mind. It's *hard.* It will make a big change, you see; there's things I've got to do, and to give up doing—and then there's the fellows to poke fun and play jokes, and—well, there's lots of things, and it took time. But I'm there all the same. Now, what's first?"

A soul on its momentous journey, inquiring the way! Inquiring of her, Doris Farrand, who was supposed to have passed that way seven years before, and to be able to direct another. Could she? One false step now might be fatal to a soul. Oh, for someone close at hand who would be sure to say just the right word! She glanced about her; most of the workers within call she did not know. Athalie was in the next room, but Athalie was hardly the one; at least she might not be. Richard would be here in a few minutes, but with a thrill of pain at her heart she put him aside at once. Richard would do for the legal points and the philosophical questions, but she felt instinctively that he would not know how to deal with this boy. Oh, for five minutes of Garrett Randall's help!

Meanwhile Ted waited, looking straight at her with hungry and at the same time searching eyes.

"Ted," she said, speaking hurriedly, almost breathlessly, "you know the way: Jesus Christ is the Way; go straight to him, just as you would to Mr. Randall if he were here. Jesus Christ is here; he never goes away. Tell him what you have decided, and ask him to do the rest."

Was she glad, or sorry, that at that moment Billy came clattering back, seven noisy boys in his train, all eager to tell her that they were glad she was there?

Just how she got through with the next half-hour she could not herself have told. She tried to take up the work she had planned for the evening, and the boys seemed interested in her effort. Ted alone asked no questions and sat as one with thoughts apart. He had more important business in hand.

When Richard came for her, Doris sent him to answer the legal and philosophical questions at the other table, which he did in a way that called out hearty approval. While he was gone Doris had opportunity to say another word to Ted.

"You understand, don't you?" she asked anxiously.

He nodded gravely.

"I s'pose I do," he said, "but it seems kind of *scary*. I don't know how to talk—not to *him*."

"Think of him as a man, Ted; down here, walking the streets with you boys, knowing all about you, and more interested in you than any man could be."

Again Ted drew that long, slow breath which indicates strong and controlled feeling.

"Well," he said, "I'll try it; it's likely he knows just how hard it will be, and that will make him kind of patient with a fellow. He is the only man in the world that was ever downright good to me, and I'd feel awful mean disappointing of *him,* even if I didn't for myself."

Ted's pronouns were mixed; evidently Garrett Randall's name was inseparably associated in his mind with that of Garrett Randall's Master.

The boy's underlying motive might have been a low one, viewed from some standpoints; yet Doris, as she turned away, felt that the highest reward there could be in this world would be the knowledge that somebody, in order not to disappoint her, was resolutely setting his feet toward the narrow road.

During the homeward walk Richard and Athalie had the talk almost to themselves, Doris joining in only when directly addressed.

"You are tired out every Friday evening," Richard complained at last. "I have noticed it for a long time."

"I noticed," said Athalie, "that she was very tired last Friday, and the Friday before."

Richard joined in the laugh at his own expense, as it chanced that on both those Fridays, society functions had absorbed Doris far into the night.

"Nevertheless," he said, "Water Street is responsible for a good deal. One of these days I am going to rebel."

Chapter 21

"I was asleep, but my heart waked."

Athalie and Richard went away together. Richard had an appointment to meet, and Athalie was to spend the night with a friend who was an invalid. Both of them besought Doris to retire early and get a long night's rest.

"Because," said Athalie, "tomorrow will be your birthday, remember, and we shall want you fresh for all the dissipations we have planned in its honor."

Mrs. Farrand opened the door of her room as Doris passed. "Is that you, daughter?" she said. "Are you alone? Come here a moment, dear, I have something for you."

Although the light in her room was carefully shaded, Doris saw that her mother had been crying. She stooped to kiss her and to say softly, "Dear mother, what is it?"

"It is nothing new, dear. Mother is lonely sometimes with a loneliness that nothing earthly can help. I have been looking over some letters that brought back the past very vividly. One of them is for you."

"For me?" said Doris, wondering.

"Yes, my dear, for you. A birthday gift, and I know you can have nothing more precious. Your father wrote it on the afternoon of the night that he went away. We had been talking about you especially, because the next day would be your birthday, and he asked for pencil and paper to write you a birthday greeting. He said he had had a quiet talk with Athalie that afternoon, but there had been no chance to see you. I discouraged his writing, I thought him too weak; but he insisted and wrote these few lines, addressing and sealing it himself. You notice that it is to be given to you on the eve of your twentieth birthday."

Doris took the package, her eyes misty with tears. She bent and kissed her mother without a word and went away.

She locked her door with a sense of relief in the thought that she was to be alone all night. She had a feeling that it was to be to her an eventful night. During that almost silent homeward walk her thoughts had been busy. Some of Ted Mullins's questions had probed her. The wonder of it, that she, a professed Christian for eight years, should be in doubt about pointing out the way! The shame of it, that she must either evade some of those questions or be a false witness for her Lord! Something was radically wrong; the contrast between her religion and that of Garrett Randall, for instance, was too sharp to be accounted for by difference of temperament or environment. She had come home with the feeling that something must be done; that, like poor Ted, there was no use in trying to live the life she was now living, "gnawed" as she often was by her own conscience. Perhaps she had even reached unconsciously the point where, like him, she "*must* have help or go under." Her newly aroused conscience reminded her with startling directness how long it was since she had been disturbed in this way. This could not be because her mind and soul approved the life she was living; was it, then, because the tendency of such living was to silence conscience?

True, these were "old-fashioned ideas," she could almost hear Richard's voice saying so, but they had been her father's ideas. Still, of course, that was not a reason for blind adherence to them: her father was but another human being, and she had been a mere child when he went away; she might not have understood his views. This was surface thinking, or rather, it was not thinking at all, but quoting the thoughts of others. Back of it, burning as a steady light, was a belief that they were the ideas of the Lord Jesus Christ, and a dim realization of the fact that in these fast days he, too, would be considered old-fashioned.

Now she was alone in her room with a message from her dead father in her hand; that dear father whose memory had lingered with her through her girlish years, and had its subduing influence on her life. What would be that father's last word for her? What a sweet thought it had been to reach forward through the years to her twentieth birthday! How like her memory of her father! There would be some sweet, strong word for her, of that she felt sure.

"Something to help me," she said aloud. "I need help, oh, I *need* help!" She broke the seal, drew out the single sheet of note-paper, and held it unopened for several minutes. A strange awe stole over her, as if she were in the presence of the unseen world. Could her father see her now? Did he know how eager her heart was for his message? At last she spread open the page. There were but a few lines, evidently traced by a hand that trembled, yet the words were distinct.

"Dear girlie," it read, "father's baby: I think I am going home tonight, and tomorrow you will be only thirteen; too young, thank God, to mourn overmuch. I want my darling to have a happy life. What shall father say for a good-bye word? It shall not be 'good-bye,' dear, it is only a 'God bless you' until we meet again. I will reach forward to the time when you are getting done with what is called girl-hood, and give you my wish for those womanly years. I will give you a life motto; I ask you, my dear, to be true to it until I see you again. 'Walk worthy of the vocation wherewith ye are called.'"

There was only one other word, feebly traced, suggesting that the effort of writing had been too much for the fast-ebbing strength, and that perhaps mortal weakness had followed it. The word was, "Amen." It came to the girl like a second appeal, a pledge which she was asked to make, or else a prayer for her from her father's dying lips.

"So let it be," had been his explanation of its meaning to her, a little girl.

She sat quiet, and the room was very still. She sat long with that message from the other world in her hand. Here, once more, almost in her father's voice, was that thought which had been now three times thrust upon her in a way to arrest attention. Was it *God's* word to her, as well as man's? She shed no tears; this was a solemn time, but not a time for tears.

She went over her life, going back once more to that summer Sunday in her father's church, when she, a child of twelve, stood at the altar and listened to well-known words: "You take the word of God as your rule of life? You give yourself soul and body, time and talents, to God's service? You do this intelligently, sincerely, freely, and forever?"

"Do you do it?" Ted Mullins had asked her that evening. He seemed to be there now, adding his probing question. History and conscience and honor met in solemn council in her heart and answered, "No." The Bible had not been her rule of life. It *had not!* It held a position of honor, it was treated always with a certain sort of deference, but—a *"rule of life!"* It was folly to talk about that. Could anybody conscientiously say that? Here was the old question with which she had quieted her heart before. She still knew no one intimately who seemed to her to be trying to live by such a test. Not even Miss Mayburn anymore, for she had finally gone away where her life could not be daily watched. And there were no others, unless—unless that young man, Garrett Randall, was indeed an exception. It was scarcely possible to avoid bringing him mentally into this solemn interview. Was not his study of that word "vocation" a vivid memory in connection with her knowledge of him? Was not his daily effort to order his life so that things would "fit" a steady refutation of her excuse? But he was only one, and he was young and uncultured. Wasn't it folly to suppose him in the right, and all her other friends mistaken? Then, suddenly, she was back in Water Street, was speaking eagerly to Ted Mullins the strong conviction of her soul, "When Ted Mullins's account is called for, will it help him any to be able to say, 'I knew what you wanted, but Miss Farrand and a crowd of others didn't do it, so I didn't'?" She could hear Ted's grave conclusion, "It wouldn't go down."

Was there not in the depths of Doris Farrand's honest soul a conviction of what God wanted of her? Was she living her daily life in accord with that conviction?

She sat long and thought. She was in the Bible class—that Bible class which she had deserted, even before Miss Mayburn went away. It was a summer morning, and the girls of the class were all about her in a flutter of irresponsible life, and Miss Mayburn was saying:

"If even one of you would choose it for a life motto, think what a difference it would make!" And that motto—how did it differ from her father's? "Walk worthy of God," said Miss Mayburn. "Walk worthy of the vocation wherewith ye are called," said her father, calling down to her from his far, safe home.

What if she had heeded the call, then, when Miss Mayburn spoke? She remembered vividly how the thought had haunted her, oppressed her summer, "spoiled all her good times," she told herself, irritably, more than once. Miss Mayburn had been true, had not left her to unrestrained heedlessness; she was always dropping quiet little words, which, if not originally intended solely for her, Doris's conscience had appropriated sufficiently to make her uncomfortable—sufficiently to make her, after a while, an easy prey to Richard's persuasions that she needed the Sunday morning rest after the hard work of the week and owed it to herself to give up the Bible class. True, she had not admitted that she was so much of a weakling as to be in need of a great deal more sleep on Sunday morning than her self-imposed obligations gave her opportunity for on other days; what she assured herself was that she owed it to Richard to yield to him in unimportant matters, since she was his promised wife. Was this an unimportant matter? Well, yes, in a sense it was. She was older than most-of the girls now left in the class, and surely she could study the Bible without Miss Mayburn's help. She remembered that it had been a distinct relief to get away from Miss Mayburn, although stern justice had even then compelled her to own that her Bible-class teacher had not been offensive nor even obtrusive in her zeal, but had governed herself always in accordance with the dictates of good judgment and a cultured heart.

Nor had her pupil, by deserting her, closed all the avenues by which she could be reached. Had not Garrett Randall more than once in the most unwitting manner, with his debates and his study of words, and his self-renunciations and his deliberate choices, opened again and again the discussion between two selves which Doris now realized had been at war within her? Nay, had not that young man's very personalities, being far removed in his mind from the thought of flattery or of compliment, served to rouse into renewed life her dormant conscience? She remembered the tones of his voice, the look in his eyes when he asked:

"Shall I tell you of whom you remind me tonight? I thought of it as soon as I saw you in that shimmering dress, 'The king's daughter within the palace is all glorious.'" Verily, how often had this daughter of a king, living her disguised life, been wooed to come boldly forward and proclaim her royal lineage. And then she realized that she had let the thought slip. She had not deliberately resolved that she would have no such motto as that which Miss Mayburn had offered her; she had by no means desired not to be known as the king's daughter; she had been indifferent and self-absorbed, she had simply—What was that chapter in the Bible she had learned as a child and recited proudly to her father? She was a child again, and it was Sunday afternoon, and her father was resting on the lounge, drawn up before the western window; and the sun was setting, and all the room was aglow with its solemn beauty, and all the sky was a flush of crimson flecked with gold, and her father's voice was saying:

"Now, daughter, for those new verses you were so anxious to let me hear." How proudly she had recited the entire chapter, without a suggestion of the time when phrases in it would serve as history! "Therefore we ought to give the more earnest heed to the things which we have heard, lest at any time we should let them slip."

That was what she had done. Not decision, not deliberate rejection, she had simply "let them slip."

Then had come Water Street, and Ted Mullins, with his probing questions, and then her father, reaching down out of heaven, to call after her.

She sat long, deep in thought; no tears, nothing visible that could be called emotion; nothing stiller than her face and manner could be imagined. Some of the time she sat as if she were carved in marble. Then, at last, she knelt. The house was very quiet, the moonlight flooded the room, enveloping the kneeling form. If the angels were there, they were invisible; she thought not of them. It may be that her father's spirit hovered near his child, waiting, watching; if it did, he knew it was as it should be; she thought not of him. One was there—He who had knelt long before in Gethsemane for her; He to whom it had been promised that He should "see of the travail of his soul and be satisfied;" and the girl knew in her inmost soul that she had not satisfied Him. Yet she knew that He was there, and was waiting.

When at last she arose, the new day was flushing the eastern sky. Her twentieth birthday.

"Tomorrow," Athalie had said, "you will put away your 'teens' and your frivolities, I suppose, and become a woman."

As the girl stood there, watching the rapidly growing glory which foretokened the coming of the sun, she realized that a new day had indeed begun.

All this time she had held clasped closely, like a treasure, the letter from her father. She unfolded and read it once more, lingering over each word as though it were a caress; then she folded it carefully, and hid it in her dress; as she did so, she said aloud, with steady voice and a face that meant decision, one single word, "Amen."

Chapter 22

"Riches are not forever."

"Here's a paper," said Miss Melinda, coming from the kitchen, newspaper in hand.

"Oh, that won't do," said Miss Harriet; "she doesn't want to go through the street carrying a newspaper bundle, and a Sunday one at that. Can't you find a piece of brown paper in this house to do up a bundle in?"

"Not a scrap," said Miss Melinda, cheerfully; "unless she'll wait till I run upstairs and get that great big sheet of brown paper that come around the tablecloth we bought this spring. I put it away because it was such a nice, big, smooth sheet it looked good enough to write on if a body had anything to write; but I can get it."

Here Doris interposed.

"Please don't, Miss Melinda. Think what you may write on it, someday. I wouldn't sacrifice it to a bundle. I don't mind the newspaper in the least, Miss Harriet. I'm not going to the village, only back to the hotel. As for the Sunday part, it won't soil my white morning dress, will it?"

"Well, I dunno," said Miss Harriet, as she folded the fluffy eider-down wrapper into the big newspaper, "whether it will or not. It's trashy enough to hurt even cloth, maybe. I never see the beat of them Sunday newspapers for stuff; how folks can read 'em week after week, as they do, is more than I can understand. I hope you don't think we take it, Miss Farrand. I wouldn't be seen taking it in at the front door with the tongs. Our grocer put the precious sheet into the bottom of the basket, Saturday, to 'protect the basket,' he said, and I asked him if he was sure it wouldn't dirty it instead. But there was nothing but dry paper parcels put in the basket, so there won't anything from them get on your dress. Melinda, she got out the newspaper to look at the pictures; I never see the beat of that girl for pictures; she'd fish one out of an ink-bottle, I b'lieve, to look at."

Doris gave the "girl" of sixty years or more, a quick, questioning glance, from the little knot of gray hair on the back of her head, down the length of her plain, short, print dress, to her stout, worn shoes, and wondered if an artist soul were hidden behind all this commonplaceness. She looked from her to the bare wall of the small, neat room in which the two sisters sat all day and every day, and sewed to earn their living. Was there a starved life behind it all, hungering for beauty? So Miss Melinda loved pictures, and flowers, evidently, for the little patch of ground under the kitchen window was gay with old-fashioned blooms that she had been told by the sterner Harriet, Melinda "fussed with a good deal."

"Pictures she shall have," Doris told herself, as she climbed the hill to the summer hotel, carrying her own package, after the primitive fashion of the village. It was hundreds of miles away from her own home, this scrap of a village tucked in among the Berkshire hills, which was hardly a village at all, only a post-office, and a red schoolhouse, and a smart little chapel, newly built, and two or three summer hotels and boarding-houses.

Once, years ago, Doris's mother and father had come up among these hills for a summering, and Doris had been eager to repeat some of their experiences. Moreover, Richard Shipley was a law student in the city near at hand, and could make the trip easily on Saturdays, even coming sometimes on Friday evenings when office business was not pressing.

Richard Shipley had profited by Mr. Holmes's experience and "given up" the ministry before he entered it. Within three months of the night vigil which resulted in a marked change in Doris Farrand's life, Shipley had been offered a position in the law office of his father's old friend, with opportunity to earn his living while he continued his law studies. The old friend was evidently unaware that the year's study of law was being sandwiched in between a college and theological seminary course, but took it for granted that the legal profession was the young man's chosen one. The offer was especially satisfactory because it included a home in the widowed lawyer's household, provided Richard's mother would come with him and assume direction of the servants. As the house was large and well appointed, and the servants understood their business, nothing could have suited Mrs. Shipley better.

"It seems like a Providence," she said to Doris, which was her usual way of acknowledging guidance.

"Not that there really is such a thing, you know," said Athalie, commenting on Mrs. Shipley's manner, "only sometimes things happen so exactly to her liking that it seems as though somebody might have arranged them."

Doris pondered the expression in her heart. Was it Providence? Was it God's way of making plain to Richard that his calling was not to the ministry? She was not so sure as she used to be that Richard must study theology; she was not even sure that she desired it. Was Richard—would Richard *ever* be just the kind of man that God meant when he instituted the sacred office?

No one could have been more elated than was Richard Shipley at finding how quietly Doris received the final decision.

"I have been an idiot," he told her gaily. "I might have known I could trust to your good sense to see what a wonderful business opening this is. Judge Bronson is the leading lawyer in that part of the country, and he is growing old; it will end in a partnership if I succeed in keeping on the right side of him, and I think I may be trusted for that. The fact is, Doris, I settled it some time ago that I had mistaken my calling in trying to enter the ministry; but your heart seemed so set on it that I tried to keep on, long after I knew it was folly, so as not to disappoint you. If I had realized what a thoroughly sensible girl you were, I should have had all my arrangements made long ago."

"What about your mother, Richard? Isn't this a great disappointment to her?" This had been Doris's only reply.

Richard had laughed carelessly as he replied that so far as his mother was concerned he believed that her affections had been set on the ten thousand dollars attached to the profession rather than to the profession itself. He made haste to add that this was because she thought it would make life so much easier for him to have an assured income while he was studying; but now that he had succeeded in proving to her that Judge Bronson's offer was worth more thousands of dollars to him than the average minister ever saw, she was quite content.

Neither of them spoke of Doris's fortune; but the girl knew, better than Richard supposed she did, that the knowledge of her many thousands was what had reconciled Mrs. Shipley, not to the giving up of the ministry, exactly, but of the ten thousand included in it.

Neither at that time nor in the weeks which followed did Doris make in words any objection to the new plans. Richard was to go many hundred miles away from her, but even this she told herself was for the best. She had her own life to re-order, and she needed to be quite alone to get her bearings and fully understand herself. If they were both to readjust their lives, it would probably be better for each to do so without the watchful presence of the other.

So Richard, at the close of that year of legal study, had gone his way, not to the theological seminary as had been planned so long before, but to Judge Bronson's law office; and now, after two years of separation, Doris had come to the Berkshire hills for her summering, partly in order to be near him.

Doris was now twenty-two, and had been graduated from college. In one more year Richard would be admitted to the bar, and then would begin, probably, their long-ago-planned life together.

It was Miss Melinda's love of pictures that made Doris look a second time at the brilliantly illustrated Sunday sheet instead of consigning it at once to the hall waste-basket.

"Think of feeding artistic taste upon such horrors as these!" she said as she gazed. "Miss Melinda shall have some pictures before the day is done. I shall give her that lovely Madonna and the little colored sunset that I found last week; then there are some charming Easter pictures left over, and a landscape or two that I fancy she would like. Oh, I'll decorate those bare walls until she doesn't know them. I wonder what the poor starved soul has to read? She isn't driven to this trash, I hope. What does it read like?"

She glanced down column after column and page after page in ever increasing disgust. Was there really nothing, in so large a sheet as that, to justify a respectable person for buying it? Suddenly her eyes were held. She read not the column alone, but half the great page, standing, just where she was, her sun-hat still hanging on her arm. As she read, the color on her face deepened and spread. What remarkable tale was this? Was it a mere made-up story? Were the localities and the hints at certain facts only strange coincidences, or had this record to do in a startling way with her own life?

The article was headed, "Truth Stranger than Fiction." The writer affirmed that not only was it stranger, but harder; and said that no weaver of fiction, however sensational his tastes, would think of foisting upon even credulous readers such an altogether improbable plot, or such an unjust condition of things as the truth in this instance brought to light.

There followed, written in the melodramatic style of the third-rate sensational newspaper, the story of a man who, years before, had been made the dupe of a "fashionable Eastern belle." He had offered her all that an honest man had to give, and she accepted it, apparently, in good faith. The marriage day was set, but never came; the young lady found a new slave more to her mind, and tossed aside the other one as a worn-out plaything. Smarting under the sense of shame, and disheartened by the "blasting of all his hopes in life," this victim of heartlessness sacrificed his business prospects, emigrated to the far West, and plunged headlong into the hardest work he could find.

His experience in taking up government land, and discovering years afterward that it was "a network of mines," was given in detail. His marriage to "an estimable woman—after years had dulled the pain of his early experience"—was duly chronicled, as also were the births and deaths of four children. Then the wife died, leaving one son who grew to manhood and was associated with his father in business. The father was represented as having been soured by his early experience, and as having an unreasonable temper from which the devoted son suffered much. Matters between the two reached a climax when the son chose a wife who, though in every way worthy, was not to the father's mind. He was threatened then with disinheritance; but believing this to be only an outburst of passion, he stayed on as business manager of his father's large and steadily increasing interests, living on a small salary, and economizing in every way as his little family grew up around him, knowing that his father was the wealthiest man in all that region of country.

Suddenly the father died; then came the discovery that he had willed every penny of his "vast fortune, not to a distant relative even, but to the daughter of the woman who had tossed him aside in her youth." His last interview with his son had been an angry argument on some political question—it was well known that the father tried to dominate his son's views, even on public questions—he had grown very angry and ordered the young man from his presence, declaring in the hearing of several witnesses that he should have reason to repent that day's folly. It was believed that under the influence of this passion he had destroyed the will known to have been made in the son's favor, and substituted for it the one drawn in a moment of weak sentimentalism, which gave to the girl who was the daughter and bore the name of his lost love. True, the will mentioned another heir whom he chose to call a stepson; but as none of his acquaintances had ever heard of a previous marriage, this was believed to be the son of a woman who had once nursed him through a serious illness. Whoever or whatever she was, neither she nor her son could be found; so the "splendid fortune, which by all the rules that govern justice and honor belonged to the son who had helped to make it," reverted to this unknown girl who, "if she had any sense of decency, to say nothing of self-respect, would be overwhelmed with shame at the thought of receiving what ought to be another's, and that other the only son of the man who had defrauded him, in order to enrich her."

This, in brief, is the story which met Doris Farrand's startled eyes and made her wade through three columns of adjectives in that much-illustrated Sunday newspaper.

Was there possible truth in it all, and truth which closely touched herself, themselves? Could she by any stretch of imagination make her mother into that "Eastern belle" who had "ruthlessly and in cold blood wrecked a life"? No language could be more absurd as applied to her mother, and yet—mother had once been engaged to the man who had left her daughter his fortune, and that man had made his money from Western mining lands, and there had been a stepson for whom search was still being made in Richard Shipley's best fashion. And she, Doris Farrand, bore her mother's name, and the man who had remembered her knew it.

But she had never heard of another son—none of them had, of course. They had gone on the supposition that there were no direct heirs, else the property would have reverted to them. If there had been a son, a man grown, and defrauded of his natural rights, would not Mr. Malcolm have spoken of it as a matter of course?

True, they had not questioned, why should they? On the face of it, it would have seemed absurd to be asking if there were no near relatives, when he had been at infinite pains to remember and have searched for that mysterious and long-lost-sight-of stepson!

It was all very strange, very startling. It was more than probable that the whole was a sensation story springing from the brain of a Sunday newspaper writer. She could seem to hear Richard say something of the kind. Yet the writer must have had some foundation in truth, else how could he so nearly state the circumstances as they fitted her experience? And yet, what motive could Mr. Malcolm have had for deceiving them?

Clearly there would be no more peace for Doris until she had fathomed the entire mystery, if mystery it was.

Instead of consigning Miss Melinda's Sunday newspaper to the hall waste-basket, Doris folded and laid it away with utmost care. As she did so there floated through her brain the opening lines of an old hymn familiar to her childhood:

"God moves in a mysterious way
    His wonders to perform."

Was it possible that Miss Melinda's Sunday newspaper was a link in the chain out of which God meant her life-story to be woven?

Chapter 23

"A good name is rather to be chosen than great riches."

"Really, Doris, this is the most eccentric of all your eccentricities; I find myself wondering what you can possibly want to do next."

Richard Shipley's tone and manner indicated strong excitement. They had come out to the east veranda, which stretched itself the full length of the long, old-fashioned summer hotel. It was the hour of the day when the verandas were for the most part deserted, those of the boarders who were not out on all-day excursions being engaged in resting or in making their dinner toilets. Only a few old-fashioned women, who did not take the trouble to dress oftener than twice a day, were in evidence, and these preferred the west veranda and the sunshine; so Doris and Richard could talk unobserved. Richard had come down the evening before, having, with some difficulty, managed a free Saturday, in order to give himself plenty of time to talk Doris out of certain ideas that in correspondence he had found alarming.

It was nearly two months since Miss Melinda's Sunday paper had disturbed Doris's peace. During that time she had carried on a vigorous correspondence, not only with Mr. Malcolm, the lawyer, but with a number of other residents of the distant town where her newly acquired fortune had been made. The results were startling and, to some of those interested, almost appalling.

Mr. Malcolm had been prompt in his replies to her questions, and plain spoken enough, now that he had been questioned.

Undoubtedly there was a son in the case; a man grown, and having a wife and children. Had there been no will, he would, of course, have been the legal heir. But there was a will, which had been executed in accordance with all legal requirements, and the firm having the business in hand had paid strict attention to their instructions. With possible heirs under different circumstances they, of course, had nothing whatever to do; their business was to see that the ones recognized by the will received their rights, and this, to the extent of their ability, they had done.

This had been the substance of a long and technically worded reply to Doris's first letter. It was followed by other letters wherein her questions were answered in detail.

Yes, the son still lived in the town where he had been reared from childhood. He had no property of his own. He was still employed in the business, much as he had been in his father's time. His salary was not large, but neither was it alarmingly small. He was a reliable man and commanded the respect of the community in which he lived.

Of course there had been a great deal of talk about the disposition of the property, and equally of course public opinion sided with the son and considered him unjustly dealt with; but in a case like this the law had nothing to do with public opinion, and it was unquestionable that every detail of the business had been legally correct. Undoubtedly it had been a hard blow to the son: a man living in the expectation of falling heir to two or three hundred thousand dollars, and suddenly losing all chance of a penny, might be excused for considering his lot a hard one; but the man in question was not one to allow himself to be crushed by such an experience; he had business abilities of no mean order and would doubtless make his way in the world. The verdict in town was quite general that he was a better man, viewed from all standpoints, than his father had been. All that talk about his children being "reduced to beggary," etc., was a bit of sensational journalism which the West produced, as she did most other things, in larger measure than the East.

There was no occasion whatever for Miss Farrand to take note of these and other reports which might reach her from time to time, as sensationalists in search of items wandered that way and had time to write up the story. There was absolutely no flaw to be found in the will, and the son was not a man to try to make trouble for others when he had nothing to gain by it.

The whereabouts of that other heir still remained among the things unknown, and, although lawyers as a rule learned very early in their professional life not to be astonished at anything and never to turn prophets, still, if he might depart from that custom for a moment, he would venture the assertion that there was not now one chance in a thousand that the said George Smith would ever be found. The reasonable probability was that the boy had died in childhood, and that his mother had also departed this life. In short, so far as careful investigation could discover, Miss Farrand had nothing to do but enjoy her entire fortune with a serene mind.

But no mind was ever less serene than Miss Farrand's after she had carefully translated from their technicalities and made her own the contents of these letters. For the first few weeks she kept her own counsel, assuring herself that it was not necessary to disturb the quiet of others with a mere newspaper story, if such it should prove to be. When she had the matter well in hand, and was slowly settling to certain convictions, she made her mother her first confidante. The aroma of the unworldly atmosphere which had enveloped Dr. Farrand's life still lingered with his widow, and Doris had a feeling that here she would find a sympathizer in views that perhaps others would call romantic and foolish. Nor had she been mistaken. Mrs. Farrand's first startled question after hearing the story was:

"Then the money isn't yours, rightfully, is it?"

Doris could have laughed, if she had not been too near to tears, over the relief that this spontaneous question gave her. Coming to her as the instinctive feeling of one who had all her life breathed an honest and honorable atmosphere, it seemed to clear the air. Yet the most difficult letter that Doris had ever written was the long one in which she told this story in all its details to Richard Shipley.

It was that letter which made him secure a free Saturday, to the marked inconvenience of Judge Bronson, and hurry to the Berkshire hills by the fastest train. Not so much because he objected to spending Sunday in talking over business perplexities, as because he did not feel equal to waiting another whole day before bringing the influence of his logic to bear upon Doris's sensibilities. There was no telling, he argued, what an emotional girl in the habit of being led by her impulses might settle it with herself that she would do, before he was able to reach her. Late experiences had taught him that Doris, once settled, was hard to move.

He brought his mother down with him on this occasion, partly because he had been long promising her an outing, and partly because he felt that she could monopolize Mrs. Farrand and Athalie, thus leaving him more time alone with Doris.

The exclamation with which this chapter commenced had been called forth by Doris's first verbal expression of the thought that lived with her. Not even to her mother had she put it into words. Richard should be the first to hear.

"Now, Richard, you know every little detail as well as I do, and I am hoping and believing that the same thought has come to you which came with force to me—that I have no moral right to a penny of this money."

It is true she had not before put it into words, but in her letters the thought had crept in between the lines for Richard to read; not in its baldness, but sufficiently to make him feel that Doris was revolving some romantic scheme of restitution.

He caught his breath over her sudden plunge into wild extravagance. "No moral right to a penny of this money!"

This was worse than his worst fears. He lost no time in making it plain to her that she had hoped in vain, that nothing was farther from his ideas of right than such a proposition.

He argued, and lectured, and moralized. He was skilful in his management of the situation.

What did she know of details, after all, he asked her. How much did lawyers tell, beyond what they were compelled to tell? Had not Mr. Malcolm shown her how completely silent he could keep concerning all that did not touch the matter in hand? She might rest assured that the father knew what he was about when he willed the property away from his son; there was a deep reason for it, no doubt. Who would be so likely to understand a son as his own father? Perhaps he knew that to leave him to his own resources would be the making of a man; and that to plunge him into wealth and unlimited control would ruin him, body and soul. Doris would better have a care how she interfered with the dealings of Providence. Oh, yes, he remembered what Mr. Malcolm had said about the son's respectability, and all that; there were thousands of men who succeeded in living honest and honorable lives because they were poor who, if they were suddenly plunged into the temptations inevitable to wealth, would go to ruin. Any student of human nature would assure her of that.

Moreover, what had become of her own personal responsibility? What was money for but to be used for the benefit of others? Did not she feel that in giving up this trust she would be guilty of gross ingratitude, when Providence had in this way planned for her to carry out work that was for His glory? Was she not now, on Water Street and in a dozen other places, furthering schemes which brought her constant evidence of what could be done with money? Could she possibly think it would be right, not only to plunge her mother and sister into poverty, but to choke all these opened avenues to usefulness, and throw back a dead man's gift to spoil a life that he had planned to save?

Richard was excited by his own eloquence, and failed to take note of the fact that he was building his logic upon his own imaginings as to the situation; but Doris saw it.

They talked long, until the sun dropped behind the hills and the girl shivered, either with the chill of the mountain air or with nervous excitement. Richard, reaching through one of the low windows, drew a gay afghan from the couch and wrapped her in it.

"There," he said admiringly, "you look like an Eastern princess. You are not cold now? Then let me try to show you how this thing looks to practical people who are used to judging in a common-sense fashion instead of emotionally. Not that I do not admire the emotional part, Doris. In fact, I presume I love you the better because of your angelic flights into other-worldness; but it is my duty, don't you see, to help keep you plumb—you are a bit in danger now and then of veering over to one side."

It was an unfortunate illustration for him. Quick as thought Doris was back on the stone steps of the old college and Garrett Randall was saying, "You see, I've kind of slanted over to one side, and Water Street is helping me to keep plumb." The memory cleared her vision again. She knew that she had, in the years gone by, "slanted over to one side," and no one knew better than herself on which side the slant had been. There must be nothing of that kind again.

Richard was compelled to return to town early on Monday morning. He went away in a gloomy, anxious mood. He had not been so successful as he had hoped. It was still uncertain what Doris would do, and fairly probable that she would do something. He hoped that he had tided her over the fancy for doing such an absurdly unpractical and unreasonable thing as throwing up her entire fortune for the sake of a sentiment. He had made many concessions to sentiment. He had himself proposed a very fine gift to the discarded son; or if she liked that thought better, a series of gifts, coming into his life at opportune moments, with just the help needed to tide him over a crisis. Something like this would be her delightful privilege if she did not put it out of her power. Then there were the children—what opportunities she might have to do for them! In just the ways, perhaps, that a far-seeing man had believed a sweet, wise woman would plan to do for his grandchildren, if he gave her the means.

In short, Richard, as he sped back to town on the Eastern Limited, told himself that he had suggested schemes enough to sink many thousands of dollars. Still, there could be no objection to them. Judiciously managed, there would evidently be money enough to do a great deal, and that Doris must have some such escape-valve was evident. Doris was not like other women. He was pleased with himself because, even then, he could feel an emotion of pleasure over the thought that she was not.

Still, there was enough to keep him anxious. He must contrive to run out again before Saturday, if possible.

Doris, after his departure, found it hard to interest herself in the commonplaces about her. Not even a new picture, brought by Richard on purpose for Miss Melinda's walls, was able to awaken the enthusiasm which it deserved. While the question she was considering still remained unsettled, all other matters must continue to seem too trivial for notice. She had promised Richard that she would do nothing rash, that she would in fact do nothing at all until she saw him again; but she had not promised not to think; some of his logic which had impressed her when he was there, seemed not so clear in his absence.

Mrs. Shipley, who had been left to complete her visit, noticed the unusual quiet of the girl and commented in characteristic fashion.

"Seems to me, Doris, you are changing pretty fast, actually growing old. Your family must belong to the type that fades early;

there's a great difference in families about that, you know. My mother used to be complimented on her youthful appearance after she had three grandchildren; but you certainly look five years older than you did when I last saw you. I believe you and Richard ought to get married, without waiting for him to be admitted. What is the use of your wasting all your pretty looks with waiting, when you have money enough to last you both for a lifetime? That is what I say to Richard. A woman wants to look fresh and pretty when she is a bride, I tell him, if she never does again, and when the first freshness wears off they can't imitate it to save their lives."

Doris laughed absent-mindedly, and laughed again, presently, over Athalie's flushed face and flashing eyes. Why should Athalie care whether or not Mrs. Shipley thought her pretty? Why should anyone care anything about what Mrs. Shipley thought? She arrested herself before this question took actual form, because it seemed not quite loyal to Richard. But she found it more difficult than usual to talk to Mrs. Shipley.

"I am going for a long tramp," she said to Athalie, while it was still morning; "a very long tramp, Athalie. I don't want luncheon, I breakfasted late, you remember, and I may not be back until dinner time; in fact, I may not be back then. I have been promising Miss Melinda and Miss Harriet that I would come some evening and have supper with them, perhaps this will be the evening. You don't mind, do you?"

"Not a bit; I shall be glad that you are having a rest. Poor child! How you are ever to endure that kind of a mother-in-law is more than I can imagine. A month of it would kill me, or else I should kill her, I don't know which."

"It would be neither," said Doris, smiling. "You would be good and patient and thoughtful of her comfort all the time. You would make an excellent daughter-in-law, and I shouldn't; when I was tired of it, I should run away for a long tramp."

Chapter 24

"All things work together for good."

It was a much longer tramp than Doris had planned. She had in mind a certain waterfall where she had been early in the season with a party of hotel friends. She remembered thinking then what an ideal place it would be to hide away in, if one had a knotty problem to solve. There, more than in any place she had ever seen, she would be alone with nature, in such guise that it did not obtrude even itself, but simply helped the soul to feel alone with God. That, she believed, was what she needed.

She had been long in search of it, but had missed her trail. Now, after much tramping interspersed by many rests, during which she had absorbed herself in her troubled thoughts and taken no note of time, she roused to the fact that she did not know where she was. In the woods, certainly, which was growing more dense with every step she took, and with no defined path anywhere. Still, of course, there was no danger. There were several trails down the mountain; she would be sure to find one of them after a little, and she tramped bravely on. At last she came to the mere suggestion of a trail and followed it for a long distance, in the hope that it was the path up which she had climbed. She kept looking for familiar objects as landmarks; instead, she passed vines and queer-shaped trees, and wild flowers that she was sure she had never seen before. Once she saw, and barely escaped treading on, a snake. This made her shiver and shudder; it was almost the one form of life which had only horror for her.

Very soon she observed that the sun had disappeared; this could not be its setting, her watch still gave her several hours before sunset, but it could be a storm—a thunder-storm, perhaps. At the hotel, safe-sheltered in the large, old-fashioned, homelike parlor, surrounded by friends, she liked to watch the play of lightning and listen to the roll of thunder over the mountains; but it was another thing to be utterly alone in the heart of a great woods with no knowledge of which way to turn in search of shelter, and feel that a storm was coming swiftly. However, if she should make all speed, she might reach the open before the storm broke. She quickened her steps, but every suggestion of a path had now disappeared, and the underbrush which impeded her way grew every moment more troublesome. It soon became so dark that it was useless to try to select her way; she could only stumble on blindly, hoping that it was in the right direction; but if it were, surely by this time she should have reached that comparatively open space.

Suddenly the wood was lighted for an instant as if in lurid flame, and there followed the crash of thunder, louder and more prolonged than any she had ever heard; it seemed to her that the very foundations of the earth on which she trod were shaken. Moreover, during that instant of light she had seen slipping swiftly across her very feet another snake. This time she screamed a little, then took herself well in hand and sternly said, "Be still." It was of no use, however, to assure herself that she was not frightened. It seemed to her that the situation justified her fright. She was alone in a great forest where people had been lost more than once and not found until too late. It was growing night and a fierce storm was raging. No one knew just where she was, yet no one would be anxious; she had herself cut off all immediate search for her by arranging with Athalie that she might not be at home until late. When at last her friends were frightened about her, it might be days before they found her, if indeed she was ever found. And at the thought of the vast stretch of woods about and beyond her, and the creatures who might roam it at night time, a cold chill took hold of her. She recalled the gruesome story of a young girl who, years before, had wandered out into this very forest and never been seen again. She recalled all the stories she had heard of people being lost, and wandering about in circles, and wondered if she were doing so. Certainly she reached nowhere; she must have been walking now for hours. Yet she was afraid to stop; it was horrible to think of sitting. Suddenly her heart, which had been beating in great thuds, seemed to give one terrible bound and stand still, and she knew that her nameless terrors had taken tangible shape. Here before her, dimly outlined in the gloom, was some sort of a hut, and unmistakable sounds issuing from it, suggesting human habitation. To be alone in the forest with snakes and other forest creatures, and storm and night enveloping her, was quite enough to fill a girl with vague terrors; but to be alone in a forest at night with some unknown man—this was definite danger. She must use her strength and her common sense to get her away from this situation. What man that one could safely meet would be hiding at night in such a center of desolation? Just then a cheery whistle from the cabin broke the strained silence and without effort of hers lessened the tension of her fears. A man in hiding would hardly whistle, she supposed; yet bad men did, probably, and he thought himself alone.

"He may be an honest laborer," said Common Sense, "who could put you on the right trail at once."

"There is nothing here to call an honest laborer," said Caution, joining sides with her fears. The fears prevailed. She would steal away very softly, as far from that cabin as she could get.

She turned from the dangerous spot and began to take cautious steps, and made almost immediately a misstep; the treacherous stick on which she tried to balance herself broke and was dislodged from its place with a noise that seemed to her excited brain louder than the thunder. The whistling in the cabin suddenly ceased. Doris, in her terror, stood still, It was quite dark now; even if the man should come out to look, he might not see her; the dress she wore was the color of the tree trunks about her; if she remained perfectly motionless, she might yet escape.

But he came with a lighted lantern, gazed for one astonished moment at the apparition clinging breathless and motionless to a tree trunk, then took long strides toward her.

"Is this an enchanted forest after all," he said, "or do I see Miss Farrand in actual flesh and blood?"

The reaction was too sudden for Doris to regain immediate control of her nerves; she sank down among the leaves and mosses, a limp heap, and cried as she had on rare occasions when a child, with her head in her mother's lap. Garrett Randall bent over her amazed and dismayed, murmuring incoherent apologies for frightening her.

"It is nothing," she said, looking up suddenly through a mist of tears. "At least it is nothing but fright, foolish fright, I suppose; but I am lost, and the night was coming, and the storm, and then that cabin—" she stopped at that, and laughed. How absurd it seemed to have been afraid of that cabin!

Mr. Randall decided swiftly that the way to help steady her nerves was to laugh with her.

"Light begins to dawn," he said gaily. "You saw the hut and heard the pounding, perhaps—I was engaged in mending my dining table—and thought that at the least I was an escaped convict hiding from justice. It is nothing so romantic as that. I am only a tramper in search of the curios of the woods. My hut is a borrowed one belonging to the lumbermen whose camp is not far distant. I don't wonder that its outward appearance disturbed you; but the interior is charming, it is decorated with some choice 'finds' of this very day; and it is a capital shelter from rain. Let me help you over there to try it, until we see just what this storm is going to do."

"But where am I?" asked Doris, struggling to her feet with his assistance. "And how am I to get where I ought to be?"

"That depends, that last. I think you will have to tell me just where you ought to be."

Thus admonished, Doris explained the situation. His eyes lighted with pleasure, and he spoke eagerly:

"So you are really staying at the Riverview, and your mother and sister are there? I wonder if I could make you understand how glad I am? That is only three miles from Brook Farm, where my mother and I are spending a whole month—think of it! I have been very homesick for a sight of you all.

"Now, as to where you are, I think you must have been traveling for some time in an opposite direction from Riverview, as you are now well up the mountain and about seven miles from there."

Doris uttered a dismayed exclamation, and he made haste to reassure her.

"But the situation is not at all serious. I am sure you will be willing to accept of my hospitality. I am not camping out, I go home to my mother every evening. Most of my days are spent in the woods in search of certain rare treasures which a nature-loving professor in our college is good enough to pay me for finding. The lumbermen at the camp yonder are all good friends of mine, and it chances that this is the evening in which they drive to Brook Farm for supplies. I am waiting to ride instead of tramping, as I usually do. Now Brook Farm, as I told you, is only three miles from the Riverview, and my friends, the lumbermen, will consider it a privilege to be allowed to take you safely there. Can you be at home in my cabin until the storm passes and the carriage arrives?

Although, to be accurate, it is you who will have to 'arrive' at the carriage. There is a zigzag path through the woods to it, not far away. I am to be shouted for when it is time to go."

The reaction from her terrors put Doris in high spirits. She accepted the hospitality of the cabin as freely as it was offered, and found it not an unattractive place. The floor was reasonably clean, and the tins and other cooking utensils hanging against the walls showed careful handling. There was even a white curtain before the one window place; it had, however, been looped back so that it could not be seen from the outside. Garrett Randall was much amused over Doris's assurance that had she seen it she would not have been afraid of the man inside.

"It shall be dropped hereafter, though I smother," he said gaily. "It is an innovation of my mother's, and it amuses the lumbermen greatly. Still, I admit it gives one a sense of security from the observation of squirrels and things."

They were very gay. The host explained that he had been mending his table with a view to serving supper, and as they would not reach Brook Farm until long after that meal was over, he would suggest that he be allowed to continue spreading the aforesaid table for two, instead of one.

"I shall be delighted," said Doris; "I hope the provisions are bountiful, for I have had no luncheon, and although I thought an hour ago that I should never want to eat again, I am discovering that I am famished. May I help get supper? I never did, in a cabin. It must be fun."

It was fun. The two bustled about the little bare room, entering with the zest of children into the situation. The mistress of Brook Farm had known Garrett Randall for less than ten days, but he was already a prime favorite, and she knew how to put up luncheons for the woods. Even without the eggs, which Garrett fried while Doris made coffee, there would have been a bountiful supper. The "table" that was being "mended" proved to be a barrel with a board nailed over the top.

"It wobbled," Garrett explained. "The cover had never been nailed on, you understand; and occasionally, owing to an eccentric fashion it had of tipping over whenever anything was placed a trifle to one side, accidents happened, so I borrowed some nails of Ben, the chopper, this morning and there is no wobble now."

It was a unique dining table before which they presently sat. The lantern had been hung from the roof in such fashion that it swayed gracefully over the table, at least Garrett called attention to its grace. Doris had the seat of honor, an empty paint keg with a board nailed over it, and a mackintosh laid on it for a cushion.

"It is not going to rain, after all," Garrett Randall remarked, as he folded the mackintosh. "That shower went over; we shall have a moonlight ride down the mountain. Did you ever go down by moonlight, Miss Farrand? Then you have an experience before you worth remembering."

She remembered it all. Never could even a woodland feast have been more thoroughly enjoyed than was that one. The Brook Farm food was excellent, and Doris's long fast had prepared her to do it justice. The pleasure it was to her to sit once more opposite to Garrett Randall at table, she made no effort to disguise—why should she?

There was much to be talked over while they ate. Mr. Randall told his part of the story in few words.

Yes, he had been graduated. Oh, yes, his mother had the pleasure of seeing him receive some of the honors. Indeed she was there; he couldn't have given the valedictory if she hadn't been sitting in the front seat expecting him to do her credit. Yes, he was going back next year; going to teach and study at the same time. Yes, he believed the opportunity offered him was rather rare; at least so they told him. Oh, yes, he meant to make teaching his work. He decided, away back in Water Street days, that what he knew himself he could teach to others; and he hoped to guard against the mistake of trying to teach what he did not know. His mother was with him, and his fine gray eyes lighted with pleasure as he told of it; they kept house in a very tiny way, a little more elaborate than the cabin style—at least they did not use barrels and paint kegs, but it was primitive. Mother made fully her share of their income by taking care of certain college buildings.

"One of these days," he said gaily, "my mother is to sit in the traditional chimney-corner and fold her hands while I take care of her. Then she says she will be miserable, and keep begging me for something to do. But I don't believe it, do you? I mean I look forward to the time when my mother need *do* only when she chooses; her life has been one of constant doing, from necessity. However, she is very happy now; mothers have great faith in their children, you know."

Then he dismissed himself as a topic and began to ask numberless questions about his old friends.

Doris, while she talked, studied him with interest. The two years since they had met had changed him. He had always been manly, in the true sense of that word; but now he had taken on an air of assurance, as one who had made acquaintance with the world and was no longer afraid of it. She could not, for instance, imagine him as hesitating over any social function. Even his manner to her had undergone that subtle change which placed them, as a matter of course, on a perfect equality. The boy, Garrett Randall, had looked up to her with a sort of worshipful deference; but the man met her on equal ground, and she liked the change.

It was very curious to be seven miles up the mountain in the depths of a forest, eating her supper at a barrel table with a lantern light, and Garrett Randall for her host, but it was very interesting.

As they talked, she found her thoughts returning to the topic from which they were never long separated; she wondered how this young man, who had somehow made acquaintance with the world, would look upon her problem? Had the world changed him? Would other men, good men, agree with Richard that her ideas were born of sentiment without foundation in common sense, and were utterly uncalled for by a sane conscience? That was one of Richard's phrases which had slipped out unawares when he was much tried.

Suddenly she changed the subject of conversation.

Chapter 25

"He that harpeth on a matter, separateth chief friends."

"Mr. Randall, you are studying law and preparing to be a teacher of law, I wonder what you would regard as equity in a matter of which I have heard? May I suppose a case and get your legal advice?

"Suppose a man had property willed to him by one not bound to him by ties of either family or friendship, and learned afterward that the—the daughter of the one who made the will was living, and ought by all the rules which govern sane and sensible people to have been her father's heir. Suppose it was found that he disinherited her in a fit of ill humor and did not live long enough to right his wrong-doing. What, under such circumstances, ought the heir to do?"

"What a network of suppositions!" said Garrett Randall, gaily. "And a truly remarkable state of affairs. Are you writing a novel, Miss Farrand?"

"If I am, will you help me to plan it so that there shall be no flaw?"

"I used to think you would be a writer of fiction. Do you remember that story you wrote for the college paper? 'Interwoven' was the title; that was a fine bit of plotting. By the way, some of it would work out in the very line you are talking about. Are you really rewriting that story for print?"

"Do you expect me to answer your questions, Mr. Randall, before you have paid the least attention to mine?"

"Oh, I beg your pardon. What ought your man to do? Legally,

do you mean? Why, your discarded daughter hasn't the ghost of a chance unless she can pick some flaw in the will; and those wicked wills are generally arranged with such care that they are hard to break."

"I don't mean legally, I mean morally, in equity, in the sight of God."

She never forgot the swift change in his face. Up to that moment he had been speaking lightly, as one would talk simply for amusement. He detected the earnestness in her voice and met it instantly.

"Could there be but one answer to such a question as that, Miss Farrand?"

It seemed almost cruel, the suddenness with which this man could reach conclusions that, followed out, would overturn her life. But conclusions for other people were perhaps easy to reach. She put the shadow of this thought into her next question.

"Do you think if this were real life, instead of supposition, and you were the heir in question, you would swiftly reach the one answer?"

"I don't know," he said, speaking lightly again; after all, it was only a story. "I never expect to be tried in that line, and a fellow can't be sure of himself under given circumstances; he can only see what he ought to do."

"And the 'ought' you consider perfectly clear?"

"Is it not? Doesn't your hero think so? If he is a follower of Jesus Christ, I would ask him if he questions what *He* would do under like circumstances. If He were living on earth, as a man, I mean. I hope your friend will see his way clear, to the heights. We need stories of that kind. If I were you, I should insist upon his seeing it; a high moral atmosphere is one of the excuses for fiction to be."

"But should even fiction take higher ground than common

sense would justify?"

"Not higher than common sense *ought* to justify," he said pointedly. "I am afraid we have a habit of using that term when we mean expediency or selfish interests. But there is such a thing as sanctified common sense, which takes into consideration the golden rule as a practical guide."

Doris rose up suddenly from the little table. No, indeed, she would have no more of anything, she had eaten very heartily.

When did he think his lumbermen would be likely to start; it must be growing late.

That mountain ride by moonlight in the lumber wagon had been fitly described to her. It was an experience which, for many reasons, could not be forgotten. Before Brook Farm was reached, Ben, the driver, had expressed his entire willingness to go any number of miles farther with a friend of Mr. Randall's. His willingness changed to supreme satisfaction when he discovered that Mr. Randall was also going down, and that he should have him all to himself for the homeward ride; it was very manifest that Ben's opinion of that gentleman was an exalted one.

Out of regard for Ben, and the early hour at which he must be stirring in the morning, Garrett Randall waited only to shake hands with Mrs. Farrand and Athalie, and promise to come to dinner on the following day. It was just as he turned to climb back into the wagon that Doris held out her hand to him, and spoke for his ear only:

"Thank you, Mr. Randall; my hero has decided. I shall make him do it."

"Good!" he said, and rode away well pleased, without even a conception of what he had helped to accomplish.

The days that immediately followed were also ones that Doris never forgot. Looking back, it seemed to her afterward that she lived years during that short space, and grew so perceptibly older that others besides Mrs. Shipley, the outspoken, might have commented.

Richard Shipley came down in the middle of the week, as he had promised himself that he would, only to find, to his dismay, that Doris's "obstinacy" had taken great strides since he saw her. He had left her doubtful, questioning, more or less open to arguments based on common sense. He found her settled in the conviction that she had no moral right to the money willed to her, and resolved upon taking prompt action toward transferring it to the rightful heir.

To say that Richard was dismayed is to put it mildly: He stood before the situation, appalled. He literally, as he told his disturbed mother, did not know what to do.

The mother's views were not as comforting as they might have been.

"It does seem strange, Richie," she said plaintively, "how you are led. It almost makes one think that there is no such thing as Providence. There you had ten thousand dollars, and might have had it yet and been a minister by this time on a salary of your own, if it hadn't been for that girl."

Richard turned upon her savagely.

"What do you mean by that? You certainly needn't lay any of that business, at least, to Doris. I clung to the idea of studying for the ministry long after I knew that I should make a failure of it, just to please her. Her heart was a great deal more set on it than yours ever was."

"Oh, I don't mean that, Richie. I mean that you thought you could afford to give up the other money because she had lots of it; and of course you wouldn't have done it if she hadn't had; and I must say, I don't think you are being honorably treated."

Richard's face was very red, but he remembered that he was speaking to his mother, and tried not to be too severe.

"Mother, how can you be so ridiculous? Do you think I sold

myself to the ministry for money, and then backed out of the bargain on account of money? You don't realize what you are saying. I gave up preaching because I knew I was not fitted for it, and I ought to have given up long before I did. Money had nothing to do with it, and I don't want you to say that ever again."

She was crying now.

"I won't," she said sobbingly, "I won't say anything, Richie dear, that you don't want me to; you know I think only of you. But I can't help saying that you are being badly treated. Think of that Silverton girl, worth no one knows how many millions, and ready to die any time for your sake, and you wouldn't look at her on account of Doris; and now she goes and makes a beggar of herself and you, and—"

But Richard had flung himself away, too indignant to trust himself to any more words. With one statement of his mother's he could not help agreeing; it seemed to him that he was being badly treated. If he had married Doris a year ago, as his mother had urged, this sentimentalism of hers would never have reached such dimensions; he felt sure that he could have controlled it. Or, if he had permitted the division of the property and given Mrs. Farrand and Athalie legal rights, the matter would have been easier to manage; it was not probable that the three women would have gone insane together; but he had really done the worst both for himself and Doris, and must stand aside and see her beggar herself.

It was certain that Richard did not appear at his best during this ordeal. His arguments took many forms.

"You seem to have forgotten one thing," he said gloomily to Doris. "Or at least it does not trouble you. How many years do you suppose you are putting between us now? Even after I am admitted, there will be one cannot tell how long to wait before I can be sure of a decent income. Do you care so little for me that there is no shrinking from this long-drawn-out separation?"

She shrank from him then, almost visibly. "I don't understand you," she said. "Do you think I am doing this because it is a pleasure to me? If I leave myself out altogether, can you suppose that I like to bring my mother and Athalie to what you call a 'beggarly condition'? Oh, Richard, *won't* you understand that there is a solemn 'ought' behind it all? That loyalty to Christ demands it of me? Believing that, would you have me hesitate? Would you love me if I did? "

He turned away from her searching eyes, and controlled his voice, and spoke tenderly:

"I think, dearest, that there has always been in you a vein of sentiment that was in danger of biasing your judgment, and leading you to do emotionally things that were beautiful and lovable, but not wise. And I believe that you would do better, in matters of business, to depend on those whom you have a right to believe you can trust, rather than on your sweet, illogical heart. Thank Heaven you were not trained for a business woman, and have no head for it. I may love you the more on that account; but I feel, because of it, all the more bound to protect your interests."

After a talk like this, Doris's one wish was to put the subject away and talk, when Richard was present, about other things. Of what use to argue with him when they lived on different planes of thought? Not alone upon this subject; during their two years of continuous separation she was conscious that both had changed. The topics upon which they now radically differed seemed almost numberless; and more than once, along with these other haunting questions, came the dull undertone of one that said, "How can two walk together except they be agreed?"

That solemn night in which Doris Farrand had stood in vision before two roads and been called upon to choose, and had chosen, had marked an epoch in her spiritual life. From that hour she had been the sort of Christian who keeps steadily before him the "vocation to which he is called." Every act of hers was henceforth to be measured by that rule which to some people seems narrow— Is this what Jesus Christ expects and has a right to expect of me? She was literally to try with each new day to "live as seeing Him who is invisible." Such living brought her into daily companionship in a new and beautiful sense with a strong and perfect life, and opened her eyes to much that had been obscure.

But about one matter there had ceased to be questionings. She had not moved a hair's breadth from the position which she took when she said to Garrett Randall, "I shall make him do it." Therefore it was of no use to argue with Richard, unless, indeed, she could bring him into her line of vision.

It was not easy, however, to escape Richard's mother, who chose to put herself into the argument after this fashion:

"I don't see how you can think you are doing right by Richie, after all he has given up for your sake. He treated that Miss Silverton almost rudely, because he was pledged to you. Of course, Richard wasn't looking for a rich wife, and I don't say that he wouldn't have preferred you without a penny to anybody else; but what I do say is that he has planned his life very differently from what he would if all that money hadn't been left to you. I don't suppose he would ever have given up being a minister, and the ten thousand dollars that went with it, if he hadn't thought he ought to take the best possible care of your money; and, of course, a lawyer could do that better than a minister could. Don't you think a girl ought to have some thought of the man she has promised to marry, and who has sacrificed for her sake, instead of following her own romantic notions?"

What reply could be made to talk like that? Meantime Garrett Randall came daily, being welcomed with heartiness by the entire family. "I don't believe I could have been more glad to have seen my son, if I had one," Mrs. Farrand said, and Athalie added:

"He has grown handsome, hasn't he? I always thought him

fine-looking, but he has developed wonderfully in these two years. Isn't it good to see him again? Dear me, we had nice times in that little house on Willow Street, hadn't we?"

The next day Mr. Randall brought his mother.

"I remember I wanted you to know her," he said gleefully to Athalie, "and you told me not to count it among the impossibilities."

"She is an old-fashioned mother," he said to Doris. "I am not always sure how she will impress some people; but I know you will like her."

Not only Doris, but every member of the family felt drawn toward the "old-fashioned" mother, whose royal soul looked at them from earnest gray eyes of which her son's were the counterpart, except that his had in them always a merry twinkle that care had stolen from hers.

Mother and son came to dine with the Farrands, and Richard was there to meet them. He had come down on purpose to make a final effort to bring Doris to reason, and was at his best. He greeted Garrett Randall with hearty friendliness and assured him that he had heard with interest of his record in college; he had been always intending to mention it to Mrs. Farrand, but believed he had not done so. He was very courteous to Mrs. Randall, joining heartily with the others in the laughter that her quaint, keen humor provoked. Evidently Richard meant to make his final effort under as favorable circumstances as possible.

On their way to the dining room they encountered the improvised clerk of the summer hotel, who stared hard at Mrs. Randall, then came swiftly after her.

"You don't remember me, do you, Mrs. Smith? I don't wonder; I have changed a good deal since you saw me, but you haven't. I knew you the moment I laid eyes on you. Don't you remember, up there at Green Cove, a tow-headed boy called Billy? I'm the chap.

Billy Forbes, at your service. I used to play with Georgie, you know. How is Georgie, and where is he?"

There was a glow of unusual color on Mrs. Randall's face. The others had passed on, and were waiting for her at their table; Garrett, but a few steps from her, also waited, and wondered. She spoke quickly:

"I remember you now; but I am not Mrs. Smith anymore, I am Mrs. Randall. My son and I are staying at Brook Farm for a few weeks. Come out and see me; I would like to talk over those times with you." Then she hastened on.

"Who was that, mother?" Garrett asked wonderingly. "He seemed very glad to see you. Is it someone whom I ought to remember, and don't?"

"No," said Mrs. Randall; "you could not be expected to remember him. I'll tell you about it when I have a chance."

Chapter 26

"Withhold not good from them to whom it is due, when it is in the power
of thine hand to do it."

One of the sudden storms frequent to that mountain region came
up while the family were at dinner, and continued with such
violence that Mrs. Randall was persuaded to remain for the night.
Then, when it was found that her son was to be away for two or
three days, the invitation to spend this time with the Farrands was
so earnestly pressed that the little" old-fashioned" mother who had
not before, for years, been outside of her own very small world,
felt herself drawn by strong cords to these people who had been
good to her son, and was not hard to persuade.

Their acquaintance made strides during those days. Doris, in
particular, was deeply interested in the woman whose strong face,
seamed as it was with the scars of many burdens and some well-
fought battles, still spoke not only of strength but peace. She
would have known, she told herself, without having heard it, that
Mrs. Randall was a woman who had found her true "vocation."

On the second day of the visit the girl was seized with a desire
to know what this quiet, elderly woman, who had probably been
hidden all her life from the world, would have to say about the
matter which was still under consideration.

Richard, to his intense annoyance, had been imperatively
summoned back to town by the midnight train of that first day, and
had been given no opportunity to make that last supreme effort.
His only word to Doris on the subject had been:

"Do nothing until I see you again; I will be back tomorrow if possible, the next day certainly."

She could not help but promise. She felt that perhaps her relations with him demanded so much; but that need not prevent her talking the matter over with Mrs. Randall.

They went out to a summer-house in the lower garden, where they would not be likely to be disturbed, and there Doris told, with a fullness of detail that afterward surprised her, the story of her later years and their peculiar responsibilities.

The keen interest of the elder woman and her incisive questions led the girl on, and she grew every moment more eager to know just what would be the unconsidered verdict of a perfectly unbiased and yet intensely interested listener. There was no long waiting before it was given.

"And so," said Doris, breaking off to reach her climax, "it seems to me that in honor, or even in common honesty, I have no right to this money."

"Of course not," said Mrs. Randall, without a second's hesitation. Then as she saw the color waves flow over Doris's face, she added:

"Forgive me, child, I'm an old woman, and speak sometimes when I ought to keep still. It is none of my business; but I couldn't seem to think of you as doing anything else."

Her son drove her home the next evening in the farm wagon, just after Richard Shipley's arrival by the late train.

She was unusually quiet during the first half mile, but as they were beginning to climb the long hill, she said, as though they had been conversing on the subject:

"She is an unusual girl, a *very* unusual girl."

"Yes," said her son with emphasis, "she is."

There were two girls in the family with whom she had been visiting, but it did not occur to the mother to explain, nor to the son to question, which was meant.

"You don't know about her puzzle, I suppose?" Mrs. Randall said, after another brief silence. "She said I might talk it over with you if I chose, though I don't think she is the least bit puzzled."

Whereupon in brief, vivid lines she sketched the story for him as an artist makes the outlines of his picture, leaving the finer work to a more leisure time.

Garrett Randall, startled, almost dismayed, over his share in the story that he had thought was being written, and which, instead, was being lived, was even a more silent listener than his mother had been. Both because he knew so little and so much, he had fewer questions to ask. Intuitively, after the first start of surprise, he seemed to know the story. He caught himself moving ahead of the narrator and anticipating what she would say next. He could see again, outlined in the shadowy moonlight, the figure of a girl who had lifted a pale, pure face to his, and said with an intensity of earnestness that he did not then understand, "I have decided; I shall *make* him do it."

His mother, having sketched her outline, waited for some word from him, and failing to receive it spoke quickly:

"Garrett, a girl like her could do no less than that."

Then his answer was quick, "Of course."

His mother's heart gave a little thrill, not only of pride, but of relief.

They had reached a bit of comparatively level ground and the horses were trotting. Mrs. Randall laid a detaining hand on the driver's arm.

"Drive slowly, will you, Garrett? I have more that I want to tell you. My boy, you have been everything in the world to your mother, and we have lived for each other; but there are hard places in my life that you don't know anything about."

His free hand closed over her old, wrinkled one and held it in a firm, tender clasp as he said:

"Yes, indeed, mother; I can well imagine that this old world has given you some hard knocks; but if God wills, you shall make the rest of the journey through green pastures."

"Dear boy," she said, with a tremble in her voice that was unusual, "you have never brought a sorrow into your mother's life, and I am sure you never will. But there is another story that I have got to tell you now. I didn't suppose that I should ever tell it; but I find that we cannot hide things in this world very well; perhaps it would be better not to try.

"Garrett, you saw that young man speak to me the other night, but you didn't hear him call me 'Mrs. Smith.' That was the name by which he knew me once.

"It is an honest name, my son," she added quickly, responding to his start of surprise. "I had a right to it; there is nothing about that to hide, only it had to do with a hard page in my life, and I thought it could do no harm to fold it over and forget it.

"You were only a month old, you know, when your father died. As soon as I could, I broke up our little home and went a long journey to the Far West, to join an aunt of mine who promised me a home if I would come out to her. She gave it as long as she lived; but it wasn't hers to give away. She died when you were two years old, and soon after, I married a man named Smith. He had been kind to me and I was all alone among strangers, and I thought it was right; but it was a terrible mistake. He was cruel to me, Garrett; and worse than that, he was cruel to you, my baby. That was an awful life, my son; it was God's mercy that it did not last long. You were not yet three, when he was thrown one night from his horse, and killed. He had been drinking, and did not know how to manage the horse. I knew he had been a drinking man when I married him; but he told me he had reformed and would never touch another drop, and I believed him. After that, I supported myself in any way that I could. His property all went for debt. The neighbors were kind, though, and I got work to do by the day, and little by little got into the way of taking care of sick people. There was no such thing as trained nursing about there, and sick people liked me, so I was making a fair living. It was in this way that I knew William Forbes, the man who spoke to me the other night. He was errand boy at the Glen Cove House, and I went there to nurse a sick man who had come on from farther west and had a very long spell of sickness. I took you with me to the hotel, and this boy did a good deal of taking care of you, with the housekeeper's help, while I was in the sick room. Your name, you know, is George Garrett, and your father wanted you called Garrett, after his brother; but Mr. Smith hated the name, and would call you George, and the neighbors got in the habit of it. Of course they knew me only by the name of Smith; it was a hundred miles or so from where we had lived with my aunt, so it was natural for them to call you 'Georgie Smith,' and I let it go; I didn't think it would ever make any difference.

"I nursed that sick man for four months; some of the time he suffered a good deal, and he got so used to me that he thought nobody else could do anything for him. He was fond of you, too; as he began to get better, he would have you in for an hour or two and get up real frolics with you. When he asked me to marry him, I thought it was God's good hand leading me, and furnishing a kind father for my boy; he used to call you his little stepson. But my one bitter experience had made me cautious. He had taken me all by surprise, and I wouldn't make any promises; I told him he must wait until he was entirely well, at least. Then I wrote secretly to the place he came from. I wrote to the minister whose name I had seen on a kind of church card that was kept because it had some figuring on the back of it. I wrote without giving any reason for it beyond the fact that the man was sick and I was his nurse. By his answer I found out that that man had a wife and children! The minister said he was glad to learn that it was illness which had

217

kept him away from his family; that there had been a difference between the husband and wife, a short time before he left home, and he being a man of fierce passions, and accustomed to doing as he pleased, some of them had feared the worst from his long absence. It was a long letter, and a good one. I knew the minister was a good man. He asked if I was a Christian woman, and if I would use my influence as a nurse to get that man to go back to his family, if he had any idea of deserting them. One thing that made them fear so was that he was known to have taken large sums of money with him, and he left things so that it was hard for the wife and children to get enough to keep them. That was the kind of a man he was. I never knew whether he was going to cheat me and go back to his wife, when he got well, or whether she was the one to be cheated all through. I went home the next night after I got that letter, to the house where I had a room, when I wasn't out nursing. I spent the first half of the night in writing a letter to him, telling him some things that I had found out, and begging him to get away from Satan and go back to his family. The other part of the night I packed up. As soon as it was daylight I got the boys downstairs to take my trunk to the station, and I took you by the hand and walked there, two miles, in time for the first train east; and I came, just as fast as the cars would take me, away back to the village where you were born.

"Of course the folks there had never heard of 'Mrs. Smith,' and I wished with all my soul that I never had, so I was glad for them to say 'Mrs. Randall,' as they had always been used to doing. And I began to call you, 'Garrett,' as your father had wanted, and as I had always meant you should be. I wasn't in hiding, for I didn't think the man would hunt for me; and yet I was kind of glad to have such a reasonable way of letting the old life, even to the name, slip away from knowledge.

"That is the whole of the old story, Garrett, and I didn't mean to darken your life with it. But it explains why Billy Forbes called me

'Mrs. Smith,' and was so eager to hear from 'Georgie.' He was very fond of you, and was good and kind to me; but I had forgotten there was such a person on the earth.

"I have another reason, though, for telling you this long, hard story. Garrett, the man who left that girl his money is the one I nursed, and ran away from, and you are the 'George Smith' that she says the lawyers have been hunting for."

Long before she reached her climax, her son had anticipated her. With the first intimation that he had ever been called "George Smith," his legally constituted and legally trained mind had leaped to the decision that his interests and Doris Farrand's were inextricably linked in this matter.

But his first words were for his mother. He put his strong young arm about her and drew her to him.

"Poor little mother," he said, "what a hard life you led in the days when I could be only an additional burden! God grant me the privilege of making it up to you."

They sat late into the night, those two, going over the surprising story, and fitting into it the links which only they two knew. Two sentences characteristic of them both were spoken.

It was when Garrett had exclaimed at the lateness of the hour and had leaned over his mother's chair to kiss her good night that he said:

"Mother, do you think there is any need for others besides you and me ever to hear our part of this story? I am not 'George Smith,' in any true sense, and naturally the people looking for him will not find him. Can't we keep our knowledge to ourselves and not complicate matters more than they are?"

"If you think so," she said, looking up at him with something more than the fond mother love in her eyes. "It wouldn't have made any difference, would it, Garrett, if you had known this years ago?"

"Of course not; the 'George Smith' for whom they were looking never ought to have been found."

Then they kissed each other, this mother and son, who lived in an atmosphere where the precepts of the golden rule were as natural to them as the air they breathed.

Athalie Farrand confessed to a sense of relief at hearing that Garrett Randall and his mother had been taken into confidence.

"Because," she said, to her mother, "Doris is inclined to what Richard calls 'other-worldness,' and we are so fond and proud of her that we may be possibly growing unworldly, too, to keep her company; but Garrett is clear-headed and logical, and goes straight to the core of things. As for that sturdy little mother of his, one cannot imagine her as being anything but keen and true."

Not so was Richard impressed, when he came down for that last word.

"Oh, if you have taken counsel with the neighborhood," he said loftily, "and if that embodiment of all the virtues agrees with you, as of course he does, I admit that there is nothing more to be said. I should like to remind him, though, that it is much easier to give up property for other people than for one's self. If the conditions were such that he was to be a loser by these inane decisions, we should see a different form of logic applied. A man can play the fool in order to curry favor with a woman, when there is nothing to be lost by it; when anything is at stake, he gives his common sense a chance."

"Richard," said Doris, white to her lips, "I think you are forgetting yourself."

He turned and went swiftly out from her presence, feeling sure that he was, and that he could not, just then, get control of himself.

Chapter 27

"Whoso findeth a wife, findeth a good thing."

It seems to be a very difficult thing in this world to hide when one wishes to do so. Here was Mrs. Randall who had been hiding successfully for more than twenty years, without a thought of such a thing, and who now found that to keep the identity of one George Smith in the background was beyond her power. Neither she nor her son had taken the summer-hotel clerk, William Forbes, into consideration. He was so small a factor in their life, with so little knowledge of them in any way, that they forgot him; but he did not forget them.

Again it was Miss Melinda's love of pictures that helped to make history. Miss Harriet and Miss Melinda had a niece who was teaching school in the Butler district, five miles from the Riverview. It was this fact which had led to William Forbes's willingness to spend summer "clerking it" in the Berkshire hills.

William Forbes was a character in his way; old enough to be called an "old bachelor" by his comrades, and young enough to have golden hopes centered about the pretty teacher of the summer school in the Butler district. William and his mother were the joint proprietors of a smart eating house in town, whose busy days were in winter; and it had been a shrewd stroke of business as well as of friendship when he decided to leave the town house to his mother's care and, for that one summer, make himself invaluable to the proprietors of the Riverview. When he had a period of leisure that was yet too brief to cover the distance between the Riverview and the Butler district, it was his custom to stroll over to sit awhile with the aunts and talk about the pretty niece. At these times, for the benefit of Miss Melinda especially, William indulged in all the harmless gossip about life at the Riverview that he could remember. It was on the evening following his interview with Mrs. Randall that he introduced her to the aunts.

"I met an old acquaintance today; hadn't seen her since I was a little chap, and knew her in a minute. It beats all how little some folks change. She is a Mrs. Smith, at least she was when I knew her, but it seems that isn't her name any more. Her boy, Georgie, used to be a great pet of mine; and he's a six-footer now, and real stylish. They say he has been to college, and all that. Mrs. Smith asked me to come out and see them, but I shan't; he ain't my kind. Why, you've seen him, Miss Melinda; he's that tall fellow who was walking by with your Miss Farrand that time when we stood on the post-office steps, remember? I didn't know who he was then. His name ain't Smith, though, now, nor even 'George.' There's something kind of queer about that, come to think of it. He used to be 'Georgie Smith,' fast enough. I'd know his mother anywhere, and she don't deny it, and now he's Randall, Garrett Randall. Ain't that rather queer business?"

"George Smith!" said Miss Melinda, holding midway the stocking she was darning. "Ain't that the very name that was in the long story I read to you last spring about the lawyers who had been hunting for him and offered a reward, and all that? I know it's the same name, because I said that whenever I met a man after this named Smith, I was going to stop him and ask if his name wasn't George, and if he didn't come from that part of the world, so I could get the reward. And you laughed at me, don't you remember, and said I might as well look for a needle in a haystack; that there were more Smiths in the world than there were weeds in the garden. I mean to go and get that paper and show it to you,

William. I've got it, I know. I saved it because there was a great big picture of a flower show on the other side, with a piny in it as natural as life, all in colors. It's pinned up over that hole in the wall, you know, Harriet. I mean to get it."

It was in this way that a newspaper story, somewhat similar to that one which had changed Doris Farrand's life, fell into the hands of William Forbes. This account, though in some respects more sensational, was also more realistic than the one Doris had seen. It ventured to mention one name connected with the story, and that name was Smith. William Forbes read the three-columned article with exceeding care, then talked it over with the aunts, then folded the paper, to the great injury of the "piny" on the other side, and walked away with it in his pocket. By the time he reached the Riverview he had reached a conclusion.

"There's some mystery about them, anyhow. And they're all mixed up together, him and her. I wouldn't lift my finger if it was to harm any of 'em, but so far as I can see, it might help Mrs. Smith and the boy, if they're the ones, and it can't do no harm to find out. And if *they're* helped, why the others will be, the girl, anyway; a fellow with one eye can see that. Billy Forbes, you better sail in. It may be too late for the reward; it's an old paper, and he may be the wrong chap; but then again he may not be. Yes, sir, I'll try it."

Before he slept that night he posted a long and carefully written letter.

Meantime, ordinary life came to a sudden standstill with the Farrands because the mother fell ill. A sharp illness, which made them fear the worst; and that was followed by many days of anxiety, even after the immediate danger was over. During this time, not Garrett Randall alone, but his mother, shone with a luster of pure gold. Mrs. Randall's ability as a nurse was fully tested, and proved royal. When the let-up from anxiety and boding fear came, to no one were the family more grateful than to her. But several weeks passed before Athalie and Doris were able to breathe freely again and to say to each other gratefully, "She is steadily gaining now."

During this time letters came to Doris which she only half heeded, important as they were; and it was not until the doctor assured them that all that was needed now for their invalid was nourishing food and good care, that she re-read her letters and brought the news to Richard.

"I have some interesting letters from Mr. Malcolm, Richard. Don't you think, they believe that that George Smith has been found!"

"Indeed," said Richard, who, now that Doris had repudiated her fortune felt that he cared very little about George Smith in any way. "What was his supposed motive for staying in hiding all these years?"

"That is one of the strange things about it; he was hidden from himself, apparently. I haven't given the letters careful reading—I couldn't, while mother was so ill. I simply took in the fact that the lost heir was probably discovered, and wrote to Mr. Malcolm to take whatever legal steps were necessary, under such circumstances. There is another letter from him today, which I haven't read. I thought it would be interesting for us to go over them together, and that we would read the first ones before going into the details of this. I presume it explains matters more clearly. Now that everything is settled, Richard, let us enjoy it. It is like living a novel."

"And being the heroine," said Richard, cynically. "And the heroine's boundless self-sacrifice is of no avail, it seems. To me, now, that would be a bitter drop. This unknown, 'George Smith' is to gobble up her fortune and be happy."

"He has only his share of it," said Doris, trying to smile. "And besides, Richard, you may be doing him injustice. Perhaps he will feel as we did, that he does not care to profit by a dead man's ill nature."

"Don't you believe it," said Richard, quickly. "Trust any *man* for seeing his way safely through such an experience as that. It is only women who allow their judgment and common sense to float off in a fog of sentiment."

"Richard, need we go through all that any more?"

"No, we needn't," said Richard. "It is too late; but congratulations are in order for George Smith, whoever he is. By all means let us live out the rest of the novel. If we knew where the real hero was, we might send for him to spend the evening with us and have a jubilee."

"Well," said Richard, as they turned away after straining their eyes for the last glimpse of the swift-moving train, "here we are. The close of the—what act? When the curtain rises again, what next?"

Athalie laughed. "We have been living an eventful life for a few years, certainly, haven't we?" she said, as Richard followed her into the carriage that was waiting for them, and gave the order to drive home.

"There is a sense in which we have swung quite around the circle, and are back at the point from which we started."

"Willow Street and all," said Richard, looking gloomily out as the carriage turned into that narrower and quiet street.

"You are not to speak disrespectfully of Willow Street," said Athalie, cheerfully. "Mother would not like to hear anything said against it. She confided to me the morning after we were nicely settled again in the little house that she felt more at home than she had since she left it, and could not be thankful enough that it was vacant when we came back. To have no more battles to fight with cook or Thomas, or any of the rest of them, has taken a great load from mother's mind, and made her feel young again. 'Some are born great,' you know, 'and some have greatness thrust upon them.'"

"And some are skilled in thrusting it *from* them," said Richard, still speaking cynically.

Athalie's laugh was as free as ever.

"You may as well forgive those two, utterly," she said. "It doesn't require much penetration to see that they were born for each other. Don't you remember that even William Forbes thought so? And they differ from us commoner mortals in exactly the same ways. Haven't you noticed that?"

"Those two," as Athalie designated them, were Doris and Garrett Randall, who had now been husband and wife for about three hours.

It was nearly three years since the Farrands had returned to the Willow Street house, and the modest income that had been theirs before Doris's fortune came to her. Or to a little more than the original income; for the enterprise in which their five thousand dollars was supposed to have been lost righted itself, and began to pay dividends in such degree that there was somewhat more to plan with than there had been at first.

As soon after Mrs. Farrand's illness as she was able to join in the family councils, all the details of what Doris called "that troublesome business" were carried out in strict accordance with her conviction that she had no right to a penny of the dead man's money.

The discovery that their friend and helper, Garrett Randall, was the missing George Smith, came about through the intervention of William Forbes, as he had hoped that it would, and he and the pretty school-teacher were made happy by the "reward" which was duly paid.

At first the news came as a kind of shock to Doris, and Athalie voiced the thought that was in her heart when she said:

"It seems a little too much like a second-rate novel to think of Garrett Randall posing, all these years, under an 'alias.'"

But they discovered early that in saying this they were being unjust to Garrett.

"It was simply one of those natural carelessnesses of an honest and honorable woman who doesn't suppose that the public are or need be interested in her affairs," he explained to the Farrands. "Mother was 'Mrs. Smith' to the man whom she cared for through his illness, and he naturally supposed that her child bore the same name. She had never spoken to him of her second marriage; they were not, we must remember, on terms of social intimacy; it was merely a sick-room episode between a good woman and a bad man. His freak of calling me his 'stepson' in his will was, I suspect, another stab at the son with whom he was angry. A man like that, it seems, is willing to defame his own character, unnecessarily, in order to hurt somebody else."

Doris and Garrett Randall exchanged a very few words about the business.

"Of course," she said, "the action that I have taken has nothing whatever to do with your half of the property."

He gave her a significant smile as he said: "Of course you know what I will make my hero do."

"Was there no question in your mind about it, either," Athalie asked him once, curiously, "or in your mother's?"

"How could there be?" he said quickly. "Miss Doris might have had questions, for the desire to give his money to her seems to have been born of the only pure friendship the man had—a vision, perhaps, of his youth. But the thought of me ought to have been associated in his mind with his insult to my mother. I could throw his money back at him, if he were living, and tell him not to dare to cover crime with gold."

"There are a couple of you," Athalie had replied composedly. She had not thought it worth while to say that she admired them both. But she did say to her mother that evening, in strictest confidence, that those two people were made for each other and ought, somehow, to discover it.

In process of time, they discovered it. There had been no sudden break with Richard; indeed, there was not at any time what looked to those outside the family circle as a break. That the loss of Doris's fortune was a trial to the young man he made no attempt to conceal; but this was never in his thoughts a reason for giving her up. It was the inevitable trend of character that drifted them apart. Religion meant something to them both; but it meant infinitely more to Doris than it did to Richard, and because it meant so much to her, and by comparison so little to him, the gulf between them daily widened. It was Doris who at last put the feeling into words. They had been having an earnest argument about some question on which they radically differed, and it gave her the opportunity she had resolved to seek.

"Richard, hasn't the time come for you and me to own that we have made a mistake?"

This was the beginning of a long conference during which Richard was the victim of almost every emotion common to human experience. Prominent among them was the feeling that he was being ill-treated. Yet it was not fifteen minutes after he locked himself angrily into his own room that night, before he had an inner consciousness that Doris was right.

The change in their relations was so natural and so far from bitterness on either side that Richard stayed out the week which he had planned for Doris, and kissed her good-bye when he went away. It was not until he was out of sight that Doris said:

"That good-bye was for old friendship's sake, mother. Richard and I made a mistake; but we have done what we could to right it, and we are always going to be friends."

When, two years afterward, Doris and Garrett Randall were married. It was Richard Shipley who not only served as "best man," but who during the two weeks preceding the marriage took in every respect the position and duties of a son of the house. He had been admitted to the bar some time before that, and was getting fairly started in business. To Athalie he confided that it was slow work, that Judge Bronson had not done in all respects as he had intimated he would, and that he, Richard, must evidently be content to go through the world at a snail's pace. Whereupon she cheerfully reminded him that snails, though slow, were sure.

"Do let us take hold of this room," said Athalie, pushing a couch into place with her foot as she spoke, "and make it look less as though there had been a funeral."

They were in the pretty parlor at Willow Street surrounded by all the festive disarray that belongs to bridals after the bride has gone. Richard laughed and seized a flower-stand that was out of its corner. As Athalie worked, she talked.

"It was a very different wedding from what I once planned for Doris, but it was pretty, wasn't it? And considering their means it was eminently sensible. Still, they have a fair enough start in life. I know you find it hard to say anything good of that mercenary man who took back his father's money, so you will not confess that ten thousand apiece for them was a fine wedding present."

"It was fine for them," said Richard; "but from his standpoint, how could he have done less? How many thousands did those two fanatics give to him?"

"Yes, but that was common honesty, or, at least, honor. But he wasn't bound by any moral obligation to give them money.

Besides, he was generous in the settlement. He wouldn't even take back that great house on St. Mark's Square. I think he did well."

"Humph!" said Richard in fine scorn. "How does his magnanimity compare with that of your respected sister and brother?"

Athalie paused in her work of shaking up sofa pillows, a pleased light in her eyes.

"That is so," she said; "I really have a brother now; I haven't given that thought the consideration which it deserves. I have always wanted a brother."

"You taught yourself to consider me in that capacity, didn't you, and worked at it faithfully for years? But Doris was right, as she always is; it was never designed that I should become your brother. It is a long time since I have wanted to, but I want something else. Athalie, you insist that Doris and Garrett were made for each other, and I think you are right; doesn't your discernment reach farther? Considered as your brother I'm a failure, won't you try me as a husband?"

Athalie stood still, a plump sofa pillow in her arms and amazement on her face.

"Why, Richard!" she said. "Why *Richard!*" but her cheeks were aglow, and there was a look in her eyes that gave him confidence. He came over to her and took her in his arms, pillow and all.

"This morning I kissed my sister Doris for good-bye," he said, "now I want to kiss my wife."

About that time Doris Randall, all unconscious of what was taking place in the little parlor on Willow Street, said thoughtfully to her husband:

"It must be hard for mothers; but my mother has Athalie, I am glad of that."

"And my mother has you," he answered, smiling; "and Athalie has Richard."

She looked up, wondering at the significance of his tone.

"Richard? Why—Garrett, you don't think—you can't mean that—"

"That Richard has found his true place in the Farrand family, even as I have? Indeed I do; I have seen that for months. Doris, my wife, we have all been under guidance."

The End

Discussion Questions

1. Doris admits that, despite being a "student of the Bible" for fifteen years, she has no idea how to apply it to her daily living. How common do you think that problem is? What actions can Christians take to understand the Bible in a way that it has a practical impact on their life?

2. The author describes Richard Shipley as an "autocrat," someone used to ruling over others. What adjectives would you use to describe Richard's personality? What kind of minister do you think Richard would be if he were to pursue his education in theology?

3. We typically define our vocation as our occupation. Garrett Randall said his vocation was to serve God with all his heart, soul and mind; and other things were an avocation or hobby. What do you think of Garrett's viewpoint? In what ways did Garrett demonstrate his true vocation?

4. With money tight, Athalie gave up her dreams of going to college so her younger sister could go. She made her sacrifice without complaint, but she sometimes felt "a kind of left-out-ness" in her life. What do you think Athalie meant by that? Faced with the same situation, how willing would you be to make a similar sacrifice for a sister or brother?

5. Richard asked Doris to marry him after he learned about her inheritance. What do you think prompted Richard to pick that

moment to propose? If you were Doris, would you have accepted? Why or why not?

6. Athalie's philosophy is, "When what you *will,* is not, then *will* that which *is.*" What do you think of that homily? Is that a philosophy you can live by? Why or why not?

7. Richard insisted that Doris Stop going to Bible class, and demanded that she turn down her minister's request that she teach a Sunday-school class. He also objected to Doris's plan to take over Garrett's Friday class at the night-school on Water Street. Why do you think Richard was so opposed to Doris's involvement with church work and helping others? If you were in Doris's situation, what would you have done? Have you ever been in a similar situation? Describe the situation and what you did to resolve it.

8. Doris and Richard argued constantly about her inheritance, prompting her to think of the verse, "How can two walk together except they be agreed?" How important do you think it is for a couple to be in agreement when it comes to money and how it should be spent or saved? Do you think a couple can succeed if they have differing views about money? Why do you think so?

9. Doris decided to renounce her fortune because her conscience wouldn't allow her to inherit property and money she thought rightfully belonged to someone else. What do you think of Doris's decision? If you were in Doris's place, would you reach the same conclusion?

10. Which character did you find most interesting? What was it about that character that appealed to you? What character did you dislike the most? Why?

My Isabella Alden Treasure Hunt

by Christian Author
Jenny Berlin

I discovered Isabella Alden's books a few years ago on a visit to my favorite antique store. In an old basket, almost buried beneath a pile of vintage table linens was a copy of *Overruled*. At the time, I'd never heard of Isabella Alden, but I liked the cover and the pages seemed to be intact. When I flipped to the back of the book, the final pages captured my attention and made me want to read more. I took *Overruled* home with me.

And it so it began. That book—once buried and forgotten beneath a pile of linen—so touched and inspired me that I embarked on a mission to find other books by Isabella Alden.

Next I found *Julia Ried* and *Wanted*. Then I read the Chautauqua Girls series and I became a genuine fan of this talented writer.

After reading a number of her books, I was surprised to discover that Isabella's reputation was founded as a writer of children's fiction. From about 1866 to 1929, under her pseudonym, Pansy, she produced wildly popular children's novels and short stories that explained Christian values in terms children could easily understand. It's almost forgotten, though, that she was a talented writer of books and stories for adults, as well.

At the time they were published, Isabella's adult novels were also very popular; and, like her children's stories, they addressed adult themes in a Christian context. She often portrayed her main character as a strong woman who—for better or for worse—affected others' lives for Christ or learned to be a better Christian because of the situations she encountered in the story.

Isabella's plots were inventive and interesting, often incorporating current issues of the day. She was a gifted writer of dialog and she used it to instantly define her characters and make them memorable. It didn't take long for me to realize that Mrs. Tyndall's helpful advice in *Julia Ried* is little more than the weapon of a catty and mean-spirited woman; or that the almost ethereally perfect Christian, Marjorie Edmonds, can say exactly the wrong thing to unwittingly incite another's jealousy and desperation (in *Overruled*). Isabella's talents shine in *Four Girls at Chautauqua*, where she skillfully used dialog to make the four main characters come alive, each with her own unique voice, sense of humor and personality.

With all that being said, it's surprising that Isabella Alden is so little read today. In many cases, modern readers know her (if at all) as the favorite aunt of Christian writer, Grace Livingston Hill; but I think Isabella Alden deserves more recognition than that.

In her books for adults she tackled adult subjects: gossip and reputation; pettiness and envy; witnessing for Christ and strength of conviction—and she did it all within the context of explaining God's plan for salvation. The characters in her books may be non-believers who come to accept Christ as Savior by the book's end; or they may be Christians who are tested or enlightened throughout the course of the story's events. No matter the premise, Isabella created true-to-life characters that are easily identifiable with today's reader.

Take, for instance, Estelle and Ralph Bramlett in *Overruled*. Their arguments, hurt feelings, and resentments are so real and so well written, they could easily be transplanted into a 21st Century novel about a bickering couple.

The same can be said of John Stuart King in *As in a Mirror*. Modern readers have no trouble relating to John's disillusionment with his Christian life. Not content with simply going to church, John realizes that the Christian life he leads is not really grounded in obedience to God's Word. What starts out for John as simply an experimental change in his life leads to the revelation that his Christian walk requires a growing relationship with God. With each obstacle placed in his path, John Stuart King—like all Isabella's characters—ultimately overcomes challenges and prevails with God's help.

Isabella included the message of salvation in each of her adult-focused books. As in her children's stories, she used plain-spoken, everyday terms that were easy for readers to understand as she presented simple but effective arguments for accepting Christ's salvation. As she said through a character in *Ester Ried Yet Speaking*:

> Will He not be pleased with even my little bits of efforts
> if He knows that my sincere desire is to save souls for his
> glory?

I think it's clear that her writings were her personal ministry to others. She was dedicated to using her talent to win souls for Christ.

She also sought to strengthen the faith of Christians who read her books. Like her character, John Stuart King, Isabella believed that simply going to church every Sunday didn't strengthen the believer's walk with Christ. She encouraged readers to engage in an ever-growing relationship with Jesus. Her characters read their Bibles, actively sought work to perform in His name, and yielded to the Holy Spirit by allowing God to take unconditional control of their lives.

One of her common themes was the sense of peace we can attain only in a personal relationship with Jesus Christ. Peace and rest and freedom from worry were recurring messages in many of her books, particularly in the Chautauqua series. One of the Chautauqua girls, Ruth Erskine, thought she had the perfect life; but inwardly, she simply went through the motions of her day, feeling nothing, bonding with no one, and rigidly holding on to her pride and society's dictates. Ruth may appear outwardly calm, but inside she's restless, spending all her energy keeping her perfect life in order but pushing away anyone who might get close enough to see under the surface of her beautiful but fragile existence. It's only through engaging with God daily and making Him the center of her life that Ruth finds peace. Peace with God is a lesson Isabella taught many times in her novels:

> You don't know what a relief it is to go right to the Lord with your worries.
>
> *The Man of the House*

> Go to Him for help, and as sure as the sun shines above these clouds, you will get just what you need.
>
> *The Pocket Measure*

> "Peace with God!" It expresses so much! Peace is greater than joy, or comfort, or rest.
>
> *Ruth Erskine's Crosses*

In my search for information about Isabella, I discovered some critics carelessly group Isabella Alden with "temperance writers" of the late 19th Century. While some of her novels (such as *Overruled, Three People, Judge Burnham's Daughters* and *One Commonplace Day*) included sub-plots that warned of the pitfalls of alcohol abuse, I think it's unfair to label her books as "temperance novels."

She wrote to win souls for Christ. Her characters abstained from alcohol in the same way they abstained from dancing or playing cards. She summarized her position in *The Chautauqua Girls at Home*:

> "It is a question whether we have any right to indulge in an amusement that has the power to lead people astray," Ruth said, grave and thoughtful, "especially when it is impossible to tell what boy may be growing up under that influence to whom it will become a snare."

In *Overruled*, Miss Hannah Bramlett vows to help Jack Taylor fight the temptation of alcohol, no matter what it takes. Later, Hannah's sister-in-law Glyde Douglass comes upon Jack just as he is about to enter a saloon. Their encounter leads Jack to confess to Glyde that he blames God for not making it easier for him to resist alcohol, giving Glyde the opportunity to explain to him the concept of free will:

> "Suppose you had a very pleasant house into which you could put your little boy, and keep him there with locked doors and windows grated, so that it would not be possible for him to escape. You could keep him from a good many wrong roads by that means, couldn't you? He would not be tempted by gambling-saloons nor drinking-saloons; he would not stand around on street corners, nor mingle with men who used evil words—oh, there are a hundred wrong roads from which you could surely shield him! Would you do it? Keep him there all his life, surrounded with pleasant things, books and flowers and

birds, and everything that love could furnish, but still a prisoner? Would you do this, instead of letting him go out in the world to choose his own way?"

Vigilance of character and staying true to one's faith were also common themes in Isabella's adult fiction. In *Julia Reid*, the heroine takes a job that requires her to leave home and live in a boarding house run by the attractive Mrs. Tyndall, who describes herself as a Christian and attends church regularly. Julia admires her instantly and falls under the woman's influence before she realizes the woman's behavior to others is far from Christ-like.

Isabella's long-time friend, Theodosia Toll Foster described her as having "great strength of character and an inflexible firmness in matters of duty and right." In her books, Isabella's characters were portrayed as people who must develop that same strength. She challenged her readers to be better people and to nurture a closer walk with God.

She was astonishingly prolific, producing over 100 books, as well as serialized stories and Sunday school lessons for children. In the year 1900 alone, her book sales were estimated at around 100,000 copies per year, and they were published in several languages.

Unfortunately for us, Isabella Alden's books are becoming more difficult to find. While some of her adult books, such as the Chautauqua series, are available to today's reader, other Alden books, like *Enlisted* and *Doris Farrand's Vocation*, are rare.

That's why I'm so pleased to see publishers bring out new editions of her works. To me, Isabella Alden's stories are treasures of inspiration. Each book helps me examine my own walk with God and challenges me to truly experience the abundant life He has promised me.

Isabella Alden's books are as true and compelling today as when they were first published; and they achieve what Isabella wanted most: "to save souls for His glory."

Blessings to you,
JENNY BERLIN

Jenny Berlin is the author of Ask Me Again, *a contemporary Christian novel. Learn more about Jenny and her books at www.*JennyBerlin.com.

Biography of
The Author

Isabella McDonald Alden was born in New York in 1841. Her mother, Myra Spofford MacDonald, was the daughter of a distinguished scholar. Her father, Isaac MacDonald was well-educated and an advocate of social reform. In her younger years, her father tutored her at home instead of sending her to public school. It was her father who gave Isabella the nick-name "Pansy" and encouraged her to write beginning at a young age. At ten years old, Isabella had a story published by a local newspaper.

When she was old enough to leave home, she continued her education as a boarding student at the Oneida Seminary in upstate New York. There she met Theodosia Toll (later, Theodosia Toll Foster), who would become her roommate, life-long friend, and co-author (under the pseudonym, Faye Huntington). Later, Isabella attended the Seneca Collegiate Institute and finished her formal education at the Young Ladies Institute at Auburn, New York. After finishing her formal education, Isabella took a teaching position at her alma mater, where she met her husband, Reverend Gustavus Rossenberg Alden. They were married in 1866 and had one son, Raymond.

Prior to her marriage, her friend Theodosia (or "Docia," as she was often called) helped launch Isabella's literary career. Docia submitted one of Isabella's novels to a writing contest (against Isabella's wishes). Isabella won the contest and in 1865 the winning novel, *Helen Lester*, was published under her pseudonym, Pansy. Isabella would use the Pansy pseudonym for all her published works.

As a new bride, Isabella devoted her energies to being the ideal pastor's wife. She called on church members, cared for the sick, taught Sunday-school, orchestrated ladies' prayer meetings and mission bands, and developed Sunday-school lesson helps that were widely used by Christian churches across the country.

With her husband, she instituted a weekly magazine for children, appropriately titled, "The Pansy." The magazine was wildly popular. Children from all over the country subscribed and devoured the stories that described God's plan for salvation and reinforced Christian behaviors. Producing the magazine was a family business, with each member contributing stories. Isabella's husband, son, father and sisters all wrote for the magazine, as did her best friend, Theodosia Foster.

Isabella was active in the Chautauqua movement of the late 19th Century. The movement was named for New York's Chautauqua Lake, which was the site of the original assembly in 1874. John Vincent and Lewis Miller began the program as a training camp for Sunday-school teachers. Over the years, the religious focus of the program evolved to include nondenominational lectures and classes, concerts, plays and university-level courses. The program proved so popular that by the end of the century, hundreds of Chautauquas had sprung up across the country, offering similar programs.

Her Chautauqua experiences sparked Isabella's interest in the temperance movement of the time. She was an officer of the Women's Christian Temperance Union; and she featured the WCTU's work in her book, *Judge Burnham's Daughters.*

With all her activities and responsibilities, Isabella still found time to write novels. She was prolific, producing an estimated one-hundred books, as well as short stories and articles. Many of her books were based on personal experience or featured characters based on real people in her life. Her childhood friend, Theodosia

Foster, was the inspiration for the main character in *Docia's Journal*. Her own life as a teacher and pastor's wife served as the model for Marion Wilbur in the Chautauqua Girls series. In *Wanted* and *Julia Ried*, her heroines boldly speak out in church—a direct and liberating reference to her own upbringing in which her father had a strong aversion to women speaking in public, especially in church.

Her books were translated into several languages, including Japanese, Armenian, Norwegian and French, and sold around the world

After Isabella's son and husband passed away in 1924, she lived with her daughter-in-law until her own death in 1930.

Isabella left behind a legacy of sincere, beautifully written books and stories that tell of Christ's salvation and the joys of living a Christian life with strength and conviction. In her memoirs, she wrote:

> "My very first little story books were written with a single distinct purpose in view, given over to the desire and determination to win souls for Jesus Christ. The longer I wrote and the older I grew, that was my central purpose."

> "I dedicated my pen to the direct and continuous effort to win others for Christ and help others to closer fellowship with him."

Isabella Alden accomplished much in her remarkable life. Most importantly, she accomplished her purpose and wrote to win souls for Christ through her inspiring stories.

You can learn more about Isabella, read free short stories and view a complete list of her published books at:

www.IsabellaAlden.com

ISABELLA ALDEN

www.ingramcontent.com/pod-product-compliance
Lightning Source LLC
Chambersburg PA
CBHW071143170626
46809CB00002B/750